PRAISE FOR *THIS LIFE OR THE NEXT*

"The novel strikes like a projectile . . . a subdued explosion that sends shrapnel in all directions—to journalism, to literary fiction, to immigration policy, to religious critique . . . This book has made my own brain work so hard it creaks."

—Morgenbladet

"The original form is the great strength of Demian Vitanza's book about the radicalization of a Norwegian foreign fighter . . . The genre increases the sense of authenticity. This is an exciting book, well written with a strong, believable narrator."

—Dagsavisen

"Thank you for telling a story full of nuances about a subject that is too often depicted in black and white. I spent time in the same area as Tariq the year before him, and met many like him. There, as in other wars, I was struck by how random it often is, which group or side of the front people end up with, and how fine the line is between being labeled a terrorist and a hero. This complexity is only visible if you are willing to light up the gray areas. Congratulations on an important novel. I hope it will be read by many."

—Kristin Solberg, foreign correspondent (NRK)

THIS LIFE

OR THE

NEXT

THIS LIFE
OR THE
NEXT

DEMIAN VITANZA

TRANSLATED BY TANYA THRESHER

amazon crossing 🌐

Text copyright © 2017 by Demian Vitanza
Translation copyright © 2018 by Tanya Thresher
All rights reserved.

Previously published as *Dette livet eller det neste* by Aschehoug in Norway in 2017. Translated from Norwegian by Tanya Thresher. First published in English by AmazonCrossing in 2018.

Published by AmazonCrossing, Seattle

www.apub.com

Amazon, the Amazon logo, and AmazonCrossing are trademarks of Amazon.com, Inc., or its affiliates.

ISBN-13: 9781503959767 (hardcover)
ISBN-10: 1503959767 (hardcover)
ISBN-13: 9781503903821 (paperback)
ISBN-10: 1503903826 (paperback)

Cover design by David Drummond

Printed in the United States of America

First edition

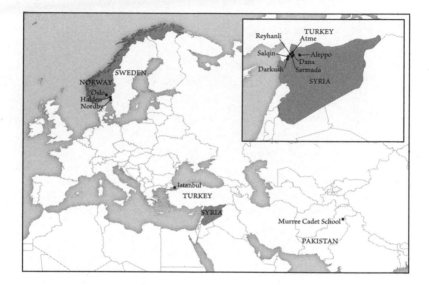

Reyhanli
Salqin
Darkush
TURKEY
Atme
Aleppo
Dana
Sarmada
SYRIA

NORWAY
SWEDEN
Oslo
Halden
Nordby

Istanbul
TURKEY
SYRIA
Murree Cadet School
PAKISTAN

PART 1

I don't trust anyone.

I don't know. It's like I'm damaged goods.

No, not even you. Don't take it personally; it's just how I am now. I've seen a lot, you know. I have to watch out for myself. Right now everyone wants to talk to me: journalists, researchers, all sorts of people. I kind of think they all have their own agenda. They want to show things in a particular light, take me apart and tell their version. Everyone has a version, a theory about who I am and why I left. I can't handle that. I really just want to lie low. Serve my time and move on. But when I read what they write in the papers like . . . you know how people are, they don't understand. I think I need to tell things the way they are.

It wasn't actually my idea. It was my writing teacher who came up with it.

Yeah, here in prison. She noticed I wasn't paying attention in class, and I explained how I just zone out sometimes. She thought it might be good for me to write, encouraged me when I handed in essays and stuff. So I thought some more about it and thought that maybe it was a good idea. That maybe it would help people understand. And then you came to the prison with your writing class, and I thought we could, well, put something together.

It has to be a novel. It can't be real.

Yeah, just the way it was. Or, not quite. It has to be a different story because it can't be with real people. Now that I think about it, it has to be totally different.

After all we're from the same town, so you could put in some of your stuff when there's something I can't talk about.

Sorry, it's just a lot to think about.

We can try. I'll start by telling you what happened, then you write it down and show me. If it works, we'll keep going. Little by little, right. I'll have to check if we can work together before we get into the hard stuff.

Well, I'm sure you writers have lots of ways of putting a story together. But do you want to know what I think? I think we should just start at the beginning and keep going. Straight ahead. What do you think?

Try whatever you want, but I'd like to see if it's OK as we go. Don't take it personally. Just remember—didn't you used to walk around Karl Johan Street as a kid and watch the different artists do portraits? Weren't you checking them out before you sat down and let someone paint a portrait of you?

You probably know better than I do exactly where we should start. By the way, would it be all right if we included something from when I was really little?

Right, I was born in Norway, but since Dad was doing time, Mom and I went to Pakistan a lot. For months at a time. We stayed with my maternal grandma in a small village. Once we were going to celebrate Eid. Grandma sent me to the barber, and I was wearing new clothes, a fancy tunic—you've seen them. All white and clean, ready for Eid. The street where Grandma lived was pretty narrow and full of stalls and dirty workmen, their fingers oily and black from fiddling with machinery and car parts. They hadn't gotten off work yet. A stream of filthy water ran down the middle of the street, something that's common in some parts of Pakistan, so you have to walk on one side or the other. And as I walked down the street, I thought I was better than all those workers. So clean in my white clothes. I was sucking on a caramel I'd been given, because at Eid there's always a lot of candy. But the sun was so bright that it kind of cut into my eyes, so I had to squint. And that was when I tripped. Not only did I face-plant, of course, but I fell right into the sewage in the middle of the street. I was howling and flailing around in the filthy water. A couple of the workers came over to help me up.

At the time it was just embarrassing, but later I thought it was God putting me in my place. That one moment you can feel like royalty, and the next be flailing around in sewage. Whatever—there's no point in going around thinking you're better than everyone else. All of a sudden you may need their help to get up out of the shit.

I could see the train tracks from my room in Halden. There was a fence between the street and the track, but Granddad, my dad's dad, had cut through it so he could walk over and sit down by the water on the other side with his newspaper and fishing pole. He'd moved to Halden a long time ago and was a shift worker at the paper mill, but in his free time he mostly sat by the water. That was before he divorced Grandma and moved back to Pakistan.

I used the hole in the fence to sneak away and put small things on the tracks to see how the train would squash them. You know—coins, toy cars, screws. I had what I'd call an almost scientific curiosity about the shape different objects would take after the train had squashed them. But the high point was the house key. The metal got rolled out and looked like . . . well, you can imagine. I laughed my head off, but then I didn't have a house key. That was the kind of stuff I got up to, the small crap all young boys pull.

Later, when I was a teenager, a friend and I would go through that same hole in the fence on warm summer days and run along the train tracks over to our swimming spot. And, of course, nobody else was there, so we could smoke a joint and lounge around watching cargo ships and small boats passing by.

I didn't mean to jump around like that.

You can put it in order later, can't you?

Yeah, I skipped school, but not a lot. Mainly gym. See, the other kids showed up with their spanking new sweatpants and gym bags, while I had a fucking plastic bag. Sure, my mom probably had the money, but she didn't get how things were done in Norway. Small things like that get bigger and bigger. OK, so you skip gym. Your packed lunch sucks? OK, then pretend you're not hungry while you watch the others eating. School trip? Don't have a sleeping bag; stay home.

I remember the first time I skipped a class other than gym, 'cause that was the day Dad came home. I'd asked Mom if I could call in sick, but she said I had to go. That didn't stop me. Right before lunch I told the teacher I was feeling sick. I walked over the bridge slowly, with my hand on my stomach, but as soon as I got to the other side, I raced through the town center, up past the stadium, and home. Of course, Dad hadn't arrived yet, so I went up to my room and stood at the window, watching for him. And suddenly there he was.

The car pulled in, and Mom and Dad got out. It was like an electric current shot through me, but I stood perfectly still and waited—zap, zap, zap—and I heard the door open downstairs, footsteps, the two of them talking. I heard them laugh down there, and I laughed quietly as well. Then Mom figured out I was home and called me, and I ran downstairs like a madman. And even though I knew it was my dad, it was a stranger who hugged me at the bottom of the stairs. There was a closeness, there really was, but it was an artificial closeness. I hadn't seen him in almost eight years, right? And nobody knew exactly what to say at first. Mom went to make food. Dad went and looked around the house, scratching his head, and I was left holding the banister just watching him.

The transition was—I don't know—abrupt. From grass to asphalt. But he did his best. You know, he thought he'd really let us down. Once he even said it straight out: he was ashamed he'd been away for so long. He thought he had to make up for all the time he'd been in prison. In the beginning it was pretty extreme. He bought me a bike, a skateboard, computer games, a bow and arrow, clothes, and crazy amounts of candy. Actually, the candy caused quite a problem 'cause Mom didn't want me eating so much sugar, but Dad just kept pouring it on. They would start discussing it, but Dad insisted he just wanted to do something nice. In the end he said it didn't matter. "The most important thing," he said all the time, "is that we're together again."

Dad had grown up in Norway, so he was the one who taught me customs like table manners, not staring into the neighbor's window, saying thanks after a meal, eating with a knife and fork, and stuff like that.

I learned customs from Mom as well, but, like, Pakistani customs, right? That was a bit different. It was Dad who showed me how things work in Norway.

We went to the movies a lot, several times a week. If a movie wasn't showing at the Aladdin Theater in Halden, we'd drive into Sarpsborg or Fredrikstad. Then Dad would play a Kishore Kumar CD. Indian music. Always the same CD and always the same song on repeat, "Aane Wala Pal."

I think the song is about how the future will soon be the past. Live life while you can, or something like that. You get the picture. Dad said he listened to that song a lot in prison. When he sang along to it in the car, I remember that I tried to watch the road in front of us. I was still quite small and had to stretch my neck to see over the dashboard. Otherwise, I only saw the sky and nothing of the road.

One time he wanted to take me to *Hannibal*; it was playing at the Aladdin. The ticket seller said it was NC-17, and I was, I don't know, maybe nine or ten. But Dad insisted that it'd be OK if he was with me, and she couldn't make those kinds of decisions. She answered that rules were rules, and in the end we had to see *Shrek* instead, which was playing the day after. We took the popcorn we'd bought and went down to the river—you know, behind the Tista Mall—and that was the first time Dad explained exactly what had happened and why he'd been in prison. Yeah, that was where I felt we really got to know each other. He became my dad again. A little, anyway.

He can tell exactly what he did or didn't do in his own book, if he wants to one day. But he'd gotten a long sentence, and that was what meant the most for me. He'd been away for a long time.

While he talked, we fed popcorn to the ducks, and I remember I was glad to have something to do because I didn't dare look him in the eye. The ducks were swimming around chaotically, fighting for the bits of popcorn, while Dad spoke with a calm, serious voice. As the story went on, I started to understand what he'd done. When we finally threw the empty popcorn boxes into the garbage and went home, he put his hand on my shoulder and asked if I could forgive him. "I hope you can forgive me," he said, and I remember that I didn't answer, but in my head I thought of course I could. We became really close after that, and it didn't stop there, because as we were walking in the dark, I pointed out some stars—you know the ones that make an *M* or a *W*—and said that I'd learned they were called . . . yeah, I don't remember anymore, but then I knew and I told him what it was. I was really good at constellations actually. And dinosaurs. When I got something into my head, I just had to find out. But anyway, the next day he gave me a book that explained all the constellations, and the following week a telescope came in the mail. He just did that kind of thing.

Our house was actually pretty big.

I don't know how I'd describe it, really—normal, I guess, with a small garden.

Did I say that Grandma lived with us?

I mentioned Granddad, didn't I?

Yeah, that's right. But Grandma stayed with us after they got divorced. Actually, she owned the house. She had her own apartment and her own entrance, but she came over whenever she wanted. Completely silent, like a spirit. We'd often walk into the kitchen and food would be ready for us, and nobody had even realized she'd been there. In that way, she wasn't typically Pakistani but silent like a Norwegian winter, always smiling, subdued.

She stayed when Granddad went back to Pakistan, and even if she was pleased he'd left, she got even quieter after that. She only ever raised her voice when she called me from the garden. She didn't like me being at the computer so much and wanted to get me outside. And I would yell something like, "Yeah, yeah, I'll be there in a minute," but I never managed to tear myself away from the screen. Suddenly, click, click, click, two hours were gone, and Grandma wasn't in the garden anymore.

She liked being outside. She had a kind of kitchen garden. She grew herbs and vegetables, and in the summer she went around in a huge straw hat and did the weeding.

No, I really liked spending time with Grandma, I really did. It was just that I was in the middle of a game.

She showed me different plants and how they grew, what they liked, fertilizer, moisture, which plants were friends and which were enemies, or you know, how you can put some plants next to each other and it works really well, but others don't. She knew all about that stuff. She knew all about gardens; she broke seashells and fermented nettles to feed the plants. And it was always calm wherever she was. I don't know why I didn't spend more time with her. Sometimes I still hear her voice calling me, sometimes in my dreams, or sometimes, just suddenly, I'm really aware of her voice.

Yeah, here in prison too. I hear her calling from the garden, "Sunflowers, rosemary," but I can't go out to her.

When I was twelve, my parents sent me to a boarding school in Pakistan.

The Murree Cadet School. Murree with two *r*'s and two *e*'s. You can look at their website; then you'll get it.

It was an hour, or maybe not even that, from Islamabad. Up against a steep mountainside. The buildings were kind of on different levels, with stairs connecting them. So many stairs each day, you have no idea. And really strict discipline: lineups, one arm's length from each side front and back, each day freshly polished shoes, freshly ironed school uniforms, clean hands, nails, straight backs, and our hats perfectly on our heads. Otherwise, you got . . . well, yeah.

The school was an imitation of a British private school, you know, but in a Pakistani military style. You can imagine that mix.

It was Mom who wanted me to go there, not because it was a military school, but because there wasn't really much to choose from if you wanted to send your kid to boarding school in Pakistan. And that was what she wanted: that I learn the Pakistani language and get to know the culture. Besides, for Pakistanis, sending kids to cadet school is a sign that the kids are brought up well. Properly. I don't think she really knew what she was sending me into. Dad had grown up in Norway, so he was more skeptical about the whole thing. But he let himself be persuaded.

No, as for me, I thought military school sounded cool, right? I was a boy after all, and I imagined tanks and weapons, big muscles, and war paint on our faces.

The welcome was totally reassuring. They'd rolled out carpets and put up a big tent for the reception, and the recruits were slowly arriving with their parents. Then there was food and drink and we got to know the other families. We met the teachers, the principal, and, last but not least, the superintendent, Kassar. He was a retired lieutenant colonel with a uniform full of stars. He smiled at all the parents and seemed to be pleasant. Us kids were allowed to play freely, and before I knew it, I was in the middle of a game of hide-and-seek with a gang of other boys. I didn't have any sense of what was in store for me. I was just caught up in the game.

After working up a sweat, I suddenly thought about my parents. I wanted to hang out with them a bit before they left; after all I wasn't going to see them for a really long time. But there were hardly any parents left when I went into the tent to find them. I kept looking around, but after a while I had to ask one of the teachers if he'd seen them. Then I found out they'd already gone. Well, I didn't understand: "What do you mean, they left?" I was sure they wouldn't leave without saying good-bye. "Don't take it personally," said the teacher, but I still didn't get it.

You know what they'd done? OK, my mom told me later on the phone that they'd been encouraged to leave while the kids were playing. The school thought it would be best that way. They were afraid that emotions might get the upper hand. That too much sentimentality would start us off wrong. Or that somebody might change their mind at the last minute and go back home with their parents. My mom said it sounded sensible at the time. So they'd left.

Yes, of course I was upset. Suddenly your parents are gone, right? And when they'd disappeared, bam, the show was over. The superintendent, Lieutenant Colonel Kassar, he completely changed: his face suddenly became hardened. He ordered the older cadets to tidy up, and then the military machine started to roll. Quick as lightning. The food was cleared, the tent packed down, the carpets rolled up. Everyone had a job and worked so fast it was as if the wind just blew everything away: the tent, the feeling of safety, the parents. So there we stood on the bare parade ground with the Pakistani flag fluttering in the wind. We were told to line up.

Those of us that were new were totally confused.

Maybe four hundred and fifty.

About seventy newbies.

Yes, we were arranged according to height, and then we got our place in the system. Were given units, each unit its barracks. Each barrack had several dorms. Each dorm, several bunk beds. And that was where you got your spot. A bed and a cupboard that, well, just looked like bits of junk welded together actually. Then that was that, OK? Now I'm here, right? I couldn't sleep the first night. It was cold because even though it was Pakistan, the school was up in the mountains, and it can get really cold there, especially during the night. Then there was a bug, a horsefly or something. No, wait. Not really a horsefly. I'm not sure we get them here in Norway, but whatever it was, it buzzed around my face the whole night, and all I could do was think about my parents and how I wanted to go home.

The next day we had to put away our personal clothes, and I got my uniform, which only had one stripe on the shoulder. The lowest rank, right? We learned that each unit had a leader, and then each room in the unit had a deputy leader, all seniors. The leaders could make up rules and punish us if they wanted, and they took advantage of that power. Or just 'cause they felt like it; some people need to feel powerful, right? Some people are like that. For little shits like me it was important to have the right friends.

In the beginning a slightly older Punjabi kid in my room watched out for me.

No, I don't remember his name, but his face was totally emotionless. He'd been there long enough to be cynical. "You're not going to like it," he said, "but you'll get used to it."

On the third day the fun began. Kassar was waiting for us. It started with a lineup on the parade grounds where we had the reception. But the atmosphere was totally different. We had to answer with "sir." "Yes, sir!" "No, sir!" Everything was in English. We learned how we had to stand, turn, march in place, run in place, and we had to keep time, understand? Everything had to be totally perfect. For example, when you saluted, the palm of your hand couldn't point down like you see in the Norwegian military, but out, like this, with your hand at the side of your head so the index finger meets the end of your eye, or the very end of your eyebrow. This is what we did, hands up and down, up and down, and the finger placed correctly. If anyone was off by a few centimeters, he'd get a sharp slap in the face, and Kassar's hand was a heavy one, I'll tell you that.

No, he didn't exactly hold back, if you know what I mean. And, of course, we were the young recruits, weren't we, so he wanted to show us how things were straight off the bat. When we didn't manage to keep time, for example, the whole unit was punished. Every morning before breakfast we had to line up on the parade grounds for inspection. And again after breakfast, before and after lunch, and at the end of the day. We had to look straight ahead. Like this.

Anyone who didn't look straight ahead got in trouble. Even the oldest cadets were afraid of Kassar, or rather, they were the most afraid, really, because they'd seen what he was capable of for so long. But to be honest, it didn't take long for us to learn to be afraid of him as well. Behind the strict discipline there was a beast that always wanted to break out and use its power. One day—it must have been in the winter because I remember it was snowing—Kassar walked up and down several times during the inspection like he was looking for someone he could yell at. Eventually he got a hold of a small dude and started shouting at him, I think because his shirt was slightly wrinkled, but I was standing too far away to hear, and there were all sorts of rumors afterward. Someone said he'd started to hiccup. Others thought his collar was dirty on the inside: Kassar used to pull us by the collar to check if it was clean. No matter what, the rest of us were supposed to look straight ahead. But after a while, as the shouting got louder several of us looked over— without turning our heads, of course, just with our eyes, so our pupils were pressed right into the sides of our sockets. Then the older brother of the kid Kassar was bullying just lost it.

Yeah, the older brother was at the school as well. He was standing farther back in the lineup, just on the other side of me. I saw him totally lose it and go over to intervene, and then, of course, the younger brother got a little more confident and started talking back to Kassar. That was it. Just that. That's what he shouldn't have done. Before anyone knew it, the lieutenant colonel had shoved his hand into the little boy's mouth and lifted him up by his teeth. Can you imagine that? Then Kassar twirled him around like a lasso and threw him up into the air. I can still see it. That small body and that gray sky full of big snowflakes, and his arms waving around as if he were trying to swim freestyle in midair or something. And then his mouth hit a concrete corner. Bam! And there he lay. Kassar just quietly dried his hands, and everyone was scared shitless and tried to look straight ahead and pretend like nothing had happened. But the kid, the one who had been thrown, that poor kid lost all his teeth.

Sorry, I didn't mean to laugh. It's nothing to laugh about, really. But it's like that—sometimes you can't do anything except laugh; it's not meant cruelly, it just happens. It was like that in Syria as well: we just started to laugh at really horrible things. We could watch someone being blown up or shot, and the only thing we could do was laugh. But I don't want to jump around the story. Or, it's the story that's jumping, not me.

No, wait. I've got more to say about Murree.

In addition to the Pakistanis, there were a few Afghani kids at the school. They had rich parents who were involved in the heroin trade and had the money to send their sons to boarding school in Pakistan. It was considered a status symbol, right, and nobody wanted their kid growing up in all that shit in Afghanistan; the country was in the middle of a war after all. But after one of the holidays, one of them, Nabi, snuck in some of his dad's heroin from home and smoked it. One morning we were all lined up on the parade grounds looking straight ahead, all that stuff. And Nabi, he was standing there like a droopy flower swaying in the wind with a stupid look on his face. It didn't take long before Kassar singled him out, ordered a full search of his room, and found the stuff. As punishment he was forced to stand perfectly upright out on the parade grounds for several days. He wasn't allowed to move, wasn't given food or drink, couldn't go to the bathroom, he just had to stare straight ahead. We counted the days. He lasted a long time. On the fourth day he collapsed. Then they took him inside, and we thought it was over, that he'd been punished and could come back into the fold again, carry on as before. But that evening, two older cadets carried him into the dorm on a carpet. Then we saw just how bad a beating he'd gotten. Lying there, he didn't even cry; he just whimpered, and when they laid him on the bed, he was shaking so much from shock that he eventually fell down onto the ground. Rolled over onto his back, crossed his arms over his chest, and carried on shaking and mumbling to himself. They'd beaten him so badly he had wounds all over his body.

A few days later he was told he'd been expelled. I still think it was weird to punish him so much if they were going to expel him anyway. I guess it was to warn the rest of us, set an example. But to be honest, we didn't need all that to know we shouldn't do heroin at school.

I think it was because Kassar liked it. He had to have an outlet for something or other, some sadistic crap that was weighing him down. Every now and again he just had to let it out.

The weirdest thing of all was when Nabi showed up again a few days after he'd been expelled. He climbed back over the fence in full uniform and asked to come back to school. At the time I thought he was afraid of what his family would say if he went back to Afghanistan. But since then I've wondered if Nabi really did want to come back to the school. Deep down I think Nabi needed the strict framework. He needed Kassar. Or he needed to show Kassar that he was good enough. Nobody likes leaving as a loser. No matter what.

No, he was chased away by the janitor. No more school for him.

I managed OK. I usually avoided trouble. The worst thing was when we had to run. I wasn't good at it because I was pretty unfit as a kid, and when Kassar sent us up to run a lap around the upper plateau, the older cadets ran behind and chased the slowest ones with a whip. Luckily for me there were a few slower kids at the back who took the brunt of it, but I wasn't that far ahead of them, and sometimes I took a few lashes. Once I saw one of the guys at the back stop to throw up. I felt sorry for the kid, right, so I thought about going back to ask him if he needed help, but then the older students were already around him beating him up. You just had to grit your teeth and run on and on and on.

Even though I did my best, I still have my own tale to tell about the lieutenant colonel. Every day at about four in the morning, nine cadets had to line up in full uniform, all perfect. Then we raised the Pakistani national flag and two other flags; I think it was a school flag and one for the Pakistani military. It had to be done according to a certain routine, with precise movements, solemnity, and so on, even if there was nobody else there but the nine poor bastards who'd been given the task plus the janitor, who was always sitting there with his gun, sleeping with a blanket wrapped around him.

The whole routine was on a rotation, one month at a time. That's quite a long time if you think about it—disturbed sleep, up every day at four. One day, the leader of my unit decided we should just run out, raise the flags, and run back in again: "Screw the uniform!" And being the new recruit, I couldn't do anything but trot along after them, right? And to be honest, what was the point of all the fuss when nobody was going to see us anyway? So we ran out, raised the flags, ran in again, and went back to sleep.

Everything had gone perfectly, and the three flags were there waving just like they were supposed to be when Kassar did the inspection that morning. But when the cadets were ordered to march to the canteen for breakfast, it came: "Those of you who raised the flag, stay where you are." Bam! A lightning bolt through my skull. Boring into my body. The first thing I thought was that someone had ratted us out. I didn't have time to dwell on who it could've been before the old lieutenant colonel was right in front of us. It was the first time I'd felt his breath on my face. "Do you see that chair over there?" he asked me, even though I was the youngest. "Yes, sir!" "Tell me, who sits in that chair all night?" "The janitor, sir!" Kassar just nodded calmly. "Correct," he said. "The janitor sits there every night, wrapped in his blanket, snoring. But last night the janitor wasn't sitting under his blanket, because your good superintendent was." I couldn't believe it: the spot check was the same night we'd decided to cut corners. We stood there like piles of dry twigs ready to snap, staring straight in front of us. I'm sure that if you'd taken a photo of us right then and there, the picture would've just been white, because we were all so pale.

No, no, Kassar was still calm. He took his time before he really started. First we got—what should I say?—a warm-up for the punishment. We had to run laps at full speed until we were dripping with sweat. Then we were told to take off our shirts. We looked at each other like, *What's happening?* before we did it. But he still didn't get the whip out, just pointed toward the ground, and for a long time we lay against the cold concrete surface, full of gravel, small stones with sharp edges, before he told us to do forward rolls. We might have managed a roll or two, but we were ordered to roll again and again, for one hour, two hours, until we were dizzy, nauseous, and all scraped up. And only then did he come with the rubber whip. We lined up with our hands against the wall, and then, smack, the merciless whack against the back, smack, or even worse, when he missed and hit our thighs or hips. Of course, we stayed standing even after the last hit, waiting for more, because he didn't say a damn thing when he was finished, did he, and we just stood there squeezing our eyes shut like total idiots. Eventually we realized it was over. Finished. Kassar had left, and we were allowed to join the others.

Then we got the official punishment.

Yes, at evening lineup out on the parade grounds. In front of the whole school. One student was told to take off one of his shoes and start hitting us with it. You can imagine how that felt on our sore bodies. By the end we had to crouch down and frog-jump in front of the others while pinching our earlobes and saying, "Ribbit, ribbit."

If we'd had a choice between the frog jumps and all the other punishments, I would've chosen the latter and gotten out of that damned jumping.

Yes, I started to miss Norway more and more after that. I remember when we were told to run up one of the hills, we could look over to some mountains. Really impressive, snow-capped mountains. And my friend explained it was Kashmir. But, like, in my head I could only think, *No, no, that's not Kashmir, it's Norway. Right over there, the Norwegian mountains.* I don't think I've ever missed Norway as much as I did then. I just wanted to go home to Mom and Dad and the house on Refne Street. It was so far away, and the only contact I'd had with them was by phone, but that was in Kassar's office.

Of course. That was the point of having the phone in the office. Anyone who complained or talked badly about the school would be given special treatment, so to speak.

Norwegian? No. Forget that. We had to speak in Urdu or English so he could understand what we were saying.

The older cadets bullied the rest of us a lot. Especially one guy, Zahir. You know I said it was the older students who were the room and unit leaders?

OK, so Zahir was the leader of all the unit leaders. He was a stocky guy, not so tall, but kind of compact with huge owl eyes. He came from a rich family in Punjab, was well-spoken, and 100 percent disciplined. Sometimes Kassar even gave him the responsibility for doing the drills; that was how much respect he got. But all of us in his unit knew that he was actually a lazy bum when there were no adults around. Nevertheless he always had to give me orders, even when the orders didn't make sense. Tariq this and Tariq that; don't do that, Tariq; and Tariq, go fetch that. At the end of each day we had an hour or two of free time before the last lineup by our beds, when we had to show all our bedclothes and clothes for the next day laid out perfectly. Time was precious, right. It was the only part of the day when we didn't have anything on our schedules. I would usually play cards with Sawab, who was staying in one of the other rooms in my unit. But Zahir nearly always hunted me down and told me I couldn't be there. I mean, what was his problem? It wouldn't have cost him anything to leave me alone. So after a while I started to look for ways to get him back.

I don't know if I'd call it a desire for revenge. More a sense of what was right. In the meantime, the world was going round as before, the older leaders carried on tormenting the younger kids, and for some reason they just wanted me to slave away for them. Fetch that, be quiet, go over there. I think they were jealous because my parents were in Norway, or something.

They just wanted to humiliate me.

Yeah, of course there were good times as well. Saturdays. That was the best part of the week. On Saturdays I was the champ. We got to go out

24

for a few hours into the small village, into Murree. Town Day, they called it, and they always reminded us that it wasn't a right but a privilege we had to earn constantly. But whatever, can you imagine hundreds of kids running around in a small village? Total chaos. One of the most popular places to go on a Saturday was the gaming room, where we played *Tekken 3*. I'd gotten a lot of practice on *Tekken* in Norway, right, so I knew all the tricks—left, right, uppercut. So I kept on playing fight after fight when the others folded. Nobody could beat me at *Tekken*.

I chose King. Have you ever played *Tekken*?

He's the one with the purple pants and the leopard face who breaks his opponents' bones. I even smashed the older students. But Zahir couldn't stand losing. When he lost, he just hit me in the back of the head and told me to move away from the machine. I was no match for him, so I just had to do what he said. But once—oh this was so good—Sawab and I were walking past his room one evening and we heard a radio. Of course, radios and music were forbidden at school. TV? Just forget it. Maybe if we were lucky, we got to see a film every other month in the common room. Carefully chosen so it didn't have even a hint of anything erotic. But the radio was bad enough. Sawab and I stood outside the door of his room for a long time and just stared. This was valuable information. Valuable and dangerous.

We discussed what we should do for a long time, and then the next Saturday, when we were out on Town Day, we walked up and told him that we knew all about his radio. Sawab was shaking while he talked but was very clear in his demands. Zahir should treat us well if he didn't want anyone to find out. Just that. Treat us well. It could've gone really badly; we had no guarantee that Kassar would believe us and not Zahir if we said anything. But we got what we wanted. After that, we had no problems with him or any of the other leaders at the school. He even treated us to a hamburger once in a while in town.

That type of positioning and strategizing has been a useful lesson. Sadly, you might say. In prison every time you change sections there's a new round of that game. Who's supporting who? What are the different people in for? What's your position? You don't have to instigate anything, but you know, you shouldn't be weak either. I can't say I like the game. But I know how to play it.

The barracks were badly insulated and had no heat. We were sent home for the few weeks in winter when it got really cold.

No, not to Norway. That was too far.

I went to stay with my maternal grandma and my uncle. They lived a few hours away from the school. My grandma was shocked at how thin I'd gotten, so she made sure to shove plenty of food into me. She was a worrier. She thought, for example, that my skin was too dry and suggested all sorts of skin lotions. Things like that. She cared.

I got to talk freely to my parents on the phone. No Kassar listening in. They told me I'd become a big brother. They sounded so happy that I didn't want to worry them about what was going on at school. I didn't want to complain. Didn't want to disappoint anyone. I thought, *Just be strong, hang in there.*

When school started again, I was scared shitless. I wanted to stay at Grandma's, but I didn't say a thing to anyone. So it was one more year of school. But by the following winter break, I couldn't take it anymore.

I told Dad everything on the phone, and he said he'd bring me home. He asked if I could hold on just a little longer. I said yes, but back at school I was just waiting, waiting, waiting. I started to not give a damn. I often got told off because I wasn't precise enough in my movements and stuff. Deep down I was already on my way home.

One day Kassar appeared at the door to my unit looking for me. I thought I was going to get boxed on the ear because I was wandering up the stairs like some slacker, not marching like I was supposed to. But I didn't get hit. He just looked at me sternly: "Pack your things and meet me at the office. You're leaving."

Then I met Dad at the office, and it was just, yeah, I remember I was laughing, I was so happy. A huge weight lifted off my shoulders.

Dad put his hand on my head and hugged me. Then he signed some papers, and I was done. School was done. As we left, I tell you, the only thing I wanted to do was piss on the school wall, but Dad asked me to pull myself together and leave with dignity.

You know that feeling you have when you round the corner above Rød Manor and see Fredriksten Fortress in front of you on the other side of town? That feeling of coming home to Halden? Twice in my life, the sight of that fortress sitting above town has touched me more than anything else I've experienced. Coming home from Murree was one of those times.

I'd almost forgotten how quiet and calm life in Norway can be. The first night I slept so deeply that, I don't know, it felt like my bed was sinking into the earth. Down into the magma, you know? And I remember I woke up and thought, *Is this real? Am I in Norway?* And I just lay there grinning.

Yeah, he was a year old when I got home.

Can we just call him Little Brother?

You know, from the very beginning I felt like I had to look after him. He'd just learned to walk when I saw him for the first time. He went around picking up all sorts of things. Mom and Dad just smiled when he threw bits of food around, but I tried to minimize the damage. The cadet discipline was still in me.

I got restless. Something about the silence stressed me out. Like, I couldn't just lie there. I was so used to training, right. After so much discipline, it makes you crazy to lie perfectly still with all the time in the world. So I shot out of bed every morning and exercised. Push-ups, sit-ups. I did that kind of thing for the first few weeks after I got home.

Maybe somewhere deep inside I was scared of falling apart. I was happy to be home, I really was. Away from Kassar's tyranny. But at the same time I missed the discipline.

Imagine what it was like when I started school again in Norway. Suddenly there's nobody who cares. You can have your feet on the table, swear, not give a shit. It's not good. To be honest, I don't think there's enough discipline in Norwegian schools. I really don't. It's even too laid-back here in prison sometimes.

In Murree you're pushed to the limits, and that's how you learn what you can do, or what you can't do—where the limits are, y'know? So in Norway I tried to find the limits, but there weren't any. I could call the teacher an idiot, no consequences. Forget my schoolbooks, no consequences. One time there was a kid in class who called a teacher— I apologize for the language—he called her a fucking cunt, and she started to cry right in front of us, you know? She broke down. Then she left the classroom, and we just let loose and wreaked havoc.

No, he didn't even get written up. I think she thought the whole episode was too embarrassing to write him up. Nobody was strict about us doing homework either. When I was at Murree, I was one of the best in the class in several subjects. Math, for example. I actually like to learn, but it just slipped away. First Norwegian went badly; I really struggled to write in Norwegian again. And math was a complete reversal. Then one subject after the other just fell like dominoes. Click, click, click. When Mom asked about my grades, I slammed the door and said the school in Pakistan had ruined everything. I secretly smoked around the corner, played computer games instead of doing my homework. I didn't give a shit about school and started hanging out with the other kids who didn't give a shit.

Mainly foreigners.

Of course I had Norwegian friends. But my closest friends were foreigners.

I don't know, when I was introduced as the new student, it was an Iranian and not a Norwegian who waved me over to sit next to him. And I started hanging out with two Albanians, Kushtrim and Liridon, from Refne Street, who I'd gone to elementary school with. We took the same route to school. They only had plastic bags for gym at elementary school too. The foreigners stick together; it's just how it is.

I don't know. To be honest, I don't know why.

Maybe birds of a feather flock together.

But that's just it: we weren't really birds of a feather. Somalis, Albanians, Colombians, Afghanis, Eritreans—all sorts.

No, no. Nobody went around thinking that we were Muslim then. Well, maybe we thought about it when Carl I. Hagen or some other right-wing politician was talking shit on TV, but it wasn't really a huge topic of conversation. And not all the foreigners were Muslim, anyway. What brought us together was that we weren't Norwegian. We felt that. Or at least I felt it. There was something about it that brought us together. And if there was any trouble at school, we stuck together against the Norwegians. I remember one day, a group of foreigners from another school got into trouble with some kids from our school—Norwegians. And when we saw them outside, we just knew, without even discussing it, which side we were on.

In the beginning I hung out with that Iranian. I shouldn't say his name. Maybe you could just make one up.

Actually, now that I think about it, no one should have their real names. Most people won't want to have anything to do with me, or be written about, or anything. But OK, the Iranian, he and I hung out a lot together at the beginning. And the Albanians too. You know, in junior high you get into a group, smoke behind the sheds. I remember I got a nicotine high and coughed like crazy.

You stumble through puberty. Try to be good, try to be bad. Try everything. In junior high I messed around with one of those butterfly knives. You know, the ones that open and close. Clack, clack, clack. And all my buddies thought it was cool. Especially Kushtrim and Liridon. They were entranced by that thing when we walked home from school. But I eventually got a bad feeling about it. So just like that, I said, "Guys, this isn't good; this is made to hurt people." And I folded the knife and chucked it a damn long way over the railway tracks and into the bushes. Kushtrim totally lost it and jumped across the tracks to search for the knife. "If you find it, you can keep it," I said and went home to have dinner.

Actually, there wasn't anything really wrong with my life then, but it's always the little things. For example, at the end of junior high I wanted to go on to high school, but the counselor advised me to apply for a vocational school instead. She said there was no point in high school because my GPA was too low. But afterward I found out that people with lower GPAs than me had gotten into high school. I'm not saying it was her fault or anything that I ended up as a jihadist in Syria. I'm not blaming anyone. But still, when I look back, you know, things could have been different if I had gotten into a good school. One plus one plus one. In the end, I had nothing to lose.

At some point I started hanging out with Carlos. The first time I met him was in the schoolyard. He'd spent a year overseas. Like me, only he'd been in Chile. Carlos was Chilean. Or rather his dad was Chilean, but he was already dead when I met Carlos. I bet his mom wanted him to get a bit of his dad's culture. Learn Spanish and stuff.

When Carlos came back in, what was it, ninth grade maybe, I'd never met the guy. I saw a group of people around someone in the schoolyard and wondered who it was. He had dyed his hair in a green-and-purple checkerboard, was wearing a leather jacket and some badass gold-framed sunglasses. I thought, *Hey, tone it down a bit, y'know. Who the hell do you think you are?*

I didn't have much to do with him in the beginning. But then the Iranian and I organized a LAN party at school to play *Counter-Strike*. We got to use one of the gyms one weekend. We were all sitting there with our Coke bottles and potato chips playing. He joined in. First he made friends with the Albanians. Then we started talking a bit, and I thought, *This guy isn't so bad.*

We started kickboxing together. Carlos came whenever he felt like it, but I liked being in a place with focus and discipline. It made me feel safe. So I got one belt after the other. But that's off topic. What were you asking about again?

Oh, yeah, Carlos. What else should I say? He liked the ladies, he really did. Constantly chatting online. He'd open his heart and go full throttle to get a woman. Like she was the only thing in the entire universe. But it didn't last long. Then there'd be another. And it was full throttle again and only her in the entire universe.

He spent a lot of time on his hair, had the biggest wardrobe—a bit flashy, you might say. But at the same time he was very spiritual. Actually, I'd say he was an extremely curious person. Had to test everything. Understand everything right away. Try everything. And he had to go to every party, always.

You grew up in Halden too, so you know how it is, what you do—drinking beer up by the cannons in the fortress looking at the town in the middle of summer. Surely you've been to those teenage house parties where everyone's running around trying to make out with each other and someone throws up off the porch and all that. I don't think my stories are any different from yours, just that I went a bit further maybe.

At one of the parties—it wasn't even really a party, we were just at some guy's house, it was right next to the mosque actually, the kids there were older—someone passed a joint around, and Carlos took a hit and made perfect smoke rings. Let's just say he'd done that kind of thing before. I couldn't be outdone, so I also had a little pull.

They were playing some awesome rap, and the world just flowed through me. I closed my eyes, heard Carlos singing along to 50 Cent: "Go Shorty, it's your birthday, we're gonna party like it's your birthday."

We always ended up trying things before anyone else. For Carlos it was almost like a science. He'd try different drugs and sit with a notebook writing down the effect it had on him. So when the other kids our age started to smoke joints, for us it was old news.

But back to the first time I smoked. After taking a couple of drags, I went out to the street. I could see over to the mosque. At the time I didn't think about it. But years later, when I started going to the mosque, I'd sometimes hear music from that same apartment when I got up early to go to morning prayer. They hadn't gone to bed yet. It's like that. Parallel universes. So close, and so far. You stand in one universe and stare into the other, you understand?

But sometimes you have to go a long way just to get across the street.

Of course we hung out with girls.

Oh, yeah, a Norwegian girl, but maybe it's not a good idea to write about that. I do want to get married one day, y'know, if I still can.

There was a carnival in town, and I'd been through all the stalls at least twice, so I was ready to go home. Then I spotted a girl. She had her hair in a ponytail, and when she walked past, I only had one thought: *Tariq, you have to get together with her.* Period. But she was hard to get. I actually liked that. That's how I am. The harder, the better.

I heard from some people that she'd just moved to Halden. She was from Ålesund, on the West Coast. And she was going to start at Rødsberg, the same junior high I went to, and I thought, *Jackpot, man. Jackpot.* I saw her at school, but I couldn't get her attention. Then I heard she played handball, right. Typical. She was actually awesome at handball. And then I got an idea. I took the Iranian with me as my wingman, and we hung around like dorks outside the gym where her team trained in the afternoons. But I didn't want to look desperate, so we hung out and pretended it was just a total coincidence we were there. We did a few tricks on our bikes and sat on some pallets. And when they came out,

I looked at her, I swear, for a thousandth of a second. She looked back, and that was that. She understood. And I understood. We have a thing. So even though we hadn't spoken to each other, we knew something was going on.

She still kept to her new friends in the schoolyard. So, you can imagine, I got more and more antsy. Finally, I just walked up to her in the schoolyard one day; even though she was standing with a group of girls, I didn't care. Walked right up, without a plan, right, and just said, "Hi." "Hi." "OK, I'd like your number." She asked me why I wanted it. I'm bad at planning, right; I could've had something ready, said that I wanted to call to invite her out to something, but what? I had no plan. Typical me. I said I just wanted it. I probably sounded like a fucking idiot, but she wrote it down for me anyway. Then she said, "Don't give it to anyone else, OK?" Like, why would I give it to someone else? When I got back to the boys, they really roasted me, you've no idea. But I'd gotten her number, so I could handle a bit of roasting.

A couple of days later, I saw her sitting alone on a park bench along the pedestrian street. She was probably waiting for someone. I stared at the back of her neck; she always had a ponytail, and between her blond hair and the collar of her denim jacket was the most beautiful neck. I thought, *Now, Tariq, pick up the phone and call her now.*

I watched her put the phone to her ear. "Hello, it's Tariq." I tried to sound casual and asked if we could get together one day. "Maybe," she said. She didn't seem that interested, but more like whatever, we could maybe meet up sometime. But she didn't know I was watching her while we were talking. She gave herself away when we hung up, because she leaned her head back and stretched her arms out with a big smile on her face. So it was obvious: she had feelings for me.

It lasted a little over a year.

I don't know.

Just write that we drifted apart. Then I got a cat.

Yeah, a little kitten. Black with white patches on its forehead and the softest fur. The best medicine for a broken heart.

I've been thinking about something since we last talked. I wonder if it's important that I haven't really had a proper dad.

Yeah, everything I've said is true. He did make an effort after he got out of prison. Took me to all sorts of things. But then it started slipping again.

He had some criminal friends he partied with and stuff.

The problem is I really don't want to bad-mouth my dad. I can say he's struggled with some things, but we don't need to go into what. I can see he's trying to mend his ways. He needs me to believe in him.

Yeah, I do.

The official version was that he was working overtime at a carpentry company. The whole thing was really hard on Mom. She got tired of him hanging out with his criminal buddies.

No, it was different for Little Brother. He'd sit together with Dad on the lawn mower and drive around, or they'd play on the living room floor. Little Brother was basically glued to him. He didn't really notice any problem apart from the fact that Dad was away a lot.

Bitter, no. I was happy that Little Brother got to grow up with a dad.

It was worse for me. I didn't talk much with Dad during that time. He was still a stranger to me. To be honest I didn't talk that much to Mom either. I kept to myself when I was home. Or I'd just pop into Grandma's apartment. But she just went around humming, so I got antsy there as well. In the end I'd put on my headphones, pull my hood up, and go out. I listened to 2Pac, "Me Against the World" and "Young Niggaz." Walked up to Rød Manor, smoked weed, and toppled statues of old, rich bastards.

Then I'd call Carlos and kill a few hours playing some game or another.

I mean, if you've got a dad, I don't know, I wonder if it's different. Someone to lean on, y'know? Or, if he's not there, a big brother. Someone you can ask about things, someone who isn't just there wagging a finger at you when you get in a fight, but who actually gets it. It's the same with Carlos. His dad died when he was little. Carlos and I were both fatherless. We had to take care of each other. We were brothers. I was his big brother.

One day when I got home from school, I saw Dad sitting in the kitchen crying. The only time I've seen him like that. He was mumbling to himself in Urdu for a long time before he looked at me, his eyes completely red. Then he explained that Grandma had died. Her heart had stopped, he'd found her in her kitchen, the radio was still on.

It was spring. She'd managed to plant some things in the garden before she died, but over the summer the weeds took over. None of us knew how to take care of her garden. Nobody took time to do it. Nobody remembered the names of the different plants.

As if that wasn't enough, things started to go downhill for Dad. He went out more and more with his criminal buddies and drifted further and further away.

We're close today.

We're trying.

We send each other letters from our prisons.

No, it won't work. I don't want to get into his case. Actually, I think it's best to just write him out of the story.

Maybe my parents get divorced, and he moves back to Pakistan or something. In a way that's not completely wrong. He was a long way away, even if we were living in the same house. It'd be a little weird because Dad had really grown up in Norway, but it could've happened. In a parallel universe or something.

OK, write this. Mom and Dad divorced. Dad moved to Pakistan, just like his father did when he got divorced.

I don't know. He just left. After that it was very quiet in the house. Period.

I started a mechanics course down in Porsnes. I already felt like I'd failed not going to high school. Those of us doing TIP, Technical and Industrial Production, had our own area in the schoolyard. You know when you're trash. It's just how it is. We hung out there, smoked. Carlos went to another school, but I got to know a Somali guy, Ali. He had a mini-Afro and always had worry lines between his eyes. The Norwegian kids joked about his pronunciation, and let's just say that the teachers didn't always stop them. In fact some of them even joined in, imitating his accent.

Especially one of the teachers. He'd been on the verge of losing his job a few times because of racism but got to stay, redeemed himself by taking the foreigners on a fishing trip. He was about to retire when we had him, so he didn't really give a shit. We had CNC class—we were learning how to program a lathe—and Ali said he didn't understand. The teacher couldn't be bothered to explain. "Well, people like you don't understand shit anyway. The only thing people where you come from know is how to blow yourselves up."

Yep, he said that.

What were we supposed to do? I'd learned at Murree that I had to respect teachers just as much as my parents, right, but then you get people like that. And there were others too. That's how it is for foreigners: you just have to swallow it. If you complain, it gets worse—then you're seen as ungrateful too. You have to learn patience. *Sabr*, we call it. So we took it out at kickboxing instead. Right, left, right. Bam, bam, bam. But to be honest, if I could turn back time, I'd have gone for the bastards' throats. So, no *sabr*.

I got to know a Norwegian guy who was also doing mechanics. A childhood friend of Carlos's. He was called Nils, or Pilla. First it was the classic Nils-Pils 'cause he could down two or three pilsner six-packs at a party. But then he moved from pilsner to pills and was called Pilla. He was short and compact, always had *snus* under his lip, and wore his hat backward. He was a son of a bitch at boxing. We bonded over that. He was always ready to put up his fists and was known for one particular punch. A single cross punch—bam!—done. You always got a few bruises hanging out with him 'cause he was always trying to prove himself, even if it was mostly roughhousing.

We hung out in Carlos's garage mostly. There was a room above the garage where we'd be left alone. Unlike at my house, his mother didn't pay attention to what we were doing. She was hardly ever home anyway. It was perfect for us, y'know; we could sit in Carlos's garage, smoke joints, watch movies, or play games, or read about the Illuminati and the Freemasons online and make up theories about the world. Sometimes we invited friends over, maybe some girls came by. When there was a party, everyone wanted to pregame at the garage. That became a thing. But it got a bit out of hand, y'know? People were doing lines, pills, and everything. Carlos could get a hold of anything, and I was no angel either.

We also hung out a bit at the ramps outside Rock House, where the young punk bands go to rehearse. I never got into skateboards, but some of the others did. Ali and Kushtrim, the Albanian, they'd spend hours doing tricks while the rest of us stood and chatted, vented about whatever we didn't get out of our systems at kickboxing. In the winter we hung out in the Lunch Bar in the square, ate kebabs, and eventually got thrown out because we were taking up a table that paying customers could use.

It was easier in the summer. We snuck along the railway tracks to our swimming spot, or we'd go to a place up past Femsjøen and Kruseter. There's a lake up there called Klaretjern that's full of bauxite or something, so there isn't anything living in it. The water's perfectly clear, like a swimming pool. We'd put on goggles and each take a stone from the shore that we'd carry as we walked into the lake. We built a cairn at the bottom of that lake.

Later on when I got a dinghy from my uncle in Oslo we went out to sea more often. It was only a four-horsepower engine, so it didn't really go fast, but we got out and fished a bit. Felt the waves. I usually went with Carlos and Nils. Carlos just wanted to smoke and sunbathe, while Nils was great at fly-fishing. You know, he really needed to show off.

No, the fish didn't bite much.

Later on I got a larger engine. Thirty horsepower on a teeny, tiny dinghy; it really lifted up out of the water. That was the end of fishing, but we got more speed.

We did a lot with motorcycles as well. You know, the little ones you can drive when you're sixteen. People showed up with them at parties and thought they were the coolest motherfuckers. They'd probably gotten them from their parents. Carlos and me, well, we didn't have motorcycles. We had pliers. We cut chains and kicked off the wheel locks. Sometimes we had to lie down and kick at the wheel to get it free. People stared at us as we lay there kicking. But we just politely said hi and that we lost the key or something. In the end the shit would come loose, and then we just had to run with the bike, jump on, and slip the clutch. Then it was our turn to be the cool motherfuckers.

It was fun for a while, but we found out one of the motorcycles we'd taken belonged to the son of a policeman. So it wasn't long before we had to say adios amigo and drive it into Iddefjord. We drove like mad up and down the harbor a few laps before Carlos did a crazy stunt off the dock and had to swim to land while the bike sank to the bottom. It's probably still there.

Trouble found us quickly when we were at a party. Especially with Carlos. He was always starting fights. Then he wanted Nils and me to back him up, but when the cops came, he ran like crazy. He almost made a sport of it. He did a bit of that sort of thing—what's it called when you run around town, climb up buildings, and jump over stuff?

Yeah, parkour.

He wasn't scared of throwing himself off a balcony or anything. But all that stuff singled us out. People started to avoid us, didn't want to hang out in Carlos's garage anymore.

It was just, like, the hard-core guys that stayed—Ali and Nils. Some others too: the two Albanians from the Refne blocks, Kushtrim and Liridon. But Liridon got into varsity soccer, so he didn't hang out with us as much. Besides, he got superstraight and was always training and taking the bus to school and back. Then there was this guy, Arbi, from Chechnya, who I practiced kickboxing with. Arbi's family had fled the war when he was little and settled in an old house in Tistedalen, which they'd spent years fixing up.

He had a stone face, Russian-style. You really had to man up before sparring with him during practice. I remember the way he looked at you, stared at you like you were some kind of prey.

Usually we just kept going 'til one of us got knocked out.

Sometimes. I knew his tricks, dodged and blocked. But when he finally hit me, I always blacked out. The coach got pissed every time we knocked each other out. Not that it stopped us: we just got tougher and tougher.

I thought Arbi was totally cold at that time, but that was 'cause I didn't know him. Arbi became a really important person for me. I'll get to that later. But he didn't get into the shady business that I was about to get into.

One day I met my dealer down by the river. As usual I bought a small bag and gave him a bill. Then I noticed the huge money wad that my bill disappeared into. That got me thinking.

I told Carlos when I saw him. About that fat wad of bills. Carlos was one step ahead of me. He'd been thinking the same thing and already gotten the address of a dealer who smuggled packages across the border. Together we went to a trashy house in Damhaugen near the paper mill. There was a thin stream of water running down the walls from broken gutters. That was where Cato lived with his dog.

Cato was a cliché of a criminal, with a gold necklace and tattoos. He had a bong ready to go on the table. He sweated and looked out the window the whole time we were there, and the TV was blaring some reality program or another. Huge TV. And the best stereo. You know, new furniture and everything, and a shotgun on the wall. Carlos and I looked at each other; we were trying to hide our uncertainty as best we could. Cato paced around the room and talked nonstop about what sort of deal he could offer us—a gram here and there, money this and that, deadlines, back and forth, back and forth. His dog—you know the ones that are illegal in Norway, the ones with the sad-ass faces—a white one, he just lay on the recliner and chilled.

It wasn't small bags; now it was big ones. And big bags make big wads of bills. After we'd sold our first batch, Carlos said we had to celebrate. You know, us guys who'd showed up to gym with plastic bags had a lot to make up for. Now we'd show them. First we bought new clothes. Put away the thrift-store style and dressed like the baddest rich kids. Only the most expensive clothes. Just pointed at the mannequins—"OK, that one there, and that one, and that one over there too." One day we were loaded up with bags, and outside the mall we walked past a Romany woman sitting on the ground. I stopped, pulled out a five-hundred-krone bill and pushed it down into her paper cup. She completely lost it—like, pulled the bill out of the cup and hid it in her pocket. Then Carlos was there with a five-hundred-krone bill as well. He made a paper airplane and flew it into the paper cup like a fighter jet.

We drank the best coffee. We bought the best video games. We went to the most expensive restaurants.

You know the Curtis Restaurant up at the fortress, Halden's only really fancy place? Well, we put on expensive new shirts and took a taxi up there. Classy place, but we didn't have any table manners, right. The waiter came over and asked which menu we'd like. "Uh, the most expensive one please." "And drinks?" "The most expensive." He looked at us a moment before he nodded. "I'll see what I can find." We weren't even eighteen, but we were so cocky and full of it that nobody even asked us for ID. Then one course after another appeared with little sprigs of this and that. Actually I prefer spicy food, right, like Pakistani and stuff, but we thought we were totally boss, and that was the thing. We'd cheated the system.

It felt good. Of course. Right then we felt like kings. But I have to say one thing before we continue. Even if I try to change my extreme ideas, I'm still a Muslim. And I try to be a good Muslim. In Islam you don't talk too much about previous sins. You repent and try to come back to God; it's called *tawba*. You pray for forgiveness and try to put it behind you. Done. It's a thing between God and me, so you really shouldn't go around boasting about the mistakes you've made, you understand?

It's OK for me to tell you some things, but I won't glorify my sins.

I kept going to school, did welding. The welding itself was pretty cool. It brought your thoughts together; you had to concentrate. Put on the leather apron and welding gloves, pull the mask down over your face, and follow the glow. I don't know, it could be two pipes that had to be welded at right angles—spot weld first, *zum, zum, zum,* check that there was nothing skewed, and then all the way around. We each had our own booth with a metal worktable. Ali was next to me, but he always fell asleep at his table 'cause he'd spent all night playing video games. You know, his parents were away all the time, and in the afternoons he looked after his younger brothers and sisters, so nighttime was his only free time. Then he'd wake up with a headache, gulp down a few too many Advil, and fall asleep on his welding table. Our favorite thing was to sneak into his booth while he was asleep with one of those flint lighters for lighting the welding equipment and bang it on the table so that sparks flew up in front of his face. That woke him up fast. Maybe not the nicest alarm clock, but better than the teacher catching him red-handed.

It wasn't only Ali who fell asleep. Even if it had been years by that point, I'd still have nightmares from good old Murree—Kassar's drills—and when I woke up my jaw would be totally clenched. For the most part I got to school, kept the wheels turning. The other subjects, I don't know; I passed them one way or another. But at that time school was mainly for expanding my social network.

Yup, sell more weed. Find people to sell for us. And Carlos was doing the same thing at his school. That was how we organized ourselves.

After school I went to the gym to pump iron. Sweat out the high and get more muscles. And all the 'roid monkeys were there, so we started dealing steroids too. Me and my friends really got buff, right. Pow! The money wasn't bad there either.

I remember that Little Brother reacted to it. Thought his big brother had become strong and stuff. I often picked him up from daycare. Then we talked, and he always asked thousands of questions. He walked so slow, it took forever to get home with him, but I never complained. Sometimes he wanted to stop at the playground in the schoolyard. Then he'd stand halfway up a ladder to the playhouse or whatever, totally alone, thinking about something or another. He played alone while I waited. Sometimes I got worried. In Pakistan I'd been taught too much play wasn't good. I was afraid Little Brother would become silly. That he'd become a wuss playing so much. But actually, he's doing much better than I am. I was totally wrong.

There was something about Little Brother that made everyone want to take care of him. We didn't talk too loudly when he was near; he had to put on extra warm clothes in the winter. When he was small, Mom bought those rubber things you put on the corners of tables. There were no soft corners when I was little, if you know what I mean, but Little Brother had to be protected.

Carlos and I ran our business. Got Nils and Ali to join us, though they were more on the sidelines. Organized a network of people around us. Bought clothes, cologne, watches. Went to a restaurant at least once a week. We went into Oslo as well. Did coke, MDMA, drank expensive drinks at expensive bars. Checked into a hotel room for an after-party and after it we all took some benzos to relax. We lived in our own world. We had our own language. Our own rules. Our own rhythm. Carlos said we were a perfect team 'cause he was good at the finances and I could use my muscles when someone didn't pay up.

I got more cynical. Cheated people into a game they didn't want to play. The trap was always drugs. I'd lend something to a guy and then tell him he owed me a favor, even after he'd made good. "I got you out of a jam, didn't I?" And then I'd demand something in return.

OK, say he worked in a shop. I'd make him give me the code to the safe, send one of the boys to empty the till. Or if someone was a bit late paying, I'd let the interest shoot up like a rocket. I'd visit them at home. "I have to eat," I always said. Then I took whatever I wanted: a gold watch, a stereo—whatever. And they could only stand and stare as their things disappeared out the door.

Carlos and I talked about the injustices of the world and about society not giving us a chance. That was what 2Pac rapped about too—that the system had betrayed you, that you had to fix things yourself. Eat or be eaten.

You always need to legitimize your shit even if it's the worst excuse ever. You need to believe that what you're doing is right. That you're an OK guy. That's what I thought of myself—that I was an OK guy. I don't know.

I got guns too, brought them to school to show off. Once I made Ali crawl around the floor in Carlos's garage while I pointed a pistol at him. He was scared shitless, but it was only a joke of course.

We really bullied Ali a lot, poor kid.

We started to help Cato smuggle things over from Sweden. Normally that kind of stuff was done by car, but sometimes they were scared of being stopped at customs, so then they got boat transportation from me. I went out with the dinghy and earned some dough. Went out along Iddefjord, under the bridges, and out to Singlefjord, either right to Strømstad or to somewhere closer. Picked up some packages. Took the boat over to Hvaler. Easy peasy.

Carlos and I were there for each other. Brothers, you know; we called each other that, *brother* or *bro*. Once when I was going on holiday with my family, I asked him if he could take care of my business. When I got home, he had an envelope full of money for me. He'd even been to the bank and changed it into new thousand-krone bills. Carlos always had style. I told him that if there was anything I could do in return, he only had to ask. "Yeah, now that you mention it, I do have a problem." Then I had to squeeze some guy. The usual. "OK, you don't have the money? Take your mom's debit card, or your grandma's. You're gonna pay, you son of a bitch."

Yeah. Yeah. We always got the money.

You'll have to excuse me, I'm not quite myself today.

You know the pages you gave me last time? One of the guards took them. All of them.

I don't know; they probably want to see what's going on. Maybe they're looking for evidence about some of the others who went to Syria. I told you, when it comes to so-called terrorists, they really stretch the limits of what's legal.

Oh yeah, I got to read it before they took 'em.

There was something I wanted to talk about. The format you've chosen, I don't know. It's fine that it's really free. It works well in the part about Murree, but afterward in the part about puberty, I don't think the style works as well. Don't you think it sounds kind of superficial? And the way you've got me talking makes me sound completely nuts.

Are you sure? OK, I mean, I'm no college professor, but I don't talk like some punk either.

You've written *y'know* and *right* a lot. Isn't it a bit too much?

You should've brought a tape recorder, then we could've checked how I actually talk. But maybe it's best to leave it. Once it's on tape, then . . . no, better keep going with the notebook. But if you can, it'd be good to be a bit more artistic, if you know what I mean.

And another thing I've been thinking about: we're always talking about me.

Yeah, yeah, of course, but I feel selfish only talking about myself. Can't we talk about you this time, then we'll carry on working next week?

Where were we?

Right, after junior high. I told you I didn't get an apprenticeship, didn't I?

As you can imagine, my Pakistani name doesn't exactly open any doors in Norway. Tariq Khan, right. We'll put that application at the bottom of the pile. Not that I had the best grades either.

I took Junior High 3 at school. It's like a substitute for kids who don't get an apprenticeship.

Yeah, I passed everything, but without a certificate from an apprenticeship you don't really have a good start on any career path. But I had to find something. Not so much for the money, but 'cause Mom started to get crazy about me doing nothing.

No, no. I wasn't really doing nothing. I was just working outside the system. I thought if I got a job, maybe Mom would calm down, right.

Since I was doing my business across the border anyway, it made sense to get a job over in Sweden.

Maxi Food in Nordby Shopping Center, Strømstad. Huge place, maybe a couple hundred employees. And Nils already worked there. A place like that's a total magnet for foreigners. Tons of foreigners work there—at the bottom, of course. The jobs the Norwegians and Swedes can't be bothered to do are left for us. And, of course, Pilla—Nils—but he's a foreigner whatever country he's in.

No, part-time.

I wouldn't say that, but it was an OK job. People need food, even if the redneck bargain hunters and the masses of meat people stuff themselves with drove me crazy. Y'know, when I had the closing shift we didn't get paid overtime, so if you were slow balancing your register, you actually ended up working for free. I thought it was unfair. I remember I told the boss—nice guy actually—but he just said that those were the rules, take it or leave it. So I got a group of us together, and we made it a competition.

Twenty minutes before closing we got everything ready, balanced all the registers except one. We found all the customers who were still shopping and asked if we could help them find what they wanted, stood and helped them bag their items at the checkout. Ran around like crazy, right, and then, when we closed, we balanced that last register together. One of us counted the ten-krona bills, one counted the hundreds, and so on. Our best time was four minutes after closing. All done.

Poles, Swedes, Norwegians, Africans—all sorts of foreigners. One day we played a game: every time the boss went out for a smoke break, someone got on the PA and said something in their own language. "Today, cat meat is on sale at the frozen counter" in Polish, or "Good morning, assholes" in Kurdish. We did that type of thing: lots of bullshitting.

No, everything was like before. I only worked a few days a week to make Mom happy. It didn't stop me from doing my own business on the side and partying at night.

One morning someone called me and said they wanted to fight.

Don't know, some rednecks from Aremark.

There'd been a party the day before, and Carlos had checked out a girl who was clearly with one of them. I didn't actually have anything to do with it, just kinda noticed what was going on. But anyway, it was me they called. Said they could take me. "We'll be at your house in a while." *OK,* I thought. Then I started to call people.

No, not them.

I called some of Cato's buddies who lived in the area. Asked them to hurry. Then I went and got Dad's old ax from the shed. Cato's people were on the way, but I was still alone when I saw four hicks walking toward me in the street. The thing is, I wasn't afraid. I don't know if that's good or bad. But I just walked straight toward them totally alone, and I was grinning, I remember, gripping the ax handle. It must have freaked them out to see a guy with an ax coming at them grinning. One of the rednecks, the king of cow shit himself, was in front and wanted to talk with me, right. He wanted to argue first, but I swung the ax right away. Whoosh. He jumped back. Then I swung the blunt end and got him on the nose. Not pretty. The others tried to close in, but I just swung the ax like a madman and they stayed back. Then, all of a sudden, some of Cato's people showed up. They did pretty well with their baseball bats.

What do you think? We chased them away.

Kushtrim didn't live far away, and he'd seen the whole thing. There was a lot of talk; the rumors spread. Suddenly it was six guys from Aremark who'd tried to take me. Then it was twelve. The myth about how I swung the ax got bigger and bigger; people began to talk about it in town. And you know what? I liked it. I didn't have anything against people being scared of me. It opened up new opportunities. I climbed a few rungs up the ladder. Took the business up a notch. In the meantime, Cato got put in jail, and I had to start ferrying dope across the border myself. Carlos and I worked with a lot of people, but nobody was the clear leader. So I grabbed the job. Got people to work for me. Carlos too. Cocky youngsters came along wanting to look cool and get some street cred. I gave them jobs. Got them to beat up my competitors in the market. Found ways to squeeze others out of business. Eat or be eaten, eat or be eaten, eat, eat, eat.

You get numb. You get cold. I didn't cut people any slack. I'd even ask Nils to beat up people he knew because they hadn't paid in time. He started to complain, but he always did what I said. Ali said I'd turned into a tyrant. We were sitting in Carlos's garage. I stood up slowly and looked at him. Just looked at him. "OK, OK, sorry," he said. Then I sat down again.

At home, Mom didn't know what I was up to. We ate dinner together, and in the evenings we often sat in the living room talking or watching

TV. She isn't like a typical Pakistani parent with expectations that their children have to be doctors or lawyers or engineers. But she started to notice things were slipping. Asked questions, you know. "Why are you out so late?" or "How do you have enough money to buy all these new clothes?" And she'd notice when I was busy with something. When we ate dinner and I was busier checking my phone than talking to her or Little Brother. She didn't like that. Sometimes she stayed up late waiting for me to come home. The worst was when some sort of fine arrived in the mail, which, of course, she'd see before me. She'd give me such a look, you know. Nobody wants to disappoint their mom.

But what hurt most was when Carlos turned on me. The day it happened, he'd hung a hammock across the garage loft and was in a good mood when I showed up. I explained that a payment was missing. It was one of our boys, a guy who'd always showed up and paid on time. He and Carlos had started hanging out a bit, they'd become friends, and he was part of the gang. It was the first time he'd fucked up. "Teach him a lesson," I said. Carlos always listened to me, always did what I said, but that time he didn't answer. Just lay perfectly still in his new hammock. "Beat him up and get the dough," I said. He disentangled himself from the hammock. Rubbed his eyes. "You know what? No way, man. No. Fuck that. He's a friend. It's just not like us to be so fucking hard." "What do you mean, hard? The world's like that. You eat or get eaten." I didn't even believe that myself anymore, that thing about eating. It was bullshit. But I continued anyway. "I don't give a fuck what you think about him. Go and fucking beat him up." He said I wasn't myself anymore. That I couldn't call myself his brother if I carried on like that.

"Fuck you." That was all I had to say.

Islam wasn't something that came to me suddenly.

Quickly, maybe, yeah. But not suddenly.

My mom isn't very religious, but my uncle had started practicing more and more. Right after that episode with Carlos, Mom said my uncle wanted me to go with him to an Islam Net conference in Oslo. She'd noticed I was feeling down and wanted to suggest something positive, so she'd talked with my uncle about how to get me on a better track. I really only went to keep her happy.

When my uncle came to get me, I was sitting on the windowsill in my room smoking a joint out the window. I was looking at the train tracks and thinking, *Two parallel lines can never meet, right, but maybe they cross each other eventually, just a really long way away. Or maybe not. What do we know about what's far away?* I thought things like that. And while I was sitting there contemplating, my uncle drove up in his gray Mazda, so I put out the joint and shut the window. I didn't really know what he was taking me to, just something about Islam in Oslo.

He was fiddling with the car stereo when I came out. When he saw me he always stretched out his arms like a starfish and shouted loudly, "Tariq, how's it going?" My uncle was always such a positive guy. Always enthusiastic, even when things were totally fucked up. He came and visited me in prison one time, and even then he thought everything was fantastic—good system, and super guards, and brilliant that I had the chance to think about life and get educated in the prison school system. It never stops really.

He was wearing his *shalwar kamiz*, prayer cap and everything. I'd never seen my uncle like that before. I remember Mom was standing in the doorway joking about his new style. And my uncle was just happy while Mom was shaking her head about her brother.

Yeah, we drove, and he eventually got his car stereo sorted out, so he played a Koran recital all the way down the E6. Talked about how powerful it was for him to have found the right path, and I was like, OK, whatever. When my uncle asked me whether I was looking forward to the conference, I just nodded. "Yeah, yeah, it's gonna be good." And then he went over to his usual jokes about blondes, which he told over and over again and which I pretended to have never heard before.

That year, the conference was in Ekeberg Hall, but my uncle got a bit lost. He's from Oslo, but he didn't have a clue how to get there coming from Østfold. I tried to tell him we should get into the left lane at Tusenfryd, but he got stressed, so I thought, *OK,* and I leaned back and let him drive through Oslo city center. Once there he took more detours, but I didn't say anything. I just looked out the window and fell into the rhythm of the Koran recital. Still a bit stoned. I stared at everyone we passed driving through the center. Colorless winter faces. People were buzzing around without any purpose. And behind it all what Carlos had said gnawed at me—that I wasn't his brother anymore.

When we finally arrived, my uncle said we were late. He parked and wanted us to hurry. But he was limping at the time—something with his foot—and I wasn't in a rush, you know; I wanted to stretch my legs, feel the winter sun. When we came in, it was time for prayer. The place was full of people, and everyone was going to pray. Because we were late, we had to stand at the very back, and right next to me was one of the famous Islamists, but I don't want to drop names.

Then it started. A guy called Green, Abdur-Raheem Green is the full name. He's actually a convert. I think he's from England, or maybe Australia, I don't really remember. He gave a lecture about 2Pac. At first I thought, *Y'know, this is gonna be embarrassing. A blond guy with a long beard and tunic standing there giving a lecture about 2Pac in a sports hall with bad acoustics. Good luck with that.*

My uncle was totally into it. He obviously didn't even know who 2Pac was. I was just shaking my head. But that guy, Green, he was smart. He took one of the songs, "Only God Can Judge Me," and went through the whole text. Discussed the theology, y'know? Who can judge whom, how, why. Took things from Christianity and compared them with Islam, showed the similarities, differences, and it was all in relation to 2Pac.

There was nothing I listened to more than 2Pac, right, so the talk was tailor-made for me. Green said there was no excuse for not pulling yourself together, even though 2Pac says he was bound to end up in the shit 'cause he got dealt a bad hand and had social problems.

That hit me. I'd say that was the seed.

I worked things out with Carlos. "You're right," I said. I think he was shocked when I said that. We were brothers again. We kept partying. Kept dealing.

One morning—it must have been after a party 'cause Carlos and I were sitting smoking a morning-after joint in his garage. When we were with other people, Carlos always found the right music. He always knew how to get a party going—just put on the right music. I'd actually say it was a talent of his. But when it was only him and me, he'd put on, I don't know, weird stuff. He'd put on opera, for example, or African music, or some eighties synth pop. Always something new he was just getting into. I couldn't be bothered to protest, 'cause he'd just say that I was narrow-minded and had to broaden my horizons. So I let him carry on. He'd hooked up some lights to his sound system since we'd last hung out. LEDs in different colors that lit up according to the frequency of the music. We had our feet on the table and were surfing, each reading our own screen. Carlos started looking up something about the brain and how it gets affected by different drugs. Found 3-D models of drug molecules and watched them spin around on the screen like spaceships. He always wanted to show me stuff—look at this, or this. In the end, he decided to find a complete overview of all the types of drugs you can take. A huge diagram, and we could check off nearly the whole list, I think. But then we found DMT, dimethyltryptamine. We didn't know anything about that. The Internet said it was supposed to be one of the sickest things you could take. You know, it could take you the furthest away from reality. Carlos read about a Native American tribe who tripped on DMT from sacred plants, while I started to read about the effects of DMT, that it was like a kind of dream, something from another world. Then I started to look for connections. DMT, dreams, and in the end death. I got goose bumps, right, because it said the brain excretes DMT naturally when we die. Injects it into our systems. And I thought, *Why? There's no reason to inject tons of drugs into your head when you're dying.*

Here it comes. I know this sounds a bit strange, but that's when I started making connections between Islam and life after death. What if DMT was actually the scientific explanation for life after death? It fit so well with what we'd read, that whoever takes DMT feels like time stops and they see things from another reality. So I connected it to Islam, you see? Everything I'd heard at the Islam Net conference, about life after death and Judgment Day.

No, Carlos just said I was way off base. "What do you mean, Islam?" He was sitting and reading about the Mayans and making up theories about DMT and the Mayan calendar, which was maybe, I don't know, several thousand years old. So we each went our way. We found our own explanations. Sometimes we stopped and tried to explain our theories, but we each thought that the other one was totally out of his mind. I got up and walked around the garage to think more clearly, felt I was onto something, while Carlos just continued searching on the Internet. When I sat down again, Carlos had already placed the order, downloaded a recipe and everything.

A couple of weeks later, I'd forgotten the whole thing, but I smelled something strong as I walked toward Carlos's garage. And there he was, standing in the garage like some badass chemistry professor in his lab, boiling out DMT from some ayahuasca plants he'd gotten in the mail. It stank like a meth lab, but to be totally honest, I think Carlos liked playing chemist. Eventually he ended up with a brown clump that looked like earwax, and that's what we were supposed to smoke.

When you smoke DMT, it only lasts for ten minutes or so. We took turns while the other one kept watch. You completely disappear. Hallucinate. I remember I inhaled deeply, sat back in my chair, and closed my eyes. Suddenly I was in a cathedral. One moment everything was perfectly silent before I shot like a rocket through the mosaics on the wall and out into space. There I saw a herd of glowing horses galloping around. The planets were singing in the background—deep vibes. There was more, but it's like when you dream, you don't remember everything when you wake up.

It's not like I think the images I saw have anything to do with Islam. But at the time I was really searching, naive, fell for all sorts of things. Put together DMT, Islam, and Judgment Day . . . it brought me closer to Islam. Gave me a little push at least. You know that saying "All roads lead to Rome"? Well, many roads lead to Mecca too.

One day there was a knock at the door. I'd seen him from the window, an older Somali guy who was going around to Muslim families and inviting them to the mosque for prayer. You know, some people are just 100 percent good. Just like there are those happy Christians, this Somali man was a happy Muslim. There's a movement within Islam that does stuff like that—*tablighi*; it's a bit like the evangelicals.

Not pushy, just nice. That was the problem really. I always felt guilty when I said I couldn't go. When I saw him coming, I usually went upstairs and asked Mom to say I wasn't home. But this time I wasn't quick enough; he'd seen me at the window. And when he knocked on the door, I didn't want to disappoint him.

So I went to Friday prayer. I saw Arbi, the Chechnyan, in the mosque. He'd actually invited me to prayer after training a few times, but I'd refused and hadn't really thought that much about him going to mosque. It was a real surprise to see him there. But the most important thing wasn't who was there. The most important thing was the feeling I got when I prayed. It was like pulling the plug in a bathtub. Glug. Then all the crap just starts draining out.

After that I started going to the mosque once in a while. Little by little. One plus one plus one. But at the same time, I kept on partying.

There was a house party at some girl's place. Huge house—her dad was a stockbroker or something. The whole place was glossy with white leather sofas and glass tables, everything was kind of shiny. Carlos and I had drugs for the whole party. Noses full of dust. We were high as kites, the usual stuff. And I remember we were sitting on those white leather sofas, Carlos and me, with a load of girls around us. The others were smiling, but I felt uneasy. Like it wasn't enough. Then I noticed this guy. Rich white trash with a slick coif. He was buzzing around like a fly, jealous of all the attention we were getting. I don't know, there was just something I didn't like about him. I called to him. Waved him over. "Hey, you, take my foot and kiss it." He didn't understand what was happening, did he, but he immediately got scared shitless. Maybe he knew who I was, what I was capable of. Then I stretched out one foot. The guy went down on all fours, and Carlos started to smirk.

Yeah, he kissed my foot. Without saying anything else I stretched out the other foot. Carlos fell into a laughing fit, and when the rich kid kissed foot number two, everyone around us started laughing too. "Right, go away, bitch." And then I pushed his face away with my foot.

On the way home I felt empty. *That's not me*, I thought. *What am I doing?* The power that had made me feel good earlier was starting to make me feel sick. I didn't go straight home but wandered around by the river, behind the Tista Mall. Walked up and down. I'd been to all the parties, I'd tried all the drugs, my wad of money was too thick for my wallet, I could get all the girls I wanted, but everything was empty.

Twenty years old, part-time job at Maxi Food, small-time crook, on his way to nothing. Well done, Tariq. I'd tried pouring on more drugs, more drinks, but the emptiness just got bigger and bigger. And in that emptiness, the seed began to grow. Totally unexpected. I actually think I prayed to Allah while I was walking along the river. It was like jumping off a speeding train.

I had to take control of my own soul, or *nafs*. The imam suggested I go to a *tablighi*, an event where people come from other towns or countries and gather to worship Allah. You even spend the night in the mosque.

Yes, almost the whole time inside. A bit like a monk.

The lights were switched off; there was a little sunlight shining in through the windows. Red carpets, almost fluffy. I liked the part about taking your socks off. Or what's the word? *Bliss*. I felt bliss. There on the carpet, barefoot. On one side there was a low bench in front of a sink with two faucets. Only cold water, and the floor was always wet under the basin. You had to crouch and do *wudu*—you know, the ritual cleansing. There wasn't actually much space in the mosque, even in the bathrooms. It was a constant reminder of our small place in the universe. An exercise in humility.

During the *tablighi* I sat on the carpet and read the Koran, but I had to keep getting up. I wasn't used to sitting still. My body needed to move. I paced around on the red carpet and then sat down again. You could hear creaking, it was a wooden building, and the imam lived in the apartment upstairs. I looked up at the clock with the six faces. The hands moved on one of them, while the other five showed the prayer times. I realized I was getting tired of sitting, so I started dhikr, when you repeat something over and over again. Praise God. I said the words aloud. All the names of God I could remember. And that's when I felt it. That the seed had grown, pushed its way through the soil, and that the bud was opening. Yes, I think I'd say it was the most wonderful experience I've ever had. Better than any drug. *This is what I want,* I thought. *I want Islam.*

When you experience something so strong, something so beautiful, of course you want to repeat the experience. You could say I was hooked. I tried to reproduce the feeling I'd had, go back to the same kind of inner peace, the same deep spirituality, but it was never as strong again.

After that I cut out drugs and partying. Mom was really happy. But she didn't like me growing a beard or nagging her to pray and wear a hijab. "I'll do whatever I like," she said.

For my part I started to get up early and go to the mosque for the *fajr* prayer. I remember in the beginning, about four years ago now, when I was on my way home from the mosque I'd see all sorts of colors in the sky as the sun was struggling to rise. The air was so fresh and I felt so clear, so pure as I wandered through town while everyone else was still sleeping. I kinda felt like, I dunno, like I was closer to God.

I still pray five times a day.

Yes, now you ask. At first I wasn't sure if I should bring my prayer mat to prison. I was paranoid in the beginning. I thought they'd watch all the little things, and it would be best not to have religious symbols or anything. You get a bit—what should I say?—you feel like they're always suspicious of you.

There are a lot of Muslims in prison, and we have an imam who comes every Friday, so we actually have a chance to worship. But y'know, a lot of the evidence in my case was about religion, and my interpretation of Islam. So it's difficult to separate one thing from another. When you're in prison because of violence, they say, "OK, he's calmed down a bit, that's progress, this guy's back on the right track." But when it comes to what I'm here for, how do you measure progress? When I stop praying? I don't know. But anyway, I shook off the worst of the paranoia, so now I have a prayer mat in my cell.

Yeah, I get up for *fajr* every day. Or almost every day.

Sometimes I go back to sleep afterward, but other times I just stay on my mat and let it be my place in the world. I still try to get back to that feeling I had in the beginning, when prayer gave me such a deep sense of peace.

But from my cell, I can only see a tiny piece of sky on the other side of a window I can't open. It's not the same. In the end I just shut my eyes and let the chaos in my head take over.

I didn't talk about becoming religious at first, but one day Carlos saw me wearing my kufi—y'know, the prayer cap. Besides, he'd noticed I was different. I was calmer, more present. Simply more human.

We'd been close friends for a long time, Carlos and I, running our businesses side by side. But when it came to money, we were all business. There was no messing around on that score. At the time he owed me quite a bit of money, but I told him not to worry about it anymore. Carlos didn't understand—so many thousands of kroner, right. But I didn't care about money anymore. I think Carlos looked up to me a bit after that. He was like, *What's going on with him?*

Later I asked Carlos why he'd converted to Islam, and he said it was that one time. He thought I'd showed . . . what was it he used to say? Magnanimity. That was his favorite word. *Magnanimity.* Whatever, he'd gotten inspired.

No, he converted on his own. It happened while I was away on vacation with Mom and Little Brother. He'd asked about Islam, and I'd recommended he check out Abdur-Raheem Green online. But other than that, he figured it out by himself. When I came back from vacation, I saw that he'd posted some stuff online where he was wearing a kufi and had changed his name to Yahya. It was the talk of the town, you might say. "Hi, did you hear that Carlos has converted?" Everyone had an opinion about it, either positive or skeptical.

Then I met him, and it was suddenly, "*Salaam aleikum*, brother." I was totally shocked, asked what had happened. And he answered, "*Alhamdulillah*, it's great; everything's fantastic, *mashallah*."

He'd been to Friday prayer, and he'd recited the *shahada*, "testimony," the first pillar of Islam. He told me people had cheered. Some people even started to cry. It was so intense he felt like a lightning bolt had passed through him and purified everything; that's how he put it. And afterward he got loads of gifts from the people in the mosque. Got invited to dinner with them. Talk about being well received. He felt like a king.

Y'know, there's a tenderness in the mosque. People care about each other. That was new to us.

To be totally honest, I'd slipped away from Islam a bit just then. I wasn't praying so much anymore. So I wasn't overly enthusiastic. Just kinda, "Yeah, yeah, good for you." But Carlos wanted me to go to prayer with him now that he'd converted. I couldn't say no, could I? Later on Carlos was the one who got lazy, and it was me who told him to come to pray. We swapped roles.

For us, Islam was like growing up. Finding a grown-up way to talk. A grown-up way to think. A grown-up way of existing. Ali and Kushtrim, for example, felt like we'd moved on, and they were left hanging in a childish place, partying and stuff. And Carlos and I were always asking if they wanted to come to the mosque, and we made sure to guilt them when they said no. I'd tell Kushtrim things like "Yeah, that chick is hot, but hell is hotter." In the end, Kushtrim and Ali came with us; Arbi had already been going to mosque anyhow.

Yeah, the Chechen. I knew Arbi pretty well, 'cause I'd seen him at training nearly every day for a long time. He could be hard during training, stone-faced Arbi. But in the mosque, he was totally warmhearted, and when he laughed, his whole face lit up.

Arbi and I opened up to each other, talked about how we could get on in life, cut out the bad habits, the parties. We even went and talked with the imam about it, wanted to talk away all our sins. But the imam didn't want to hear about every single mistake we'd ever made. He told a story, that one about the father who takes his unruly son to a wise man who then asks the boy to pull up a small plant. All right. The boy grabs it and pulls it up. Then the wise man asks him to pull up a slightly larger plant. OK, a bit harder, but fine. And in the end, he asks the boy to pull up a tree. "Don't give your vices deep roots," the imam said.

I think it must have been late summer, because on the way home Arbi tried to pull up a little tree, and the leaves were still green. So . . . late summer 2012? Several of us had gotten into Islam then and had started to practice more regularly.

It was taboo to smoke weed, especially in front of the others. But some of them still did it anyway, secretly. Two guys would kinda wink at each other and go around the corner and smoke. When they came back, eyes totally bloodshot, they'd say they'd been shopping or something. But we always knew and scolded them. You know, people falter. We were a bit half-baked. We weren't quite there. Actually, I don't think we were ever totally there, so it's not true to say there was an Islamist environment around us, really. Yeah, maybe in Oslo. They were more organized there. But in Halden, we faltered, we doubted.

Nils was totally uninterested in Islam. Religion wasn't for him. But we still hung out together. We went out with the boat and stuff. Carlos, being the new convert, tried to get Nils interested too, but had to drop it. "You'll burn in hell, Nils; you'll burn." But Nils didn't care. "Let me burn, then. Does it look like I care?"

Carlos and I were in touch with the leaders of the mosque, volunteered when they needed help. Why not? It's God's house after all, so we might as well clean and vacuum and stuff. One time we were up on the roof with a third brother getting rid of some moss, and that third guy, a Norwegian convert, he slipped off. It looked totally sick because he did a sort of somersault as he fell. Carlos went over to the edge and called down, "Brother, what happened? Are you OK?" But the guy had landed on his feet. He was in total shock that he hadn't hurt himself, couldn't quite believe it. So, as you can imagine, he went straight inside to pray. We laughed our heads off up on the roof; the whole thing was so crazy. Carlos thought Allah must've helped the guy do the somersault.

The thing with Carlos is that when he first starts something, he's 100 percent into it. He read the Koran like crazy, even got quite good pronunciation after a while. At one point, he got it into his head that it was his duty to bring Halden back to religion. He talked about Allah to people on the street, knocked on doors, and started to correct other Muslims about how they were praying in the mosque. He stepped over the line sometimes. I had to have a word with him about it once. You know, those new converts.

I read about Islam online. My family's actually more Sufi, to the extent that you can even call them religious at all, but there isn't much about Sufism online. You find more about Salafism. Besides, Sufism is complicated. Or it's what I'd call abstract. It's difficult to understand what they actually mean. Salafists, on the other hand, are more concrete; do this, don't do that. They're easier to relate to. Besides they have a strict, literal interpretation of Islam. I felt the stricter it was, the more truthful it was. Salafists want to get back to the roots, to Islam in the time of the Prophet.

If you're searching for something online, it sends you in a certain direction, doesn't it? The system stores information about you, what you last searched, puts in cookies, works out its algorithms, and then suggests videos for you based on your earlier searches. You go two steps along one path or another because you're curious, and then the system pulls you even further along. For me, that path was Salafism.

I was given more responsibility in the warehouse at Maxi Food, drove the truck around, was more independent. Moved stuff and was in charge. In the end I didn't even think of it as food—more like playing *Tetris* on a huge scale. Products in, products out, left, right. I'd drive around in the truck working totally on my own. And when it was time for prayer, I had a vibrating alarm on my phone. I'd completely stop. Leave the truck where it was and go to pray.

In the locker room.

In the corner.

Sometimes other people were there too, but it depended on what sort of shift it was. I especially remember a Senegalese guy. Earlier in his life, he was on his way to becoming a really great soccer player, had lots of women, partied all the time, and made good money. But guess what? He started to feel the whole thing was fake. Felt he was indebted to God somehow. So he dropped the charade and started at Maxi Food instead. You know, the guy used to be a street kid in Senegal, right, and he'd prayed and prayed and prayed for a better future. Then he hit the jackpot, ended up in Norway as an adopted child. He figured he owed God something.

Whatever, the Senegalese guy and I and two Somalis, we always went to pray when it was time, and afterward in the store we felt really great. It gives you a sort of spiritual boost when you pray, you know. The other Muslims that worked there didn't practice so much, but when they saw us coming out from prayer, they felt a bit guilty, always said they'd join us the next time. Some of them did join after a while. But that Senegalese guy, he never missed a prayer. I remember he said we were doing halal work and that we had to do it right. Not to please the boss, but to please God. "God sees everything, but the boss doesn't even notice if you're paying attention to the details." And that made an impression on me. Just stupid things like when there was some plastic garbage under one of the racks, or people were careless with the cleaning, the boss would never have said anything, but I still did everything as well as I could.

One day the shit really hit the fan. Someone had drawn a swastika in the staff bathroom and written *ALLAH* over it in huge letters. To be honest, I thought it was really sad. Nobody knew who'd done it, and I really didn't want to talk about it with any of the Swedes or Norwegians. I let it go. But then, in the break room during lunch, we heard someone shout, "What the fuck is this?" It was the Senegalese guy, who was usually so calm. He'd completely lost it. "Hey. Who the fuck wrote this? If you're man enough, identify yourself, you cowardly pig." And then I remember he said something like, "Just wait, this is gonna blow up in your faces one day." He was freaking pissed, that guy, but the union rep went over and tried to calm him down. There was also a Somali guy— God, what a hypocrite—who tried to say, "Brother, brother . . ." and ease the situation, but he was one of those people who didn't really care about Islam, and then there he was with "Brother, brother." So yeah, things like that. You notice tension everywhere really.

I was allowed to wear headphones when I was driving the truck around the warehouse. I'd gradually stopped listening to music as I became more of a believer. I listened to debates and the news instead. Nearly everything was Islam, Islam, Islam, right—cartoons here, terror there, and in the middle of it all there was one of the many debates about freedom of speech. Again and again, it's their problem if they feel offended and so on. That really bothered me. I wondered why. Where does the urge to offend come from? While I was thinking of those things, I realized something. Why is this being discussed really? I thought it had to be because society wanted to get rid of us. Weed us out. Do you know that feeling, when you realize you're a weed?

The whole point of stirring up debate was to create hate and distance between Norwegians and Muslims. And then came, well, I don't remember if it was the newspaper *Dagbladet* that printed the caricatures, or if it was the film, y'know, *Innocence of Muslims*. And I remember that a group of Muslims gathered after prayer in a parking lot, and we discussed what was going on. One of my friends made a parallel to Breivik and the mass shooting at Utøya. He reminded us that the reason Breivik shot all those kids was because he felt they were supporting Muslims coming to Norway. Then he started to draw parallels between Breivik and all the shit we had to take as Muslims. "Is this country just full of Breiviks?" We felt under attack, you know?

Yeah, then I came across something on Facebook about a demonstration in Youngstorget and decided to go and support it. It was in September sometime, in 2012. I got Kushtrim, the Albanian, to come with me, and we went to Oslo. The whole journey we talked about how the focus should be on criticizing terrorists, not religion.

We arrived early; there were only a few people there, but the police were everywhere. They were standing and watching, and there was a helicopter buzzing over us. They'd even hired security guards. Talk about feeling under suspicion. I thought it was going to be a really bad turnout. But then he arrived—what's he called again, the one from the Rabita Mosque? Aftab—with a few other imams. And they played a song over the PA system, a *nashid*, in honor of the Prophet, peace be upon him. In five minutes the square was totally packed. People flooded in from all corners.

I don't think they were particularly religious people. Just normal Muslims who felt hurt. One group was really angry; it was a group of slightly older people; they shouted some words to praise the Prophet, but otherwise, they were quite normal Muslims. Then Aftab started speaking: "I understand we're all angry"—y'know, he was trying to calm people down. What a sellout. And the mayor of Oslo, Fabian Stang, was there. And that priest, or bishop—the one from the cathedral. He said he shared the frustrations of the Muslim people, blah, blah, blah.

I dunno. It was as if the people up on the podium couldn't really express what those of us listening were feeling. Suddenly I heard someone right behind me yell with all his might, as loud as he could, *"Allahu akbar,"* and it felt much better to hear his call than listen to the people at the podium being fake. Then I remember a guy walked by, a druggie or something, on the upper part of Youngstorget, where all the policemen were standing. He managed to sneak past the police, and in a moment of silence he yelled, "Freedom of speech!" across the square, and then he went and hid behind the police again like a coward. Really funny when there are six thousand Muslims in front of you. What a guy. But this was a diversion. The point was that we felt we were being watched by the police, suspected, with helicopters and stuff.

The day after there was almost nothing about us in the papers. All of the press had been outside the American embassy where the hard-core Islamists had their demonstration. At that time, I knew almost nothing about them. I hadn't even realized they were arranging their own demonstration. They got all the attention, even though they had only about one hundred people and we had six thousand. There was just a short article about us in one paper, y'know.

In one way I thought the people who'd gone to the embassy had more of an impact than we did. And that gave them more credibility, because their opinions were much clearer than the sellouts at Youngstorget. And the media's clever; they don't publish things that don't fit into their picture of the world. They're really happy if they can portray Muslims as violent extremists. Who listens to a peaceful demonstration anyway?

I forgot to talk about the Arab Spring; it was around that time. Or maybe a bit before, because it started before I began practicing Islam more seriously. You can sort out the order afterward. Whatever. When the protests started—Tunisia, Egypt, Libya—I read about the leaders in those countries, and I thought what was happening was good. *Bring them down. They're sucking the blood out of their people.* We heard that Norway was going to support the protesters, and I thought, *Hey, it's awesome that Europe's following this. Europe's supporting the protesters. Down with the dictator pigs.*

By the time I got more into religion, it had been a while since the government troops in Syria had fired the first shots against demonstrators. It had started getting really ugly down there, and it got worse and worse. At the same time, I was having what I'd call my Islamic awakening. So it was religion on the one side and politics on the other. But they still hadn't mixed together.

At Maxi Food I was always listening to my headphones. It was about Syria all the time. The stories trickled in. Mass murder. Rape. Children dying here. Children dying there. Just things like that. One day I got asked to help bring the meat into the meat department, and I'd just heard on the radio that Assad had bombed his own people with planes. And there I was standing in front of a bunch of slaughtered animals hanging right in front of me.

Wherever I went, it was Syria. TV, Syria. Facebook, Syria. Radio, Syria. Meeting other people, Syria. Friday prayer, Syria. I remember one of the imams called Assad the son of a donkey and raged against how he was slaughtering his people. I went into the mosque in Oslo a couple of times with my uncle, and it was just the same. Syria, Syria, Syria. Collect money. Collect clothes. I gave what I could. I also started doing a collection box myself. Again, not to impress other people, but for God. God sees everything, doesn't He? I even took responsibility for handing out collection boxes to other people. I was a collection box pusher. Every time we had a visit from family, I asked if they wanted to take a collection box and do a round as well.

We started hearing about the first people who went down there—first one, then two, five, nine, twelve, suddenly fifteen, suddenly twenty. And you know what? I thought it was good they were going. May God have mercy on them. It's a big thing to sacrifice your life to help someone in need. In the beginning there were a lot of Norwegians who thought that too, that it was good to go there and help.

One day, before visiting my uncle in Oslo, I went into the Islamic Culture Center Mosque to pray. And guess what the topic was? Syria. After prayer I noticed a group of young people sitting in a circle in the corner. As I walked by, one of them looked up and smiled. "Brother, come and sit. We're discussing something important." I really didn't want to disturb them, but as I was invited, I said hi, *"Salaam aleikum,"* and sat down. There were maybe ten of them, most with beards—some long, some short—some wearing tunics, others in sweatpants, and I remember they were staring down at the floor almost all the time. There was a serious atmosphere.

They were talking about how they would collect money and help people in Syria. One of them said a new organization had been set up to send money. And then they asked me where I was from. "Halden," I said. There was a Kosovo Albanian, Burim, who said he would come to Halden one day and we could maybe collect money together. Asked whether I could help with stuff. I gave Burim my number, and that was that. Then I left for my uncle's.

My uncle was also devout, so later in the day we went to the mosque again. A different mosque, a little more Sufi, the one on Akerberg Street if you've ever been there.

Yeah, the blue one. There were some young people there too, sitting in a circle, and I got to talking with them as well. But the only thing they were concerned with was how best to practice Islam in their everyday lives. It was totally detail oriented. How to live most like the Prophet. How to hold your fingers around your arm when praying. How to eat. How to cut your nails like the Prophet. It was bordering on irritating. A little pushy. I guess I thought Muslims today have more important things to discuss than how the Prophet cut his nails.

The worst thing was that the Police Security Service, the PSS, later questioned those guys.

Well, we'd exchanged phone numbers, right. They'd asked if I would come to the next meeting. And I tried to say that it was a long way from Halden and stuff, but they texted me like crazy. So when the cops got me and went through my phone, they found loads of old messages from them and pulled them into the station—you know, the nail-cutting group.

No, no, I don't mean to be nasty about them. Seriously, they were good people. But you know, people were being massacred. It was hypocritical to pray for Syria for two or three minutes and be done with it. It's kinda like Islam is a body. If there's pain in one place, then the whole body suffers.

Feet apart. Shoulder to shoulder. Lay your head, the most holy point, down low. Stand side by side and submit to Allah. That strengthens the brotherhood.

It was Carlos, me, and Arbi, and then Ali and Kushtrim joined us. Liridon had moved to Sweden to follow his soccer career, so he'd been out of the picture for a long time. We gradually saw less of Nils. But yeah, a group of, what was it, five people. We got closer. We pushed each other to pray and to observe Islamic rules. We stopped partying entirely.

When you get down to it, Islam wasn't the glue that held us together. The glue was collective frustration. Or *anger* is maybe a better word. We were all angry. Of course, Ali didn't graduate high school. He was working in a food store and got a lot of crap from his boss. Before we'd tell him, "Hey, Ali, just screw that son of a bitch; he's garbage." But then we changed our vocab. "What do you expect? He's *kafir*, so he doesn't know any better." *Kafir*, that's like an infidel. And in the end that changed to "He's an enemy of Allah, may God curse him." The day after we'd said that, his boss had a stroke, and half his face was paralyzed.

Yeah, it's true. And Ali was like, "Shit, it works."

We were, or we thought we were, oppressed, right, and that God was for the oppressed.

Arbi also had a tough time at work. He was an apprentice in an asphalt business, and they got pissed every time he went to pray, even if it only took, what, a few minutes. They threw Muslim jokes around. When Arbi told us about it, he wasn't really complaining, he just said, "They probably don't mean anything bad by it." But I noticed it stressed him out. And he got zero support from the union reps; they mostly just kept needling each other. "But you don't complain about your landlord," Arbi said. He'd come to Norway as a refugee; he figured he'd move to a Muslim country if it all got too bad. Actually, it was only Islamic rules that kept him from laying into them at work. He took it out at training instead. Nobody wanted to spar with Arbi when he'd had a bad day at work.

Yeah, we all did kickboxing together. Arbi and I had started with Thai boxing and mixed martial arts as well, and we did weights. Arbi got really hooked on MMA; he was good at wrestling and pinned me all the time.

That New Year's Eve, into 2013, we decided to ditch the celebrations and work out instead. We didn't want to follow the Christian calendar. So we ran up the hill by the fortress in the middle of the night, Arbi, Carlos, and I, while the fireworks lit up the sky, and we pretended like we didn't care. We were totally pumped, red in the face, and then Arbi wanted to wrestle at the top of the fortress. He grinned and said, "Come on, you wimps." Carlos gave it a go, but he didn't stand a chance. So I jumped in to help Carlos, and Arbi totally lost it. He let out a roar and nearly managed to pin me as well, but eventually we glued the Chechen to the cold ground. I lay diagonally over his torso, and Carlos had his ankles. "Cowards," Arbi said. But when he was on his feet again, he grinned and wanted to wrestle more.

Arbi was a die-hard fan of MMA. He invited Carlos and me home to his basement to watch the fights, broadcast live from the United States, at, like, four in the morning or something. It was a large basement with a Persian rug and dimmed lights. Just one light-brown leather sofa, which Arbi sat on, a glass table, and a couple of chairs. Bare, not much furniture, that's how we liked it. The simple life was the Salafist ideal. We sat there, ready with our halal treats from Sweden and popcorn. While we waited for the program to start, Arbi went on about how merciless the Russians had been in Chechnya, and how passive the rest of the world had been. He called the US wimps. "They look after their own interests over there," Carlos added. Classic contribution from him. Carlos had a handle on all sorts of possible conspiracy theories about the US. It wasn't something that started with Islam, even if that added fuel to the US criticism. But before Carlos started on one of his tirades about the US, Arbi got out his laptop and showed us a clip of the Chechen leader, Putin's pal. He was standing and saying something like, "I'm a good Muslim. Look, I even have a beard." We laughed and watched the clip a couple more times, but in the end we got knots in our stomachs because we knew how awful he was making life for the Muslim brothers over there.

The sugar from all the treats started to wear off, and when it was time for action, we struggled to stay awake. Arbi connected the laptop to the TV and put on pay-per-view. The MMA fighters thrashed each other, and when we could be bothered, we commented on their techniques. Arbi had a dry joke every time someone was knocked out, while I struggled to not fall asleep between each fight.

We were thirsty for knowledge. There wasn't just one imam in Halden; new ones came all the time. People from other towns. It rotated. And we asked about everything, y'know, practical things. "Should we do military service in Norway?" "What if you're visiting someone and they don't know if all the ingredients in a dish are halal?" "What's the right way to react when someone speaks badly about Islam?" But most of all, Syria, that was the thing we always asked about. How could we contribute? The answer was always the same: Pray. Collect money. Send clothes. That was all. That was what they said we could do. So we carried on with that, even though the collection boxes I handed out to my family always came back empty.

Some of us started to think the situation was deplorable.

There were totally different opinions online, more radical opinions. This was during winter, so we had a lot of time to sit in front of a screen. We sent each other videos and figured out which ones were *haqq*.

That means "the truth."

OK, can't you just put a vocab list in the back of the book?

But yeah, back to *haqq*. The videos shouldn't be pro-US, should they? Not pro-Western, not pro-Saudi either, because that was the same as being pro-US. And then there were the people who were too friendly, who didn't take the situation seriously. We ruled them out too.

We got more anti-US, but also anti-Russia. And so, naturally, we got curious about the people the Americans and Russians condemned. Who were they really? What had they done wrong? And then jihadist ideologues appeared—Maqdisi, Abu Qatada, Awlaki. The first two mostly spoke in Arabic, so we didn't get much from them. But Awlaki was American, so we could understand him. There were some old videos from when he was an imam, and he talked about the exact things I was feeling. He dared to say it out loud: Muslims had been too tolerant all through history. At the same time he was humble, with a sweet voice, not yelling like some of the Islamists do in this country. And he often started his speeches by talking about Paradise.

Yeah, he was killed by the CIA in Yemen. The first American citizen to be killed in a drone attack. And then you get extra curious. From Awlaki it's only a short step to sympathizing with Al Qaeda. Or the Taliban.

Yes, y'know, for us they represented resistance to Western oppression. It felt good to hear that the Taliban had shot American soldiers. It healed wounds in our psyche.

Sure, you could call it hate.

Turn it upside down. Take the Bataclan terrorists in Paris. Remember two of them escaped but were shot by the police a few days later? Don't you think it healed the wounds of the French people, deep down in the darkness of their hearts?

It was like that for us as well.

Right, so infidels are *kuffar*. Then we started to classify Muslims as well. Gave them labels. A *munafiq*, for example, is a hypocrite, someone who pretends he's Muslim but doesn't really care and just thinks about himself. One of the characteristics of a *munafiq* is that he doesn't keep appointments, doesn't show up, or drops out. Originally it was used when someone betrayed Islam, right? But we also used it for small things, like when someone came late to a meeting or something, especially Carlos. "Hi, Tariq. Do you actually know how to recognize a *munafiq*?" "Yeah, yeah, sorry. I know I'm late."

We used *mushrik*, or "polytheist," among other things, for Shia Muslims; we thought they worshipped not just Allah but Ali as well. Actually, we didn't really think Shia were Muslims. That was something we talked about; some people even said straight out that they were *kuffar*. Then other people said we shouldn't be *takfiri*, people who cite law to decide if other people are Muslims or *kuffar*.

We had other classifications when the talk was about Syria. Madkhali, people who blindly follow scholars and think it's wrong to overthrow a dictator. On the other side you had the Kharijites; they were a group who'd rebelled against the caliphate shortly after the time of the

Prophet. They were serious practitioners. Picky. Strict. But they were hard toward other Muslims, called them apostates and *kuffar*, killed them if they thought they'd sinned. Kharijites had little respect for scholars or authorities. They thought it was their religious duty to over-throw tyrannical leaders. But they were without scruples. You know, in the end the Kharijites ended up killing more Muslims than *kuffar*. So someone put that label on the most extreme Islamists.

Carlos threw himself into all sorts of debates without really knowing what he was talking about. One time he was totally confused after having a conversation with a Shia Muslim at a forum, talking about how they whip themselves: "The Shia are completely out there." But then he was checking out some Shia woman at the same time, right. He did that kind of thing. I told him, "You're totally nuts," but I think he was just struggling to find his way. You know, he thought he'd started to get the hang of religion, get more knowledge, but he was a bit overenthusiastic about debating, having opinions, discussing. It's just how he is. Or was.

At home Little Brother started to ask why I had such a long beard and always wore a cap. He thought it was funny. I explained it really simply. I didn't want to push anything on him. Even if he laughed at my beard, I think he liked me being home more. He was having lessons in the Koran and Urdu on Skype with an imam from Pakistan. Something Mom had arranged, but it was much more Sufi. Like Sunday school. He always lay on the sofa and dangled his legs while he Skyped with the imam, and I thought that he couldn't possibly be learning anything. But I was wrong again.

One day that guy Burim, the one from Oslo, called. He asked if he could come to Halden so we could do another collection for Syria.

I met him in the mosque in Halden. He was wearing a *shalwar kamiz* and was reading a book when I saw him. Burim knew a lot about Islam, y'know, and you respect a guy who's trying to understand his religion.

Yes, a Salafist. One hundred and forty percent Salafist.

We talked about the West, the pressures we felt, how to survive being a Muslim in Norway, how to serve Allah. He was actually most concerned about quite basic things: keeping away from bad people, going to the mosque, being good to your parents. That was that. But even though he smiled a lot, he also harbored an anger I recognized in myself. And he talked about *al-wala wal-bara*, that you should love and hate for the sake of God. You should love what God loves, and hate what God hates. In a way that was a guiding principle; we should love our Muslim brothers more than *kuffar*.

No, actually not so much about Syria apart from how it sucked and that Assad was a tyrant. He gave me two packs of collection boxes to pass out to friends and acquaintances. But I could tell by the way he spoke that he admired people who went there. But it wasn't such a huge topic between us at the beginning. The point is more that he inspired me to take my beliefs seriously. And then you knew that, OK, with him you could talk about going there and be met with understanding.

I did that, yes. But later.

It was time for the next annual Islam Net Peace Conference. I tried to get the guys to go with me, but they were all busy. I didn't want to go alone, so I went to see Carlos to pressure him. He was playing video games in the garage and tried to give me all kinds of excuses. "Wait, wait. I just want to finish this game." Said he was busy, that he was supposed to help his mom with something. Carlos hadn't helped his mom with anything in years, so I didn't buy that one. "Help your mom? Right!" Then I started saying things like, "You know the Prophet, peace be upon him, said . . ." "Yeah, yeah, I know the Prophet said that to search for knowledge, you should travel as far as China." I said that I'd already bought us tickets. Then he couldn't say no. I picked him up in the car the next day. He was ready in his tunic and kufi, and because he'd agreed to come with me, I treated him to kebabs.

That year, the conference was in the old Hasle factory, which they'd turned into an event center. We found the entrance for men. It was completely full and they'd already started, so we sat down quietly. The room was divided according to gender. Men in the front and women behind. But Carlos had to check out the women, so he kept turning around to look where they were sitting. I don't know what he was looking at, because most of the women were totally covered anyhow. But it was something left over from the old days. It takes time to get used to a new lifestyle.

From the podium? The usual. Be a good citizen, don't take loans that are interest based, live correctly in the West—things like that. But then there was one speaker, an African. He'd spoken highly of the Taliban earlier in his life, but then he'd realized that they were slaughtering people left and right, so he thought, *Wow, I'm going to take it back.* Anyway, when it was time for questions, someone in the room stood up and asked if people ought to go to Syria. Bam! Mic drop. The room went as quiet as a mouse. Then came the standard answer. "You young people should focus on your education." But the guy who'd asked the question didn't give up: "What about people who've already gone? What do you think about them?" Then the African answered that the people who go to Syria are deviants, misfits, that they're fools. That's how he labeled them. Done. But without giving any reason whatsoever. And that really hit me. He didn't justify it using the Koran or anything. Just labeled them and stopped talking. Carlos and I, we were at a place where we wanted to discuss things based on sources, right? We wanted knowledge, not personal statements.

Afterward a new scholar came to the podium, but Carlos got sick, went completely white in the face. "Hey, I need the bathroom," he said and ran out. He stayed in there forever. Maybe an hour. Eventually I went in and knocked on the bathroom door. "Are you OK, brother?" When he opened up, my God, you should have seen his face. I figured we had to get back in the car and drive home right away. No more Peace Conference for us.

On the way home, Carlos, the poor guy, asked me to stop. "What do you mean, stop?" We were in the middle of the E6 freeway. But I pulled over to the side, and Carlos got out of the car in his tunic, bent over, and threw up over the crash barrier. It would have been quite a sight for anyone driving by. And then I started to laugh. Carlos looked at me with his pale face. "What are you laughing at?" So, as you can imagine, I pulled myself together. But then he mumbled something about the kebab. That the guy who'd made the kebab was probably a Shia and wanted to poison him. Then I broke down and laughed again.

Yeah, we got home all right, but I did think about what that scholar had said, that those who went to Syria were fools. Why did imams always say it was wrong to go without giving any proper theological reasons? Suddenly I saw the logic in it. What if they aren't saying what they really think? What if the imams, the scholars, what if they're afraid to say what they really mean? I thought that if I'd been a scholar and said that people should go to Syria, and it had led to young people actually leaving, think what a huge responsibility to have weighing on your shoulders. Responsibility for all the families, for all those who died. Besides, you might get in trouble with the authorities, lose your job; maybe the police would come into the picture, maybe you'd lose your residence permit or something. You know, it's a really big responsibility to tell people that they should leave and go to war. The logical explanation had to be that the imams said one thing and meant something else. Purely and simply to protect themselves. To avoid the responsibility.

In the Koran it says that you shouldn't think of your teachers as gods, that it's only Allah who tells the truth. So, I dove into the Koran myself. I read more and more. And then I read about the Prophet's life, started to draw parallels from history to today. For example, I read that the Prophet sent a messenger to a tribe that was under the control of the Byzantine Empire. The messenger was killed on the way, and as revenge the Prophet sent three thousand men. Do you understand? To avenge one single person.

I've met a lot of people who try to sugarcoat the Prophet, to dress up his story. The Prophet was fair, he truly was, but he was no pacifist.

How far have we gotten?

OK, 2013, yeah. Spring slash summer. By then I was fed up working at Maxi Food. They wouldn't give me a full-time job, and since I didn't have my business anymore, I needed a full-time job. So I quit. But it was harder than I thought it'd be to find something new. So I started working for a temp agency. A little better paying on the Norwegian side, but mostly it was because Kushtrim and Carlos were working there. It was tough, lots of hauling and lifting.

No, we never knew if we'd have a job on any particular day. There might be a lot or none. After a month of working there, we got assigned to work in Rakkestad, far away, in a huge cold storage facility. I asked our boss at the agency if we would have to work with pigs, but he said that there wouldn't be any problem. He did make it pretty clear that the job was really hard. "Only real tough guys can handle it over there." That didn't scare us. A little free training. So we took the challenge and drove off—Carlos, me, Kushtrim, and one more guy who was actually the son of an imam in Oslo. Out in the country it was warm, but nothing was growing in the fields yet, so the earth was still bare. It was farther to Rakkestad than I thought, so I really floored it, took some risks. At one point I was passing a truck, and suddenly a car came speeding along toward me, but instead of slowing down, I sped up. Pedal to the metal, holding my breath while the son of the imam completely lost it and started praying like a madman.

We met the boss at the cold storage facility, and I swear he looked just like a zombie, pale and huge and with short, crooked bangs. Maybe he'd been in the freezer too long, you know, completely dead-faced. And completely lifeless in everything he said. Not one single degree of warmth in the guy.

"Well, boys." Like, that's how he began, even though we'd showed up on time and everything. "Hope you've dressed warmly 'cause it's cold in here. Overalls are hanging up there for over your clothes."

To be honest we didn't know exactly what we were getting into. Cold storage, OK, but it's hard to imagine how cold it really is, you know, on a beautiful day, summer on the way—sun, and then into a winter world. Lamb carcasses hung in the freezer. The zombie pointed at the dead animals and said we had to pack them in plastic, like this, lift them onto a hook, and pull them along tracks in the ceiling to the end. All right. We started, and it never seemed to end; you have no idea. It's one thing to work outside in the heat, but in there your muscles get cold. And the zombie was really tough. He didn't give us any breaks. Said we should work until we tasted blood in our mouths. What a fucking Nazi. But we kept working. Really hard. In the end our joints were completely stiff, and when we finished we were exhausted. But y'know, two minutes later the zombie boss with the pale face was there again. "We have a new shipment; get started." We had to throw packs of meat into boxes. Take the packs out of black plastic bags and chuck them in. But Carlos started sniffing around. "Brothers, I think this smells of pork." I just said, "OK, don't complain." But you know Carlos—typical convert, right. He was crazy about everything. Had something to prove. He ripped open one of the packs and screamed, "Pork, guys, pork!" I thought, *Hey, calm down. You were eating pork your whole life up until a few months ago. Don't be so fucking dramatic.* Besides, we weren't going to eat the pork; we didn't even have to touch it. It was wrapped in plastic. But I didn't know enough then to say 100 percent whether that job was halal. Even the son of the imam wasn't sure. Kushtrim on the other hand, he was pragmatic; he just kept working and wanted to be done with it. "We'll have to find out what the rules are for next time," he said. But Carlos went over to the corner. "You know what, I can't do this." The rest of us kept working while he watched us and amused himself by pushing the truck backward and forward, backward and forward, backward and forward. In the end he couldn't take it anymore. "Hey, I'm getting sick of watching you guys doing that. Three Muslims loading pork! May God forgive you. *Astaghfirullah.*" He wouldn't leave us alone, but we just kept working.

Then the boss came in. He thought it was going too slow. Stared at Carlos with his zombie face. "And why are you just standing there?" Carlos tried to say he was a Muslim and stuff, but the boss just said, "If it's that bad, you can at least pick up the black plastic bags the others are throwing around." Carlos picked up two of the plastic bags. Stood there and looked at them. A long time. And then he said, "You know, this isn't OK. I can't do this. The plastic has been too close to the pork." Then the boss lost it. "Just get out! I don't need people like you." And believe it or not, at the worst possible moment, Carlos suggested that the zombie look into Islam, that maybe it was something for him.

Yes, of course he was told to get the hell out. And that's putting it nicely. But we'd driven together, so he didn't have a car. Rakkestad to Halden, that's a long way. I felt bad, so at the lunch break I took the car and went looking for him. And there he was, walking along the road with his coat under his arm without a care in the world. He hadn't even made it to Degernes. As I drove up alongside him, he shouted, *"Allahu akbar,"* because he'd been praying to God that we would get out of doing the pork job. I said we hadn't gotten out of it, but that we'd finished hauling the pork. Now there was a new shipment of lamb, and I got him to come back with me. The zombie boss wasn't happy to see him again, but he needed the manpower, so he let it go. Just glared at us when we got back. Carlos was totally revved up again, ready to load lamb.

That cold storage facility didn't give us any more work. Neither did any other place. The temp agency wasn't thrilled with us after that, so they didn't call for a while. They took us off their list. The thing with working for a temp agency is that you think you're free to take the jobs you want, but it's the opposite: they're the ones who are free to ditch you whenever they want, and you have to say yes to everything, or they don't call anymore. Or maybe they just don't need you anymore. Who knows? What do you do then? Suddenly we had a lot of time to practice Islam and talk about the developments in Syria.

Ramadan. I think it was in June, or no, July. It started in July that year, in the middle of the summer. You know, each time you fast, you strengthen your spirituality. You awaken a different type of awareness.

We all went to pray *tarawih*, a prayer you do during the fast. A long prayer. Maybe two hours. Even though it wasn't mandatory, we went every day. There weren't any jobs, right? So we had time. Feet apart. Shoulder to shoulder. The fast really strengthens the feeling of—how can I explain it?—we call it *iman*. It strengthens *iman*. In one way it's the power behind your belief. Afterward we would stand outside in the sun and talk, and something started happening.

The bonds between us got stronger. Something happened with the intensity. Usually we would've just messed around, but now we were serious. We didn't only talk about Syria, we talked about how Muslims were oppressed in many places. How the Russians and Americans had devastated Afghanistan, for example. Or think about Bosnia. Iraq. Palestine. Arbi showed us videos from Chechnya. Brutal stuff that he'd found online. We saw a pattern and realized what was happening in Syria was part of that pattern. And yes, the whole time it's Muslims who are fighting against it. Local people, of course, but often jihadists who went to help as well. People who can't bear to see the tyranny and who bow to no one but Allah. I began to think of them as heroes.

To be totally honest, I think there are plenty of examples of injustice against Muslims in this world. Pick up a history book or just spin the globe a little. If you want to eat from that tree, the fruit isn't hanging too high, so to speak.

Things about Bashar al-Assad were posted on religious Facebook groups. And about his father, Hafez. He'd bombed people in Hama in the early 1980s and slaughtered twenty thousand civilians. Violence wasn't anything new over there. At that time I met a Syrian who was collecting clothes for refugees from his country. When I asked about the history of Syria, he confirmed how terrible Assad was, how he ruled with an iron fist.

We didn't actually know much about IS at that time; they'd only just appeared on the scene. It was more an attraction to jihad than an attraction to a particular group.

When it came to going there ourselves, we were split. Fifty-fifty. Carlos thought it was wrong and that we should listen to the imams we'd talked with. Ali thought that too. Kushtrim changed from day to day, while Arbi thought we should go.

I was for it.

No rational person wants to go to war and die for someone they don't even know. I understand why people prefer to sit on the sofa. We discussed it a lot, called each other cowards, *munafiqs*, hypocrites. "Humanitarian help is all well and good, but someone has to get to the root of the problem," I said, "not just trim the branches."

During *tarawih* one day there was a guy who led the prayers. I'd never seen him before because he was from another town. Big guy, and I remember he read the Koran perfectly. There was something about him; he was really engaged. After *tarawih* he continued praying in Arabic for the people who'd gone to Syria, the mujahedin. Asked God to give them strength and things. Later we found out that only a few weeks after he'd been in Halden, he'd gone down to Syria, thrown himself into the war without any training, and been killed. I was totally shocked, but at the same time I thought what he'd done was a great thing. That you have to have a big heart to do something like that for other people.

People who knew him at the mosque said he was a kindhearted person. Some people online thought he was a hero. Between ourselves we said that he had become a *shahid*, a martyr. Burim called from Oslo. He wondered if I'd known the guy, but I couldn't say I really did. Just that I'd met him in the mosque. He invited me to Oslo to talk about it. I don't know, I was actually pretty uncertain about the whole Islamist community in Oslo, but I'd been following what they were posting online and stuff. There was an attraction. So we went. Me, Arbi, and Carlos.

We met Burim in the ICC Mosque in Oslo. It was just the three of us and him.

The people at ICC wouldn't have been happy if they'd known what we were talking about, but y'know this was still before a lot of people started going down there, and the mosque is an open place. It takes a lot before they throw someone out. So we sat there on the carpets. Burim thought it was right to go to Syria. Or he put it this way: "Personally, I don't think you should go, but the Koran says something else."

Of course, Carlos couldn't let it go. He wanted to know exactly where in the Koran, you know, which sura, which *aya*, which interpretation.

I don't remember all of them, but there's a verse in the fourth sura that says that unless they are sick, believers who stay home are not equal to those who struggle on behalf of Allah.

Jihad, yes.

But the strongest argument was that you should fight against those who fight against you. So the question was whether Muslims were under attack or not, and it was hard not to agree on that. Burim listed off all the military attacks we'd already seen videos of online: Chechnya, Bosnia, Kosovo, Iraq, Afghanistan, Syria, and so on, in addition to all the psychological attacks Muslims had to endure in the West. "Wouldn't you say we were under attack?" he asked Carlos.

Yes, as for me, things started to get clearer. But then there's everything that holds you back. Your duties at home, to your family, a life that still has to be lived. The point is you shouldn't worry so much about what you give up in this life. "This is only a bus stop," said Burim. "We will be rewarded in the next life." Besides, in my life there wasn't really that much to give up.

After that meeting we merged with the Oslo community. People from Halden got the phone numbers of the people in Oslo and vice versa. There were some people out there who believed it was the will of Allah to travel to Syria.

You know in Oslo it's clearer because it's bigger. You have more isolated groups that think in one particular way. Halden is small, so everything is more mixed. Shia, Sunni, liberals, conservatives, Sufis, or Salafists— everyone goes to the same mosque. You could say that our contact with the people in Oslo meant we could cultivate a certain way of thinking, both in religion and in politics.

When I saw videos from Syria, I really felt I had to do something. That was what pushed me most of all. But I have to mention Yusuf al-Qaradawi as well, a scholar from Egypt. I found videos on YouTube where he was talking on Egyptian TV with English subtitles. The TV host was asking if the rumors were true, that Qaradawi had encouraged violence against Assad. And he replied that it was legitimate to kill soldiers and federal employees in Syria. It was the first time I'd heard a scholar say something like that.

Right after I'd seen that video, I was visiting another Østfold mosque to hand out collection boxes. Someone had taped up a sheet of paper at the entrance that more or less said that we could combine the two last prayers of the day, *maghrib* and *isha*, because it was hard to figure out when *isha* actually was in the summer so far north. I'd heard other people say that before, so it wasn't anything new. But at the bottom of the sheet I saw a signature. And guess who'd signed it.

The leader of the Islamic Committee in Europe, Yusuf al-Qaradawi.

So they'd taken one of Qaradawi's fatwas and put it up in the mosque, but they didn't take up his call to fight Assad. That's not how it works. Either you listen to a scholar or you don't. You can't just cherry-pick the statements you think are most convenient.

That set off a train of thought. What could I say in my defense when I stand in front of God and he asks what I did while my brothers and sisters were being slaughtered? Everything you get is from God after all. Or, at least, that's what I believe as a Muslim. If you win the lottery, or earn money through hard work, everything is from God, y'know. Life is from God. And when I thought about how lucky I was having grown up in Norway, I suddenly felt guilty. We sat there like cowards. Slack. Lazy. I couldn't sleep. I felt like I was a *munafiq*. When I first thought about leaving, I thought it was what God wanted. That was why he'd put the idea in my head.

The PSS called me. They asked if I could come and have a chat down at the police station. They assured me it was a voluntary conversation. So I thought, *OK, let's hear what they want.*

We met in the break room at the station. It was a guy in his sixties and a slightly younger guy. They said they were Peter and Paul, but afterward I thought that was too ridiculous; they must have been cover names.

They said they were worried about some stuff I'd put online.

It was a video with a jihadist *nashid*. Part of the video showed an American soldier seen through a telescopic gun sight. Peter and Paul didn't like that.

They asked about Iraq. About Syria. What I thought. Of course I didn't tell them that I was thinking about going there myself. But I told them straight out that I was against the dictators. "I hope they get over-thrown," I said. Peter—he was the older one—said that Norway was also against dictators. In that sense we agreed. But they were worried that people who traveled down there would come back totally fucked in the head and gun people down or blow themselves up. To be honest,

I couldn't imagine that scenario. Since then there's been a lot of focus on stuff like that, but at that time I thought they were two totally different things.

They asked if I'd tell them if someone was planning an operation in Norway.

"Yeah, yeah. Of course." And I meant it.

Actually, I think the conversation with Peter and Paul was mostly about me having to change. Change my opinions. I asked if it was wrong to be against Norway's involvement in Afghanistan, for example. They said it was no problem at all to have different political opinions, that their concerns were only about security. But I don't really know where to draw the line. Some things were obviously not OK about my opinions, and that made me nervous. They made me feel like I'd done something wrong, stepped over the line. *Now they're going to put me in prison,* I thought.

Yeah, seriously, you get a bit paranoid. Think the worst.

They played on that fear—the fear I had of having done something stupid—and they made me feel the only way I could make up for it was to cooperate. I said I needed a little time to think it over. But what I really needed to think about was something totally different.

I felt uneasy. I remember I saved their number under *KUFFAR*. I said I was busy when they rang. Got nervous about the whole thing. Then I stopped answering the phone altogether. Eventually they called from a blocked number, and I was dumb enough to answer. I couldn't be rude; that would just create more suspicion. And those people, they always know how to get the upper hand on you psychologically, so I agreed to meet them again. It wasn't at a police station that time, but in a car that was parked outside the train station. A black Audi, I remember. I didn't exactly hurry to that meeting.

Paul drove. Peter talked. I sat in the back like a kid. They were respectable people; they kept to a nice tone and everything, even if the whole thing was totally fake. We drove past the square, past Immanuel's Church and up toward the fortress. "If any of your buddies see you in the car with us, you can tell them it was a job interview." I really didn't understand why we had to drive anywhere. Maybe so I couldn't just jump out of the car. So they'd get to decide the length of the conversation.

It became clear to me that they didn't really care that much about the group in Halden. They were more concerned about Burim and the people in Oslo. They said they wanted me to carry on meeting people up there and report on what they were talking about and that they'd eventually give me instructions. "You want me to spy on Muslims?" I asked. They wouldn't use that word, *spy*. They said that I should carry on as before but tell them if there was something they should know. We were in the parking lot at the fortress. They'd stopped the car. "What do you say?" asked Peter.

I needed to buy myself some time. Now that I was thinking of going to Syria myself, I wanted the PSS involved as little as possible. They made me feel you were either with them or against them. And you don't want to be on the wrong side of the PSS. So I said I'd let them know what people in Oslo were talking about.

Yeah, I was in Oslo a few times after that. The first thing I did was tell them that the PSS had contacted me.

They didn't get stressed out about it; it wasn't news to them, so to speak.

I got nervous about the whole arrangement; I had to tell Peter and Paul something. So I made things up. "They think Sharia is better than democracy," or "They're angry at several Muslim organizations in Norway because they're dipping into the state coffers and have been led away from true Islam." I whispered as if it was top secret, but I only told them things I'd found on Google. "Listen, there are some Norwegian converts that have gone down to Syria."

No, they weren't that impressed. "What else?" they wanted to know. They were fishing for concrete plans and contacts. "I'll see what I can do," I said.

No, no, it's important that it's totally clear I didn't help the PSS. I'm not a snitch. I just needed to buy myself some time.

One day I went to the mosque and saw Arbi crying while he was praying. There were some other people there as well, but he was the only one I could see. He was holding his hands up in front of his eyes, like we do when we pray, and I thought he wasn't seeing the tough skin of his palms but dead bodies. Like he was looking into the Syrian darkness. When he was finished with *dua*, he put his hands over his face, like some people do after prayers, but it was as if he was washing his face in the darkness he'd seen.

Holding your hands over your face after *dua*, that reminds me of something about Arbi. You know, Salafists don't usually do that; it's considered *bid'ah*, or "innovation," so it's a deviation from the tradition of the Prophet, Sunna. Among all of us, Arbi was the one least concerned about details like that; he wasn't so picky, didn't have such a good grasp of the scholarship and the different types of faith. You could say he was more moderate. But Arbi had a huge heart. He took things personally. And as a Chechen, he knew what war was.

I remember I looked around the mosque that evening. Most of the people were old, or in any case adult. Pretty established, people with families and children. I thought they surely wanted to help the Syrians, but they didn't have the strength for it. What could they do really? We're the youth. We have the strength, and we have the will. We have the responsibility.

That evening Arbi and I left the mosque together. It was starting to get dark, but the moon was shining brightly and there was a warm summer breeze. I suggested going for a walk. Halden was totally empty and silent. We walked past our old junior high up in Rødsfjellet. Eventually he said, "Tariq, you know what? I can't sit back anymore." I'd been having the same thought for a while too, but when he said it like that, it was kinda liberating. So I said, "OK, let's do something." We didn't say more than that. Didn't need to, y'know. Just stared at the town and felt the weight of the words we'd said.

We forgot everything. We forgot we had a family. We forgot we had a future. We forgot we had dreams. We forgot ourselves, who we were. Forgot everything. That was the only way we could keep to the path we'd set for ourselves. What we were about to do couldn't be wrong. That was what we told ourselves. That Assad was the face of evil.

Then came the planning. It would be cold, we thought, so we had to have some good clothing. We bought the best wool long underwear we could. Walked into the store in the middle of summer and only wanted to buy wool. But it was even more embarrassing when I went to buy combat clothes. I went to a store in Ski that mostly sells equipment for the police and military. And it isn't exactly great when a Paki with a long beard comes in wanting combat clothes. There was a military man in front of me in line: I was sure he'd seen action in Afghanistan or something. He gave me a dirty look when he saw me. Probably thought, *Shit; I go halfway around the world to fight the bastards, and now they're here too.* When it was my turn, the salesperson asked what I was looking for. I said I wanted a vest. "A combat vest?" asked the guy behind the register. I nodded. You know, a combat vest is the kind that holds a magazine plus a water bottle on one side, and first aid equipment on the other. I pointed to one of the vests, beige, because everything in

Syria is beige. The guy in the store told me the dark-green ones were cheaper. "No, no, it has to be beige," I said. "Why do you want that color?" "I'm from Pakistan," I said, "I'm gonna sell it there; that color is really popular." The guy went really quiet, looked at me for a while. Then he gave me the vest. But I wasn't done; I wanted gear for both myself and Arbi. Gloves, pants, jackets, water bottles, thigh holsters, elbow protectors, knee protectors, and ballistic glasses. The full package.

Before I went to pay, I tried to be a bit more casual, you know, made a bit of small talk and asked what kind of customers they had. "Well," he said, "most of them are police or military, but there are some who end up in Syria as well, of course." I tried to look interested and nod politely. "Oh, yeah, Syria you say?" Of course he understood what was going on. It was awkward. I was covered in sweat by the time I'd finished shopping.

I hid the gear in an old camper van that was in one of the gardens overlooking Halden Stadium. I knew an old woman lived in the house there. The camper van hadn't been used in years, so it was OK.

Arbi and I hid everything. We didn't say anything to anyone. Not our families. Not our friends. It hurt to not be able to talk about what we were thinking, what we were afraid of. But whatever, we had each other. We met in secret. We often walked up Rødsfjellet. The view is so amazing, down over the city center, but at the same time it's far from everything. And quiet. It was a place we could share our hidden thoughts.

One day Arbi's family asked him if he'd ever thought about going to Syria or anything. "You've become so religious," his dad said. He'd been reading the papers, stories about young religious guys going to Syria. But Arbi denied it, said that the people going to Syria were naive idiots.

My mom also noticed I'd been watching a ton of videos about Syria online. She asked about it and got more worried when I didn't have a good answer. She started to pay more attention to me. I remember a few times during the news when something from Syria came up, she'd stare more at me than at the screen.

The closer we got to leaving, the more my head spun. The absolute certainty we'd had at the beginning disappeared. We started to doubt. How would our families take it if we got shot over there? I started to think about Mom. When I first decided to go, I managed to suppress any thoughts about how she'd feel. But then I started to notice. I felt bad and made up for it by being nicer when I was home. Cut the grass, sat and drank tea with Mom. I played a lot with Little Brother, kicked a ball around or went out in the yard to wrestle.

Remember that cat I got when I broke up with my childhood sweetheart?

Well, I made Little Brother promise to look after it.

I consoled myself by reading verses from the Koran that say someone who dies in the service of Allah will be forgiven everything and enter into heaven. It even says that his family will get into heaven. It helped to believe that. Especially since Mom wasn't that religious. If I died a martyr for Allah, maybe I'd help her into Paradise as well. That's what you hope for.

I'd stopped listening to music a long time ago by then, but there was something 2Pac said that I never forgot: if you don't find something to live for, you should find something to die for. That's how it was. We didn't have much to live for. But we'd found something we were willing to die for.

That's what we wanted. Martyrdom.

To be sure that you get into heaven as a martyr, you have to have the right intentions when you fight. So we had to find a rebel group that was practicing true Islam. That's what we thought. In a way that was our guarantee into Paradise if we got killed. We looked around a bit and tried to find out what the different groups stood for. Some wanted Sharia, some wanted democracy, some wanted Sharia through democracy, some just wanted to overthrow Assad and let the Syrians sort themselves out after that.

To be honest I have reservations about democracy over there. Here in Norway, sure, but I don't know if it would work in Syria. Just look at what happened in Egypt. While Arbi and I were looking into what the different Syrian rebel groups stood for, we found out that the democratically elected president of Egypt, Morsi, had been overthrown by the military because he wanted to move his country more toward Islam. OK, so democracy only works as long as those who are elected think just like the West. You get it? That made things clear. Democracy has become a dirty word in the Middle East.

Yeah, I was for Sharia. After all, that's God's law, I thought. God created us, so he has to know what's best. But honestly I have to admit I didn't really know that much about Sharia, the different interpretations and stuff. I didn't have any clear idea about how to establish Sharia law either. I just thought, y'know, it had to be the right thing. Deep down it wasn't Sharia that made us leave. When we were in doubt about leaving, it was the news from Syria that pushed us forward.

The sarin gas attack in Ghouta happened just before we left. Have you seen the videos? Kids who have the most terrible cramps, images the news won't even show—you have to go online. We saw that and knew we had to do something. And then the feeling of hypocrisy disappeared, you know?

I say "we" because we talked a lot about it. Arbi felt the same way I did.

We started sleeping better. We started to look at the world around us. Noticed the flowers, trees, insects, the shape of the clouds, even the face of an old woman walking through the shopping center with her walker. I'd say we were cherishing creation, every step, every breath. And then I started to forgive people I'd argued with. Went to old friends and asked for forgiveness for things I'd said or done. Both Arbi and I trimmed our beards so we wouldn't arouse too much suspicion on the way there. We killed two birds with one stone because it calmed our parents down too.

We didn't have a plan, didn't know when we would leave. We hadn't set a date. The whole thing was random. We just did the things we had to and trusted that God would lead us, that he would open doors.

You know Paulo Coelho? I borrowed one of his books from the prison library, and it's sort of the same. When you really want something, the whole universe opens itself to make your wish come true. I believed something like that. That it would sort itself out, as long as I trusted in God. In a way it wasn't even a choice. We just followed where fate took us.

One day we emptied our bank accounts. We borrowed what we could borrow. I sold the boat. We got cell phones for one krone down, and then resold the phones. I registered for an online course to finish my high school diploma so I could get a student loan.

Arbi got a small van.

We visited Burim in Oslo as well. We told it like it was. Said we were on our way. He'd been busy collecting clothes for refugees, so we filled the whole van with clothes that the locals there could use and took ten cans of gas with us so we wouldn't need to stop on the way and risk leaving traces. I remember he patted us on the shoulder. "Look after yourselves," he said. "Don't get mixed up in anything you don't agree with."

Then there was nothing left to prepare. We were ready. The day had come. We drove past my house. I saw Little Brother in the window with his iPad. Arbi asked if we could drive past his house too. Totally quiet. And then we went to Carlos's garage. As usual he was busy playing video games. "Hang on a minute, guys. Just want to finish this round." He was sweating like an animal over his console. We said we were on our way to Trondheim and that we'd be back in three days. Said we were going to help out a mosque up there. It's weird saying good-bye to someone without them knowing you're doing it. I remember Arbi said to him, "Be seeing you, *inshallah*, in this life or the next." Carlos was a bit taken aback, but he didn't ask any questions. Just wished us a good trip to Trondheim.

It was early September 2013. We got in the van and put Istanbul into the GPS. Then we changed our minds. If we got stopped and they saw Istanbul, it wouldn't be good. So we did it one country at a time, crossed the Svinesund Bridge and drove down along the Swedish coast. It was evening, and I think it was totally still, because none of the wind turbines were moving. After a few hours we pulled in behind a gas station and slept. Arbi was quick to get into the back seat, so he slept best even though I was the one who'd been driving. I pushed my seat back and got a few hours' sleep, but then I woke up just as someone was sticking a ticket on our windshield. Arbi woke up too and wondered what was happening. "Ticket," I said, and he started to laugh. "Ticket, yeah, right." He moved up front while I went out and ripped up the ticket right in the face of the parking enforcement cop, got back in the car, and started driving.

We drove on, stopped for prayer and to eat falafel in Malmö. Then we crossed the Øresund Bridge, past Copenhagen, and eventually took a ferry to Germany. When we drove on board, I told Arbi that we shouldn't be too serious. People could get suspicious if we seemed nervous and isolated. Better to mess around and joke a bit. Arbi took me at my word; he went totally overboard. He jumped into a ball pit for kids and swam around in all the colored balls. Then he went to the arcade and got on this bike with a screen. Seriously. This big guy on a tiny motorcycle. We also ate really good food in the ship's restaurant. We figured there wouldn't be too much feasting in Syria really.

We hit trouble when we drove off the ferry. We realized it right away. Two guys in a van, and one looks like he's from the Middle East. That sets off all the warning bells in any police station, so of course they waved us over for inspection. Our trimmed beards didn't really help that much either. Rolled down the window. *"Guten Abend, Polizei."* And they asked in their broken German-English, "Yes, where are you going?" Arbi totally lost it, started mumbling and stuttering. In the end he said, "English, no good" and bailed out, but the officer pointed to the side and said we should park the van there. Then they came toward us. Three huge German cops. The thing was we hadn't thought about what we'd say if we were stopped. I told Arbi I'd do the talking. He nodded, glad to escape. First they were very polite, but then they started to sniff around and said they wanted to look in the vehicle. I had to let them, and they found the cans of gas and masses of kids' clothes.

"Aha. What are you doing with all this?"

"We're driving a long way," I said.

"Where to?"

"All the way to Bulgaria," I said.

"And the clothes?"

"Charity," I said. "We're handing them out to street kids; you know there are lots of Romany kids in Sofia."

But while I was talking with one officer, the other officers found our military clothes.

"*Kampfwesten! Kampfwesten!*" The polite tone suddenly disappeared. Now the one I was talking to moved in close and looked me in the eye. "And what about the military gear?" he asked.

"We're going to a big paintball game."

"OK," he said, "let me see if I understand this correctly. You're going to Bulgaria and brought gas with you for the trip from a country where gas is surely much more expensive than anywhere else, and in Bulgaria you're doing charity work and playing paintball, and for that you have expensive, high-quality military clothing."

"Yes, we're from Norway; look, here are our passports—rich country," I said.

"Do you think I'm a complete idiot?" He stared hard at me, and I thought that our trip was over for sure. Just like that. Finished. Game over. But what could they arrest us for? On what grounds? So I stuck to my guns. He asked, and I answered paintball and Romany kids. He kept pushing and I still insisted on paintball and Romany kids.

In the end I asked straight out: "What's the problem?"

"The problem is that we don't believe you."

"Oh," I answered, "but what you believe is your problem, not mine." And it really was, because they had no real reason to stop us. They tried to psyche us out, stared and shouted. But it was still paintball and Romany kids. In the end they just had to let us drive on. They did take pictures of our passports and the gear we had with us.

"If you get into any shit in Germany," he said, "we'll know who you are."

We stopped as little as possible. German autobahn, keep on driving. Arbi said he could drive a bit, but he didn't have his license, and I didn't want any more trouble. For the most part he sat with his legs out the window and got bored, while I drove mile after mile. We played this one song from a CD Arbi brought. A Chechen *nashid* by a guy called Timur something or other. Well, it wasn't really a true *nashid*, because that's only supposed to be singing and max one drum, but this one had guitar as well.

Yeah, it was OK because it was a song about following God's path.

It was called "Jerusalem." We had it on repeat the whole way; it became our road trip anthem. Arbi translated the text for me a few times. It's something about the world being shrouded in evil, and that we must prepare ourselves for a difficult fight, but through jihad we would find clarity.

He sings that Muslims one day will retake the Al-Aqsa Mosque in Jerusalem. I hit the gas a little more whenever he sang, "Jerusalem, Jerusalem." We sang along. I almost taught myself Russian with that song.

We only stopped a few times to empty our bladders, drink coffee, eat, and, of course, pray. Bowed down on the asphalt and listened to the hum of the freeway beside us. We slept in the car again, somewhere in Germany, I think. Just drove into a rest stop and slept for a few hours. In the morning we drove into Austria and then to Hungary. I got tired from the long, straight roads on the plains in Hungary, but Arbi kept me awake talking about the war in Chechnya. As we approached Serbia, the talk shifted to the Bosnian War and how Muslims suffered there, so we weren't really feeling kind toward Serbs when we reached the border. And that was where the EU ended, so we had a full inspection there as well. Took out all our stuff. Showed our passports. They also found our combat vests and started asking questions. "Palestine?" Then the guard made a pretend gun with his hand and said, "Bang, bang, bang" and laughed. He said we had to pay customs on the clothes. *Customs on used clothes,* I thought, *how stupid is that?* But it was better to avoid trouble. The shack that was supposed to be the customs office just had a few payphones and a money exchange window. Arbi knocked on the window, and a guy came over. "We have to declare some clothes," I said. It took a while before he got it. "Declare? What do you mean? Oh, yeah, of course, declare, yes." It was clear they were going to fleece us, so I went out and told the border guard that we wouldn't give them a cent. He frowned. Said that was OK, we didn't need to pay if he could have our military pants and our boots. "Listen," I said, "we're not giving you shit, and you let us drive on. Does that sound good to you?" He completely backed off. Or rather, not completely: he still wanted a pair of boots for letting us pass, but I told him to go to hell, and he said the same, and off we went. Farther along there was another crossing, with another border guard, an old guy with a fat, corrupt belly and a sad face. Then it was the same thing all over again, and that ended with me giving him the finger and stepping on the gas.

131

The customs people in Bulgaria were nicer. They just told us it would be better to keep our combat knives in the back of the van rather than on the front seat. That border was full of hookers; I have to say I didn't get a great impression of Europe on that trip.

Maybe it's just along the highways and border crossings, but whatever. Garbage, corruption, and hookers. To be totally honest, it was nice to get into Turkey. There's probably a lot of shit there as well, but we couldn't see it.

Incidentally, we got asked to empty the van there as well. That was the fourth time we got inspected. What a pain. We just threw the things out. "Look, a combat vest! Look, a knife!" The thing is we didn't give a shit anymore, and when you don't seem nervous, you're treated completely differently. But they also wanted to know if we were going to war. "Soria?" they asked. We just pretended like we didn't understand what they were asking about. "Soria? What's Soria? Don't understand." They also let us drive on.

It was nice to be in a Muslim country. Arbi wanted to stop at a mosque just past the border crossing, but I insisted we should drive a little farther into the country first. "It's like holding your breath," I remember he said. In the end we found a mosque, washed, and did *salah*.

Everyone has their own style when they pray. You can recognize Salafists because they stand straight and take up a lot of space, while Sufis, for example, usually do the opposite, almost curl up entirely to show their submission to God. One is more extrovert and the other more introvert. Sufism is more prevalent in Turkey, so I tried to fit in and not stand with my legs so wide apart and stuff, but Arbi didn't understand it at all. He stood there like he was a soldier on parade, straight back and chest out, not so much because he was a Salafist, but because that's the type of person he was. Afterward I told him maybe it would be better to not stand out like that. That it might give the wrong signals. But he just laughed it off, said I shouldn't be so paranoid all the time.

Istanbul was like, we came, we saw, we left, and what I remember best is a shish kebab from a little restaurant, a hole-in-the-wall in a market in front of a mosque. The guy behind the counter also asked us if we were going to Syria. "You go Soria?" And we just shook our heads. "No, no, tourists." I still don't see how he knew. OK, so there are a lot of people who travel through Turkey to Syria, but there are also masses of foreigners in Istanbul who aren't doing jihad. Maybe stuff like that is just plain as day. Maybe it just shines through.

Our timing wasn't good. We left Istanbul in the middle of rush hour. I remember the exhaust fumes and the heat, and our van didn't have AC. We sat there and sweated. We only got a breeze when the traffic moved a bit. I wasn't used to the way they drive and struggled to get into the right lanes. One guy gave me the finger, another blasted his horn. It was noisy and dusty, and in the middle of it all, I saw a traffic cop standing outside his booth in the street, in the middle of all the traffic and everything. He'd rolled out his prayer mat and was praying. Totally focused. Totally at peace. I remember I admired him. Like, how did he manage to find the peace to pray in the middle of all that chaos?

Then the traffic cleared and we carried on. Drove through the country. I was surprised at how beautiful everything was, the countryside, buildings, roads. The infrastructure was much better than I'd imagined.

There were automatic toll stations set up in some places, just like we have in Norway, but you needed a transponder or something because when the other cars drove through there was a green light, but when we drove through a red light flashed and it beeped every time. Arbi started to joke that it was the Devil trying to stop us. "Shaitan, it's Shaitan again."

As we were driving, Arbi's phone rang. He looked at the screen but didn't answer it, just turned and stared out the window. I wanted to say something but didn't know what. Not long after, my phone rang too. *MOM* lit up the screen. I didn't answer either. Just let the phone ring. It was totally silent in the car after that. Everyone around us on the street or in their cars, they were on their way to the shops, on their way home or to work, maybe they were going on vacation, to the pool or to soccer practice. The kids were on their way home from school in their school uniforms. One of them, a little guy walking along the street totally alone, reminded me of when I was in Pakistan, not at military school but before that, when I was really small and ran around the streets. It's weird how much of our lives we recognize around us. Suddenly you see an echo of yourself in a small Turkish village. We just drove past all the people, sitting in our van, a spaceship on the way to a totally different planet, where bombs are raining from the sky and people are ripped apart.

Right then we didn't really find comfort in each other. What comforted us in the end was the landscape. It changed. We went up into the mountains, and it got more rocky and sandy. The earth turned deep red; it started to look like the color we'd seen in pictures of Syria. We were getting closer to God, and that was what lifted our spirits.

The GPS counted down the miles, and once in a while the apathetic voice would say, "Turn left," "Take the next exit on the left." Arbi always giggled when the voice said something, but I wanted to leave the volume on so we wouldn't miss an exit. Evening came, the roads got narrower, and civilization disappeared little by little. We came up to a mountain plateau, totally flat. A sign said not to stop along the road: danger of highway robbery. Gangs operate in that area. There were no more cars, just a truck once in a while. And it just went on forever. Desolate. The road was totally straight, with one single gas station. We were completely exhausted, so we decided to stop there despite the warnings.

Even though the gas station was closed for the day, we felt safer stopping there and not at some random place along the road. The gas station had its own prayer room on the side, but we didn't want to leave the car unattended. The sun had started to go down, and I got the same feeling I used to get when I was up early in the mornings in Halden to pray. That same sky, lit up, glowing. Suddenly you feel thankful again. Remember why you are where you are. Remember God.

We went to sleep in the car. Arbi jumped in the back as usual. Lay on top of the bags of clothes Burim had given us and fell asleep right away. I lay down up front with the seat belt cutting into my side.

I woke up in the middle of the night. A strong wind was rocking the van back and forth. The only light was from a little lamp above the door of the gas station. Otherwise, just endless darkness in every direction. Beneath the howling of the wind, I thought I heard something, a call to prayer. I got out of the van and felt the wind pushing me and the sand whipping my face. I went to the prayer room, but nobody was there. I was about to get back in the van when I thought I heard the call again. *Allahu akbar.* I don't know if it was curiosity or fear, but I started to walk along the road in the dark. The wind clawed at my face, and I hunched my shoulders as I walked. And y'know how in the night your thoughts come all at once, you have no shield. I started talking to myself. "What are you doing, Tariq? What are you doing out here?" I stopped and tried to listen for the call to prayer, but there was nothing there. What if I'd misheard, you know? What if it wasn't really a call to prayer? Just the wind sighing. And suddenly, right there, I fell apart. I don't know,

I thought the wind was laughing at me. The night was laughing at me. I crouched down at the side of the road and just shook my head. "It's going to be OK," I told myself. "Go back to the van now, go back to Arbi, it was just the wind."

When I got back in the van, I realized that I wouldn't be sleeping any more that night. I might as well drive on. The road continued straight for several hours, no turns, not even a curve. After a while a dark-blue light appeared out of the black landscape on the horizon. The light of the day got stronger and stronger. I breathed deeper, felt safer, and just around dawn Arbi's Caucasian face peeked out from the back seat. He'd slept really well and was in great form.

Then the GPS started acting up. All of Turkey was supposed to be in the system, but it didn't cover all areas equally well. Maybe it couldn't get a satellite signal or something. We got sent the wrong way, went on detours, drove down dead ends, torn-up, crumbling roads. We came to some villages that could have come out of any Western movie. Just one street with some houses along it. Max one or two side streets. We started seeing the Kurdish flag. Someone had tagged *PKK* on the wall of a house. *YPG* on another. Even though the bloodiest battles hadn't happened yet, we already knew that the Kurds and Syrian rebel groups didn't have the best relationship. Best not to stop there. If they found out where we were going, it could get ugly. Luckily we had our cans of gas, so we didn't need to talk to anyone, just kept on driving.

We saw the ocean.

No, a long way off. We were already at the Hatay Mountains, and on one of the summits we could see the ocean far below us on the right. Arbi said he'd read that the US was moving an aircraft carrier into the area.

After a lot of up and down, the landscape started to flatten out. On the horizon we saw black smoke. *That's gotta be Syria,* we thought.

We arrived at Reyhanli; it's still in Turkey but close to the border. That was where Arbi had a contact. We pulled over at a rest stop by a gas station to call, but our phones didn't have any coverage. One of the pump attendants was staring at us. Staring at the van. There we were with Norwegian plates, green ones no less, just to make sure we got everyone's attention. So we moved. Drove on. In the town there were military jeeps with huge guns on their roofs, and every time they drove past, we lay down in the car 'til they'd gone by.

Before we did anything, we had to find something to drink. You know, it's really hot in Turkey in the middle of September. We hadn't wanted to stop in the Kurdish villages, so we'd run out of water and were so thirsty that we couldn't think of anything else at all. At the same time we were scared to death of exposing ourselves, and skeptical of the kiosks selling the jewelry with the blue eye, the *nazar*. Y'know, the Turkish can be superstitious and have those amulets with a blue eye to protect themselves. But for us it was *shirk*. That's not the kind of thing that can protect you; only Allah can protect you. Arbi joked that we were in Shirkistan, and even though my mouth was totally dry, I had to laugh.

In the end Arbi went to a hotel to ask for water. I waited outside and lay down in the van in case military cars were on patrol. After a while Arbi came back with two plastic bags full of water bottles. What the heck was going on?

He'd walked into the reception area with those dry lips of his and asked for water, right, and the people in the lobby had yelled, "Soria! Soria!" Arbi freaked out, he thought they'd figured him out, but no, they thought he was a refugee. They shouted and cried and hugged him and gave him as much water as he could carry.

I looked at those things, y'know, things some people would call luck, as a kinda bonus from God.

But yeah. Now we've almost gotten to the border, and this is where it starts to get hard to talk about things.

People could get into trouble if I say the wrong thing. Or I could get into trouble myself; people might get angry. Every word is a risk.

It doesn't really help if you paraphrase and make it anonymous and everything. You know, the PSS is obsessed with finding something to nail people with, and because they have almost no evidence, they'll try anything and hope it sticks.

No, I'm not joking. Even if it is a novel. All right, maybe I am a bit paranoid, but it's not without reason.

Well, yes, yes. I do want to talk about it; it's not that. I just need some kind of assurance that you're not gonna publish anything without my approval.

I just don't want to end up getting screwed over. That's happened before. With other people, I mean.

Sorry. Then the story stops here.

PART 2

OK, from now on you won't know exactly what's true and what isn't.

No, just some details here and there. I don't want to get anyone in trouble. It's best for both of us.

Should I start?

OK, so we were in Reyhanli, still Turkey, but Arbi and I, we didn't know where we were going. Or rather, which group we should join. It wasn't easy to decide from Norway, y'know? We'd tried asking people online which groups practiced authentic Islam but didn't know who we should trust really. It's not like standing in a supermarket trying to pick which toothpaste you want. It was a question of who you wanted to die with.

At first, in 2011, the rebels were all FSA, Free Syrian Army. They're the most secular. They were ruled out from the start for us because they didn't follow true Islam. The next year Jabhat al-Nusra came on the scene and became the obvious jihadi alternative.

Yes, putting it simply, Al Qaeda's arm in Syria.

IS—they were called ISIS then, but we just called them Dawla. It means "the state" in Arabic. We had them in our sights, but we didn't really know much about them. They'd been in Syria for less than six months. The establishment of the caliphate, all the videos of beheadings, the propaganda mill, terrorism in Europe—all that came later. Then they were just a religious group fighting against Assad. I didn't know about their brutality then. They were actually related to Nusra and Al Qaeda; they collaborated with other groups and stuff. But things were starting to get totally confused.

I just didn't know. After our research at home in Norway, we were choosing between Dawla and a group called JMA, who we thought had the proper understanding of faith, *aqida*.

JMA was led by Chechens, so Arbi really pushed for us to join them. He liked the fact that the Tajiks, Uzbeks, Dagestanis, and most importantly the other Chechens all spoke Russian like him.

It stands for Jaish al-Muhajireen wal-Ansar, "the army of warriors and helpers." The warriors, or emigrants, are those who come from abroad to carry out jihad, like Arbi and me. The helpers are the local people. That's from the time of the Prophet, when he did the hegira to Medina and the local people there helped him establish himself.

Arbi had made a contact in the group because he spoke Russian, but just before we left we heard there were internal problems in the JMA.

Yeah. A split. The leader, Omar al-Shishani, took a lot of other people and went over to Dawla. Some stayed in JMA, and others went with a guy called Sayfullah. That was where Arbi's contact had ended up. But at that time we didn't really understand what had happened. Arbi said,

"They almost started shooting each other." And then Arbi wanted to go to this Sayfullah guy. The whole thing was a bit too random.

They just called it Jamaat Sayfullah. "Sayfullah's group."

You know what? The whole thing was confusing. Who was this Sayfullah guy anyhow? What did he stand for? I'd seen videos of him in which he looked really angry. OK, you can fight, but do you have any knowledge of the religion you're fighting for? There was a guy from Norway, a Norwegian convert actually, who said to me once, "Remember that a mujahed without knowledge is just a bandit." Besides, what would it be like to hang out with a bunch of Chechens in Syria? In JMA there had been an English-speaking division, but in Sayfullah's group they all spoke Russian.

The bad feeling I had got worse and worse. Whenever we talked about it, my voice had gotten tight. Arbi was clear. He wanted to join them. Period. But I decided that I'd wait and check out the groups first.

Yeah, sure, if I'd had contacts in Dawla, I might've ended up there. But to get in, you needed someone to recruit you. Someone they trusted to put in a good word for you, but I was there on my own.

We met Arbi's guy in a parking lot in Reyhanli. A young Caucasian with a narrow face and messy hair. Arbi explained that he wanted to join Sayfullah's group but that I needed to get across the border as well. "Tell him I'm interested in the English-speaking part of JMA if it's still around." Arbi explained and Mr. Bad-hair-day nodded, said he'd see what he could do. Then he talked on his phone for a long time. Stared at me with the phone to his ear. The whole thing stressed me out, and I was irritated with Arbi, who was just leaning against the van being totally chill drinking his bottled water.

Not long after, a car drove up. The guy with the messy hair nodded to me; this was clearly my contact. The man who got out of the car looked at us suspiciously, like, "What do we have here?" He was wearing a light-blue polo shirt, a cheap knockoff of Polo Sport or something. Short beard and a birthmark right at his mouth. *"Salaam aleikum,"* he said eventually and held out his hand. He said he was called Abu Saad. Syrian. He could help me cross. "JMA?" I asked. *"Inshallah,"* he answered. I looked over at Arbi. "What do you think, brother?" "Trust in Allah," he said.

That was that. Arbi and I each went our own way. We thought we'd be thrown into combat as soon as we'd crossed the border. Done.

Martyr. We didn't know if we'd see each other again, not in this *dunya* in any case.

Yeah, Arbi took the van and the clothes. People from Sayfullah's group got it later. I dunno, it could still be driving around Syria with its green Norwegian plates.

I took my bags and sat in Abu Saad's rust bucket. He could only speak a little English. Broken, but OK; we understood each other. He was still serious, frowning. We drove to a Turkish military checkpoint. Five soldiers were there with huge machine guns, and I thought, *Damn it, he's going to turn me in.* A soldier wearing a skewed beret came over to the car and talked with Abu Saad, while I waved my Norwegian passport. "This is me, look."

No, no, they didn't even want to see my passport. They just looked the other way, let us pass. That's how it works there. Voilà!

Still in Turkey. So first you come to masses of checkpoints, and then you get to the actual border. Totally normal people live between each point. Abu Saad drove toward some farms and stone houses. There were those low dried-mud walls around the yards. And there were always some animals, hens usually, some sheep and a cow here and there. Cow shit was pushed against the walls to dry and use as fuel. I recognized that from Pakistan, drying cow shit. Masses of dirty kids were in the streets looking at me curiously.

Abu Saad took me to one of the houses. "Border guide," he said. "Wait here until dark; he'll help you across."

No, he had papers and could cross the border the usual way.

A clean-shaven Turk opened the door. Abu Saad exchanged a few words with him before slapping me on the shoulder. "See you on the other side." Then he disappeared back into his car, and the Turkish guide invited me in. He showed me to a large unfurnished room—just mattresses at the sides of the room against the walls, and six or seven other guys. Most of them were Arabs, a few Chechens. Two of the Arabs were dressed entirely in black; I figured they were going to join Dawla. Nobody talked much. I sat there silently too. Prayer time brought us together a bit, but the Turk who owned the house didn't pray. For him, this was pure business.

We were fed a couple of handfuls of rice and a little meat. Sat on the floor, on those thin plastic woven mats. One of the Chechens said he was thinking of going to a rebel group called Ahrar al-Sham. His accent reminded me of Arbi. I already missed him. I wondered where he was now. We'd shared the whole journey, and now here I was with strangers.

New round of prayers, the last of the day, *isha*. Then it was totally dark. After that, someone said something in Arabic. He talked for at least a couple of minutes, but the only thing he explained in English was "*inshallah*, we'll leave in one hour."

We walked in the dark. Single file, 'cause the path was narrow, fields on either side. Each of us had our own bags. Of course, I'd brought too much, a large backpack and a heavy duffel bag. I heard someone praying to God as we walked. I was out of breath from all the weight. Nearly fell over. One of the Chechens came up beside me, took my bag, and put his arm around my shoulders. "*Akhi,*" he said—that's "my brother" in Arabic—"*Akhi*, it's gonna be all right."

The border was fenced. As we approached, the smuggler asked us to wait. You know, the Turkish police shoot at anything that moves out there. So we had to wait until it was safe. And then he called, "Now! Run!" We raced toward the fence. It was a lot higher than I'd expected. We worked in pairs to throw the baggage over. Someone had pulled aside the barbed wire there. We climbed up. I stood and swayed at the top and jumped awkwardly. I scratched my arm on the barbed wire and fell to the ground. It wasn't an elegant entrance, but I'd gotten there.

Yup, then I was in Syria.

We couldn't really see each other. Just walked on in the dark. We eventually got to a group of cars. None of them had their lights on, but we could hear the hum of the engines as we got closer. And suddenly there were loads of people. Not just the people I'd been in the house with—tons more. I saw a real rebel for the first time. You know, the total stereotype. Camo pants, beard, Kalashnikov, and a black bandana on his forehead with a declaration of faith, just like in all the pictures we'd seen at home.

It was like the arrival terminal in an airport; tons of people appear, some pretend to know where they're going, others are totally honest about how confused they are, and in the middle of it all people are standing there waiting. I almost expected signs with people's names. All the groups found their people. An FSA group was there and picked up their members. Dawla was there too. The two black-clothed Arabs went with them.

The recruits were driven away in pickups and trucks together with more experienced soldiers, many of them heavily armed. Some had sniper rifles slung across their backs. Kalashnikovs. RPGs. Grenades in their belts. Welcome to the war zone.

I didn't know where to go, just stood there like an idiot 'til someone tapped me on the shoulder. I quickly turned and saw Abu Saad. Now he was smiling. At last. "Welcome to my country."

Yes, I ended up back in Abu Saad's rust bucket. In a way it felt totally wrong, but I didn't exactly have a choice.

We drove in the dark. Almost no lights anywhere. No streetlights. Our headlights were off too. I talked with Abu Saad the whole way. Told him about Norway and Pakistan. That I'd gotten closer to Allah in the last couple of years and couldn't stand watching what was happening on the news any longer. He talked quietly, nearly mumbled his questions, nodded once in a while and added *mashallah*, and *alhamdulillah*.

I tried to ask about the JMA and when he was going to take me to them. "Things are difficult with the JMA right now," he said. After all the shit with the leaders and the split, he thought it would be best to wait and see how things developed. Besides, it wasn't clear who would lead what was left of the JMA anyway. Maybe it was best if I went home with him first.

On the way we stopped at an FSA joint. It was just a bus stop, but some rebels were using it as a kind of kiosk slash checkpoint. There were three guys there. One of them was sleeping, the other two were sitting on plastic chairs watching a small TV. They had a generator humming along, powering the TV and a refrigerator full of soda. I didn't understand. Coke and Fanta in a war-torn country? Like, where did they get it? The news was on, and one of the FSA people swore and pointed at the screen because, of course, the news was controlled by the government. "Look at that fucking shit," he said. I remember he wore a military bandana and was smoking. Abu Saad exchanged a few words with them, you know, people were brothers at that time. The different rebels talked with each other. Abu Saad bought us some chocolate that was way too sticky and just tasted of sugar. Then we got back in the car and drove on. Pickups with mounted guns were parked along the road. And there were checkpoints everywhere. "Who are you?" "Where did you come from?" "Where are you going?" But then there were fewer stops; we reached some villages, drove through a little town called Darkush, and eventually got to Abu Saad's house, just outside the town.

We got out of the car in the middle of an olive grove. His house had one of those low dung walls around the yard like I'd seen at the border guide's place in Turkey. It was really the boonies.

It's weird arriving somewhere in the dark; your imagination takes over and sketches out what you can't see. I felt like this would be my home for a while, even if nobody said it straight out. Inside, Abu Saad's son came running in his PJs to hug his dad. Then he said hi to me. He talked to me as if I could understand Arabic, but I really only caught that his name was Saad. When he realized I didn't understand, he just stopped and started to laugh.

He was six years old, with crooked bangs and stripy PJs. I barely saw Abu Saad's wife, because she'd realized that her husband had a visitor and had gone to make food for us. At my trial the prosecutor picked at that. Why didn't I know the wife's name and stuff? And when I explained that was how it worked, they thought it was a sign that Abu Saad was an extremist. I eventually didn't know my left from my right with all those terms, what they meant and didn't mean. But to call Abu

Saad an extremist really isn't right. But it still didn't mean that I could just walk in and start chatting with his wife.

Yeah, of course. I saw her when she came in with food and stuff. She had light-brown eyes, plucked eyebrows. If I know Abu Saad, he'd probably tried to get her to wear a niqab but hadn't managed it. She wore a Turkish hijab and a robe with a zigzag pattern.

We ate and he showed me around. That went quickly. The house wasn't big. The most important thing was that I felt safe there. I can thank Abu Saad for that. You know, he and I talked the whole way in the car, and we thought the same way. He was for Sharia and thought God's laws were better than people's laws. He included praise to Allah in every sentence. When I heard him speak, I got a taste of his heart. I was in the right place.

Abu Saad went to make up a bed for me. I got my own room, about the size of the visiting room here, or maybe a little bigger. There was a stove in the middle with a slanted steel pipe coming out of it. They used the room for storage, so Abu Saad had to move some things to get the mattress in. Then he wished me good night, and I was alone in the small room.

The room hadn't been fully painted; you could pull cement bits from the walls. The door was metal. When it was windy, the wind came sighing under the crack at the bottom. I kept the window open because it was still hot even at night, and there were always a couple of mosquitoes that found their way in past the screen. A bit like when I was in Murree in Pakistan and I couldn't sleep because of the insects. When I lay down on the mattress, I saw a lizard as well. It was sitting quietly on the wall. It was probably waiting 'til I turned off the light before it crept on its way. Later Abu Saad told me it was Sunna to squash lizards with your fist. I tried once, but it was too fast.

No, that first night I just lay and watched it sitting there. And then I heard the grasshoppers outside. My thoughts were all over the place.

I dreamed of Arbi that night, that he was over the border too. I remember I only saw him running and running and running. It never ended.

I was woken by a rooster that couldn't keep its damn mouth shut. When I got up and went outside, I saw what the place was really like. The pomegranate trees had ripe, bursting fruit even in September. There were those circles of stones on the ground around the tree trunks. There was a trellis sticking out from the house with grapes on it, and in the yard there were some sheep and two goats that looked completely stoned. Farther along the gravel path, you could see rows of olive trees and a few neighboring houses dotted among the dry fields and yellow grass.

Abu Saad found me outside and pointed to a bench in front of a faucet. He washed first and then stood and watched me do *wudu*. He probably wanted to make sure I did things right, that I was a practicing Muslim just like I'd told him. And the water was cold. The air was hot, but the water was freezing—oh-ha, it woke me up. We went to pray *fajr* up on the roof of the house. I looked out over all the olive trees. "Those are my trees," Abu Saad said and smiled. He'd started to build a second floor on the roof, but it looked like he'd given up halfway through. Now the war was getting all his attention.

Abu Saad led the prayer. It felt good. I was there, I'd made my hegira. I was where I was supposed to be.

Later we went into Darkush. The town lies on a river called the Orontes, but Abu Saad told me most people called it the Asi River; *asi* means "the rebel." I asked if it was named after the rebellion against Assad, but he laughed and shook his head. He liked my suggestion, but it was because all the rivers in the area run south, like the Euphrates, for example. But the Orontes runs north. "It has its own ideas about things," he said.

We drove into the town center. Well, it's not really much of a center; the whole town is on the side of a mountain by the river. Still, it was bustling with people. Some people were sitting at outdoor cafés or eating outside the kebab shop. Nothing reminded you of war actually, apart from some guys wearing military pants or something, mostly to show solidarity with the rebellion. The women went around in hijabs and *jilbabs* for the most part; one or two wore niqabs, but not many. Some of the younger girls were wearing jeans and sweaters. Abu Saad had a system to classify the towns according to how much they made you struggle spiritually. How great the temptation was, if you know what I mean. It's called *fitnah*, a test. So some towns were *fitnah* towns. Course, I'd seen all sorts of nudity in Norway, so I didn't exactly lose it if I saw a woman in jeans. But I pretended I agreed with Abu Saad. Darkush was *fitnah*-light, y'know; it was controlled by the FSA, so it was really liberal. It was a pretty town, and even though a lot of people looked somber and suspicious, life was nevertheless OK. At least at that time.

We went to the butcher's first. The meat was hanging in the street, with flies buzzing all around it. Abu Saad ordered, and I waved my dollars and said I could pay, but then Abu Saad gave me the worst look. Don't even think of it! I learned that you can't pick up the check for an Arab just like that.

Yeah, you could pay with dollars; the local currency had crashed, so you'd need huge amounts of cash to pay with that.

In the grocery store Abu Saad pointed at a refrigerator with a glass door filled with soda. "This here is the mujahedin's favorite drink," he said. He pointed to a box of energy drinks, Jack Wrestler. It gave you indigestion for hours after you'd chugged it down, but still, it wasn't too bad by Syrian standards. I learned that after a while. And it woke you up in the mornings. I bought one. Abu Saad got some flour and nuts and, um . . . oh, y'know, the stuff you give to birds?

Yeah, seeds. They eat bags and bags of sunflower seeds there.

We stood in the shade outside the shop and chewed on seeds. Abu Saad asked if there was anything I needed. I said I'd like to call Arbi, hear how he was doing. "Difficult," he said, "there's only coverage in some places and at certain times, and even if you get a signal, it's not sure your buddy has one." Man, the communication there is just a mess. It took a long time before I got in touch with Arbi.

I asked if Abu Saad could wait while I went into the barber's. I thought it was cleaner to have short hair since I was going to war. "The one on the corner is good," he said and went to buy some fruit. Without Abu Saad I struggled to explain how I wanted my hair cut, but they have these posters with models, so I pointed at the one with really short hair. Like that. The barber understood, so he started cutting. When he was finished, he put his scissors on what was left of my beard. "Yes?" And I just said, "No, no, no," but when I saw his face in the mirror, I realized he was joking.

Before we went home, we sat down in a kebab shop and ate. I wanted to ask when I'd be taken to the JMA, if he thought it'd be a long time, but I didn't want to nag. *It happens when it happens,* I figured.

I got into a kind of routine at Abu Saad's. Probably a week went by without anything much happening. I read the Koran, prayed, learned Arabic words from little Saad, and picked pomegranate seeds from the pomegranates.

At least once a day, I went on a walk with Abu Saad. Sometimes Saad came too, even though he didn't understand English. He reminded me of Little Brother, but kids there are different than in Norway, more grown up I'd say. He was a really sweet kid.

Abu Saad asked me about my life in Norway. I told him I was a qualified welder. He frowned. Y'know, there it's people on the street who are welders. Maybe he thought I should've been a doctor or something. I tried to explain that the class differences aren't so big in Norway. Welders respect doctors, but doctors also respect welders. He liked that. But he liked other things less, like me having done kickboxing. For a while he must have thought I was a criminal on the run or something. He also wanted to hear about Muslims in the north. I told him straight out that many don't practice. "But if they don't pray, they aren't Muslims," he said and quoted a hadith that says that the difference between them and us is prayer. Abu Saad was very strict about that. "There is no religion without prayer," he used to say. When he asked about my family, I tried to avoid the question. I thought it was embarrassing to say that my parents had divorced, all that about Dad having been in prison and Mom not wearing a hijab or anything.

Once when we were coming back to the farm from a walk, little Saad wanted to show me his lambs. There were three lambs. He got ahold of them and flipped the animals onto the ground to look tough in front of me. Then Abu Saad lifted his son up and asked what he thought about the president. "He isn't a president, he's a dog," replied Saad. Kids already have hatred planted firmly in their heads.

I started to get restless. Abu Saad noticed. After praying *dhuhr* on the roof one day, we went for a walk among the olive trees. He got ahold of one of the branches and looked at the olives. "They're ripening," he said. Then he started to talk about the war. What the different rebel groups stood for and how the conflict had been developing. He didn't think any of the groups were perfect. "Nusra operates a lot in the wings," he said. "You never know where you'll find them." He'd been in contact with the JMA a lot himself, but they'd been weakened by internal problems. He didn't even know who the leader was anymore. He wasn't particularly excited about Dawla either.

No, more because of the Sharia courts. Abu Saad was for Sharia, but one of his relatives had gotten into trouble in one of Dawla's courts.

I think it was his cousin, but Abu Saad never told me what he'd done or how he'd been punished. Just that a foreign soldier had gotten off for doing exactly the same thing in exactly the same court. "They treat us worse than people like you who come from outside," he said. "It should be the same for me and you." I was embarrassed when he said that. He compared it to Saudi Arabia, where a normal guy can be executed for something or another while the son of a sheikh would just get three weeks in jail for the same crime. Not that I felt like the son of a sheikh, but I did agree that people had to be treated equally.

Abu Saad didn't want to ally himself to any particular group. He had the contacts he needed for making himself useful. "Allah doesn't want us to be divided and take sides with different groups," he said. He thought all Muslims should stand together.

Yes, the Sunni Muslims, then. He didn't count the Alawites like Assad and the Shia Muslims. They were the enemy after all. But the Sunni Muslims had to stand together.

Abu Saad seemed to have given up when he talked about that. As if the words were difficult to get out. He said that having so many groups had become a problem. "If we have a common desire to fight against Assad, why should we be divided?"

I asked where he thought I should go now that the JMA was in a mess. He was silent. We continued walking between his olive trees. Then he stopped in the shade of a tree and explained he was waiting to get an ambulance that he was going to use for some kind of transportation scheme. He said it'd be good to have two people for the operation.

I said yes. I didn't really have many alternatives, to tell the truth. But I liked Abu Saad. I decided to give it a try. At least at first, until I got a better idea of what was going on.

OK, you read my court papers?

No, I understand. I would've checked too if I was writing a book about a guy in prison.

Yeah, they say I was in Dawla at first. That Arbi joined Sayfullah's group and I joined Dawla, right?

It was an email or something Arbi sent to Carlos that said I'd joined Dawla. But Arbi didn't really have a clue where I was then.

No, honestly, I don't know. He probably thought I had ended up there.

Listen, I swear, and I pray Allah punishes me if I'm lying. I never swore allegiance to Dawla. I was curious about them—that I readily admit—but I never joined IS.

I joined Abu Saad.

Y'know, it was possible to shop around at that time because the groups were working together. For example, one town could be controlled by several groups at the same time. They rotated guard duty. Dawla was already kinda in the wings by then, but there was still some cooperation.

After that walk in the olive grove, Abu Saad took me to his room. He opened a chest of drawers, and hidden under a cloth was a Kalashnikov. I'm sure he saw that I was fascinated, because he laughed at me.

I like weapons, I really do. Have you ever tried shooting?

You should go out on a range and try, then you'll know the feeling.

It was Czech. Abu Saad gave it to me. It was a bit like, y'know, like the first time you hold a baby; you're a little afraid and clumsy and wonder if you're holding it right and everything. But once I got it right, I felt like I was holding a tool in my hands. A tool for, y'know, yeah, killing. But also a tool for changing the world, making a difference.

I thanked Abu Saad. Tried to give the gun back, but he waved his hand. "Take it," he said, and showed me how to use the strap and carry the weapon over my shoulder.

Abu Saad got a couple of empty cans of that jihadist drink, Jack Wrestler. Then we drove out to a deserted area, where he put the cans down and told me to take aim. "Don't shoot before I tell you," he said. I was shaking like a leaf; I'd never shot anything before. Or, well, that's not quite true; I'd been on a rifle range once in Norway. But this was in Syria, and I was holding a Kalashnikov, y'know? The thing is, when he finally said shoot, nothing happened. I didn't squeeze the trigger hard enough. My palms got sweaty and stuff. I squeezed again and suddenly felt the weapon jerk. Bang! And then a whistling sound. Ringing in my ears. Abu Saad said something to me and I nodded, but I couldn't hear a thing. He explained that you could also put the gun on automatic, but that it was on single shot now. Ah. OK.

I'd missed, so the first shot rang out, but then I got less nervous and hit the cans with the second and third shots. Abu Saad came over, put on the safety, and took the weapon. "Good," he said. I could've kept shooting all day, but he said the bullets cost a little over a dollar apiece. "It's expensive to wage war," Abu Saad said.

That night, as if it were punishment for having played with weapons, I heard Assad's artillery for the first time. I awoke to rumbling. Then it came again. It's like waiting for the next clap of thunder; you lie still and try to hear if it's coming nearer each time there's a boom. It was. And the sound echoed off the mountains around us. I broke out in a cold sweat. Got dressed and went out of the house. Abu Saad must have heard me, because he met me outside. He said it was nothing to worry about. "It's a long way off. It's Assad shooting from Idlib to psyche us out, to wear people down."

We had to prepare ourselves. We were going to get to work soon. He asked if I wanted help calling my family at home first. I nodded but didn't tell him that I hadn't been in touch with Mom since I'd left.

It had been maybe a couple of weeks or so.

He drove me to a little hill and said I had to walk about halfway up the slope. "You should get a signal up there," he said. So there I stood in the scorching sun while I dialed the number. It took forever to connect. Then the ring tone sounded; I was so nervous I bit my lip. She answered with a calm voice. I allowed a moment's silence before I responded. "Hi, Mom." And then I could almost see it, how she clenched both hands around the phone, an anxious look in her eyes. "Where are you, my son?" You know, she pulled herself together so she wouldn't be too hard on me. She said she'd tried to call so many times, and the last times she had gotten some Turkish message. "I'm right on the border," I said, "but on the Syrian side." I could tell that really hit her hard. She wanted to know why I left without saying anything. I gave her the obvious answer, that she'd never have let me go. And then I had to explain why I left, about the brothers and sisters who are suffering here and all the Muslims in Norway who only care about their own stuff, who boast about the jobs they have and the houses they've bought, all those who climb that damn social ladder. Everything I'd been thinking just poured out. Eventually Mom asked me to stop. I could hear she was fuming, but she still spoke softly, calmly. She switched from Urdu to Norwegian as well. She was probably trying to reach a different side of me. "So it wasn't enough for you to collect aid for the refugees?" she asked. "No." "I understand," she said. The phone started burning my ear. I looked down at Abu Saad, who was sitting in the car waiting. "I won't be long," I said. "I'll come back." Then Mom broke down and started yelling into the phone. "You have to come back now. You have to come back right now!" She was shouting and crying. I didn't say anything. After a moment I took the phone away from my ear. Looked at the screen. I could still hear her crying as I pressed the red button. And then it was completely silent. I stood there for a while after I'd hung up, even though the sun was scorching. Just holding the phone. After a while I walked back to Abu Saad. He put his hand on my shoulder but didn't ask any questions.

We went to a town called Sarmada. They called it "the car town" 'cause people went there to get cars. We saw a couple of fighters dressed in black on the road, and I asked Abu Saad if they were soldiers from Dawla. "Yeah, probably Saudis," he said. "They have a lot of money." He told me Dana was just a couple of miles away. At the time it was the only Dawla town in the area. They'd even established a functioning Sharia court there.

We got the ambulance from a house just outside town. It was a nineties Ford. White and red, with chrome bumpers covered in rust. A few old ambulances had been donated to Syria, I don't know by who, and they'd been distributed to different groups or trusted people, like Abu Saad.

We drove back to Darkush separately. It's crazy driving there, total anarchy. In the rebel-controlled areas no one cares if you have a license or not, so there was a lot of really bad driving. I'd gone there to become a martyr in the fight against Assad, not get killed in a traffic accident.

I parked the car at Abu Saad's and joined him in the ambulance. Then our mission started. We drove to the Turkish border, picked up medical supplies, and took them to different pharmacies in the Idlib Province.

No, it was farther south than where I'd crossed. Remember the river that goes through Darkush, the one they call "the rebel"? It flows toward Turkey, and a ways up it marks the border between the two countries.

On the way we had to take this dirt road between two olive farms. The women were working on the harvest. They were covered, but you could tell by their eyes they were absolutely gorgeous. They laid blankets out, shook the branches, and collected the olives in a cloth pouch they had attached to their waists. "The best olives are the ones that have just fallen," Abu Saad always said. "Those black ones." At the end of the field we had to park and walk the last stretch along a narrow path. We got down to the river, where there was a huge bucket, more like a tub, on a pulley system they used to get people and things across the water. It was no more than a stone's throw across, but the current was strong. FSA people were just standing around. They were never armed. Camo clothes were OK, but bringing weapons to the river was forbidden. If they saw a weapon, the Turkish military would shoot in the air as a warning. They tolerated the smuggling, looked the other way, but they didn't want people wandering around with guns.

The first time I was there, I remember seeing a woman with her two sons and a school-age daughter waiting to flee into Turkey. You wouldn't believe the crazy amount of luggage they had. Cases and bags. And I just thought, *How are they possibly going to get all that across?* It was so easy to imagine how they'd sat at home and realized that, *Shit, now we have to pack up and leave,* but they hadn't managed to leave what they really should have left behind. I helped load the baggage into the tub and watched them get pulled across to Turkey. Since then I've seen a lot of people cross that river, so many that I don't remember the individual faces anymore. They just become a blur. During the day refugees were pulled over to Turkey, and smuggled goods came back into Syria. But during the night, in the darkness, fighters came over.

And then there were the people in wet suits. You see, gas was cheaper in Turkey than in Syria, but diesel was actually more expensive in Turkey, or maybe it was the other way around, I don't remember. Either way, people brought down barrels of fuel, tied them together, and floated them across the border. Diesel one way, gas the other. That's how they did their business.

We loaded the ambulance full of medicine and drove to the pharmacies in the nearest towns. They often functioned as small clinics or hospitals as well, maybe with just one bed or two. Sometimes we also transported food to different rebel groups that were guarding the checkpoints. Back and forth, back and forth.

A couple of the pharmacies we delivered to were in a small town north of Darkush called Salqin, where we always stopped to buy ice cream. It was a big thing, ice cream in Syria. You couldn't drive through Salqin without stopping for ice cream.

One of Abu Saad's best friends lived in Salqin as well, in the center, in a townhouse with narrow steps and a small living room behind a green metal door.

Abu Hajer.

Yeah, he has to be included.

You can cut out some of the other people if you think there are too many, but not Abu Hajer.

Solid guy, or maybe chubby is more precise, with a long beard and a crazy scar running down the side of his head across his face. He didn't talk much; the war had crushed him. Sometimes Abu Saad had to repeat what he'd said because Abu Hajer kinda disappeared—I don't know, just disappeared into his own thoughts. A bit like me now, just much worse.

He got mixed up, forgot things, but he did make an effort to stay in the moment. Later I found out that he'd lost nearly all his family in the war. Eight people. The scar was from an Assad soldier. He'd been cut up as punishment after one of the early demonstrations. Abu Hajer and Abu Saad had been friends before the war, and they looked after each other as best they could.

Abu Hajer was affiliated with Ahrar al-Sham, one of the largest rebel groups. They're Islamists, want Sharia law and everything, but they want it to come gradually and preferably democratically.

On the wall in his living room there was a framed poster of the *Ayat al-Kursi*, the Throne verse in the Koran. It's supposed to protect you. On another wall there was just a nail sticking out. You could tell by the mark on the wall that a picture had hung there earlier, before the war.

Y'know, Salafism had filtered into the rebel-controlled areas. People had become more conscious about religion, about Islam, about not having pictures on their walls and stuff.

There were those plastic mats on the living room floor. That's where we sat and talked politics. Or rather, they talked. I tried to understand as well as I could when Abu Saad wasn't translating. Abu Hajer didn't like the FSA. "Criminal pigs," he called them. "Bandits." He said they smuggled alcohol and drugs and ran brothels. Besides, some of the FSA groups had ties with the US. He really didn't like that. He shook his scarred head when he talked about them. Abu Saad tried to say that not all the FSA groups were bad, there were a lot of them, and some were even Salafists, but Abu Hajer just kept shaking his head. Still, Abu Hajer was more moderate than Abu Saad. First and foremost he wanted democracy, "And then we can talk about Sharia." Suddenly, you know, in the middle of the conversation, he'd turn, point at me with his whole hand, and talk to me in Arabic. Abu Saad had to translate so I could understand. "What can you do, *akhi*? What are you going to contribute?" I didn't really know what to say, but to be honest, it didn't seem like he expected an answer.

One time after we'd visited Abu Hajer, we made the obligatory ice cream stop in Salqin. As usual, I wanted chocolate, but this time Abu Saad insisted I try the mango. Well, all right. Mango it is. So there we stood with our mango ice creams in a cone. Y'know, the people who ran the ice cream store were FSA people. Not very religious. They had tattoos, smoked, and had a TV showing music videos. The ice cream man was happy; he swayed and sang along to what was probably a popular song. While we were standing there, three guys got out of a car. They were Dawla. One had a suicide belt on, I remember—it was the first time I'd seen one—with wires hanging down and a button fastened with a pin. They wanted ice cream too.

While two of them were scratching their beards wondering which flavor to have, the third one pointed to the TV and asked the guy to turn it down. The ice cream man ignored him and started on the order he got from the two others—vanilla for one and pistachio for the other. Dawla didn't have any control in Salqin, so he probably thought that he didn't need to obey. Then he got told a second time "Turn down the TV." A guy farther back in the shop turned and looked at the soldiers. But the ice cream man just carried on scooping his ice cream. He didn't give a shit. Gave some smart-ass answer. Then the soldier went ballistic. He took out his gun and emptied his clip at the TV. Sparks and glass flew everywhere. In the end the TV was totally gone, just a hole in the wall and a ringing in our ears after the shots. The soldier grabbed the ice cream man by the collar and pulled him over the counter. They pushed him into their car and drove away. And Abu Saad and I were just standing there with our mango ice cream slowly melting.

No, two or three days later we drove by and he was back, without a scratch. They'd taken him to a Sharia court, but he didn't get tried. The TV, on the other hand, was gone. They never put in a new one.

The muffler on our ambulance rattled, the motor whistled on left turns, the odometer had stopped, the speedometer didn't work, the seats were ripped up, the siren was broken, and one of the side mirrors was smashed. The vehicle wasn't 100 percent, to put it bluntly. There was only one thing that kept that ambulance from falling apart, and that was Allah. It had been stripped of all its equipment apart from an old clumsy defibrillator and an oxygen mask attached to the wall. Since it didn't have a bed, Abu Saad had put cardboard on the floor in case we had to transport any wounded people. There were loads of buttons on the dashboard, but only one worked. It blew a lot of hot air straight at us. It stank of burning plastic, but we never figured out where the smell was coming from. You had to really rev the engine to get it started. I asked Abu Saad whether our jalopy maybe needed some oil. "Oil, no; cars here don't need oil." *OK then,* I thought.

Fuel was a constant issue. You know the barrels of fuel that they smuggled over? They were delivered to places along the roads, and children would sit with funnels and canisters, ready to fill up your car. *MAZOT* and *BENZIN*, diesel and gas, was always written on a little sign. But before it got into your tank, they'd dilute it with something to make more money. We always tried to look at the color, check the smell, but the kids just stood there and told blatant lies, that the gas was 100 percent pure. But they didn't really earn anything if they didn't dilute it, so it was never totally pure. This was the type of thing we dealt with, finding the best possible gas. When the smoke from the car was black, you just thought, *OK, those brats tricked us.* Then you don't buy from them the next time around.

No, of course not. The cars were totaled, one after the other. Toyota engines were the only ones that lasted. The Japanese engines can stand quite a beating; they just keep going on whatever fuel they get. Our Ford on the other hand barely spluttered along. But we loved it. Or we came to love it. One day we found a sticker in a kiosk that said *Allahu akbar,* and I stuck it on the windshield. Abu Saad beamed when he saw it; I'd almost never seen him so happy. *"Mashallah,"* he said, "now we're driving with Allah."

Once in a while Abu Saad would start to hum a song while we were driving. Then he'd catch himself and stop. He thought I was a really strict Salafist, and I thought the same about him. In the beginning we kinda competed to see who was the better Muslim, but eventually we started to get more relaxed.

I learned more and more Arabic. Each time we stopped to have a drink, I tried new words I'd learned. The most important were *ana uridu,* "I need." After a while I was able to upgrade to *anta turidu.* "You need." Then it started to click; I need something, you need something, everyone needs something.

We weren't exactly busy; Abu Saad would often take a small detour to show me Byzantine ruins. There was a ruin of an old church nearby, certainly over a thousand years old. It made me think of everything the country had seen in the past. For a farmer with no formal education to speak of, Abu Saad was really knowledgeable when it came to history. He could talk on and on about trade routes that had shifted to the east and west, about the Umayyad Caliphate that took over, and why the Byzantine villages were deserted.

In the end I felt more like a tourist than a jihadist. Of course, what we were doing was useful, but I asked myself if I shouldn't really be contributing more, making a bigger difference. Was this my jihad? Sitting in my Norwegian combat vest driving around with supplies? It wasn't exactly how I'd imagined it. And at some point I started to wonder if it might be better to take up arms and just throw myself into war, no matter where. You know, I was lacking something important there. I was lacking *sabr*. You think war is full-on fighting day in and day out, but for the most part it's waiting and relocating and logistics. You have to be patient.

Abu Saad was a sensitive person. He understood that I was restless. At least he gave me responsibility for the Kalashnikov, which we always carried with us when we were driving around. That felt a bit better. For a while at least. I'd sit and poke at the foam in the seats in the ambulance while Abu Saad drove. I shoved a bullet from the Kalashnikov as far into the foam as I could and tried to imagine the pain.

People at the checkpoints were often suspicious of me 'cause I didn't know Arabic. Even though I'd learned some words, they figured out immediately that I wasn't one of them. There were more foreigners elsewhere, but around Darkush there were very few, so they were skeptical. "Who's that guy?" "Does he support the regime?" People were paranoid, y'know. Things like that stressed Abu Saad out, so he preferred to go alone on some deliveries. But he had a job for me, he said. We went to the hospital in Darkush. They needed a security guard at the entrance.

The job was pretty simple really; I had to ask people to leave their weapons before they went into the hospital. They didn't want to give Assad any reason to bomb the hospital; it had to be a weapon-free zone. Not that it mattered—Assad bombs everything anyway.

The hospital had simple, old beds with plastic curtains between them. I got to know a Moroccan doctor, Karim, who spoke fluent English. He'd volunteered and rented himself a little house next to the hospital.

No, he was completely independent of any organization. I didn't see any signs of relief agencies while I was in Syria, not where it was all happening at least. Or rather, I did see UNHCR; they were distributing food and clothing. And the Red Crescent of course. Otherwise, nothing. But there were people like Karim. I admired him coming here with his medical knowledge. Sometimes we went out and got a cup of tea together when he wasn't too busy with patients.

One day when he saw me, I had a table full of weapons that had been left by soldiers as they came in. "How's it going, soldier?" he asked. "You've got a lot of weapons to look after today." And then he decided that I should be called Abu Silah. "Weapons' Dad," or "Father of Weapons." I got my *kunya* right there, my fighter name. Everyone's called Abu something there. If you have kids, you call yourself Abu and then the name of your eldest son, just like Abu Saad. But if you don't have kids, you make something up. I heard of a guy who was working as a florist who was called Father of Flowers, Abu Zahra. And I was Abu Silah.

No, the guard job didn't go well. It was totally wrong. You can imagine how an armed Syrian soldier feels taking orders from a foreigner who can't even speak Arabic. I just felt like an idiot, went up to the armed soldiers, and used the few words I knew. *"Akhi, la?"* And then I pointed to the gun and indicated they had to leave it on my table.

Once there was a huge guy with a gun on his back who wanted to go in with his pregnant wife. When I went up to him and said my thing, he waved his hand and just kept on walking. So I called to him again. Then he turned, gave me an icy stare, and threw his gun on the table. Bam! And then the pistol out of its holster. Bam! And yet another pistol from his ankle. Bam! Then he went in with his wife. That was when I'd had enough. At the end of the day, when I saw Abu Saad, I told him I couldn't do a job where I so clearly needed to know Arabic. He nodded and said I might as well join him in the ambulance anyway. But I felt like I was in the way, y'know, that I was more of a burden than a help.

We'd delivered food to soldiers from Ahrar al-Sham who were guarding a checkpoint. On the way back to Darkush, a car suddenly appeared heading toward us, swerving and honking its horn. We pulled over and felt a rush of air as it passed. Abu Saad put his head in his hands. I didn't understand what was happening. Then another car from the same direction, at top speed, horn blaring. One more, and then another. On the way into Darkush, we saw thick, black smoke rising from the center of town. We stopped at a gas stand and asked a boy if he knew anything. "Car bomb," he said.

The cars that had passed us were probably transporting the wounded. "It must have been a big one," Abu Saad said. We drove toward the market square where the bomb had exploded. There were people everywhere. Like when you poke something into an anthill and the ants crawl out all over the place. We got out of the ambulance. The air smelled acrid, like gasoline; it stank of chemicals. The walls of the surrounding buildings had collapsed. The air was thick with dust.

I couldn't recognize any of the shops or buildings. I almost couldn't orient myself because it was all so unrecognizable. People were running with buckets and throwing water through the hole in a wall. It took a while before I realized that was where the kebab shop had been. The metal chairs had twisted in the heat and looked like maimed animals. I spotted the blast crater; it was huge. People were screaming. The screams merged and triggered new screams. Abu Saad grabbed me and asked me to follow him. We walked toward the hospital. Blood was smeared all over the steps. Doctors and nurses were running back and forth. They had way too much to do. Abu Saad asked the director of the hospital if we could help with anything, but they'd already transported the wounded who needed to be moved. They only needed medical personnel. I saw Karim run past. His forehead was covered in sweat and he looked focused. He was treating a woman who had shrapnel in her hip. Her son sat by the side of the bed, just a little kid, holding her hand. I could see he was squeezing her hand, and she was squeezing back. The air was heavy in there. I knew I had to get out.

I went back to the market square. Just stood there and looked at all the confused faces. Mine was one of them. A backhoe was moving walls that had collapsed, trapping a family. A grandfather was walking in the rubble, calling for his grandchild. The boy had been completely blown apart; the grandfather was standing over him but didn't recognize him. It took a long time before he realized it was his grandson. As he screamed toward the heavens, someone came over and wrapped the boy up in a white sheet and put an arm over the old man's shoulders.

I'd seen videos of these things online. That was why I'd come, after all. But it's different when you're standing in the middle of it all with your own body, your pulse and your head not working, and hands you don't know what to do with. And you want to do something, anything, but you just don't know what. Your soul gets diluted; you feel like a nobody.

I'd lost sight of Abu Saad. I stood there feeling useless. I'd traveled the whole way to Syria to help people, but when I was actually needed, I had nothing to give. I felt dizzy, sat down on the curb, clenched my teeth, and cried.

When I pulled myself together and looked up, I saw a pale-white guy walking by. He had blue eyes and a Kalashnikov on his back. He was talking with a Syrian, but in broken Arabic. I went over to him. I hadn't actually seen any Europeans since I came to Syria. He asked something in Arabic, but when he saw I didn't understand, he switched to English. "Where are you from, brother?" "Norway." Then he switched to Norwegian. But that wasn't all. Holy shit. The guy, or Rudi as he was called, was from Sarpsborg! Like, what are the chances of two guys from the same little region in Norway meeting at a bomb crater in a Syrian village? At first we were both happy, but then I realized I was embarrassed. Here you've met an ethnic Norwegian who came to Syria, and before you've even gotten your shit together, he already speaks Arabic, he's gotten himself a weapon, and he's ready to defend Muslims. What had I been doing?

Rudi wanted to know which group I was with. I said I was still looking around and trying to get an overview. I asked what he thought about the JMA groups and Sayfullah's group that Arbi had gone to. "They're hardcore," said Rudi. "Y'know both of those groups are full of Caucasians; they're still worked up from the jihad in Chechnya. They were some of the first to throw themselves into Syria to help the rebels." When he said that, I started to wonder whether I should've gone with Arbi, if I was in the wrong place.

Rudi was with Dawla.

Yeah, of course. I asked him where he was based. He couldn't tell me, but I got his number. "Get yourself a weapon and we'll talk."

He'd held back, so I didn't want to dig too much. You shouldn't ask too many questions. He said he was in the Dana area. He'd come to Darkush when he'd heard about the bomb.

If I'd really wanted to, I could probably have gotten into Dawla right then. But what I'd seen of them made me uncertain. That, along with what Abu Saad had told me about them treating Syrians worse than the foreign fighters. At the same time I knew, y'know, that in the middle of all the brutality, I'd be safe with Rudi. Can you imagine? There I was with my tearstained, worn face, and I meet a guy who's completely calm in all the chaos. I knew that he'd seen worse. Much worse. He was quite simply prepared for war. He was there, but he didn't let himself be broken down by all the suffering. Rudi had everything I lacked: calm, presence, focus. It was Rudi who helped me understand that I still wasn't ready for war. I had to pull myself together and look the beast in the eye.

All the shops in Darkush were closed now. People either had their shops blown up, or they were too afraid to open. So we went to Salqin a lot, the ice cream town. They were open there. I especially remember the vegetable seller. He was always sitting there in his military pants daydreaming. I bet he missed how things were before the war. I always bought a little extra to make him happy, and he always put a little extra in the bag.

Because we were in Salqin so much, I got to know Abu Hajer better. I didn't like him a lot at first. I thought Syrians should be grateful that people like me had traveled from Norway or wherever to help, but I was just cannon fodder in his eyes. Like, OK, so here's another new guy who's just going to go out and get himself killed. He never laughed. Maybe smiled sometimes, but we never ever got so much as a giggle from him. Not even when Abu Saad made fun of the FSA soldiers. "They run into empty houses waving their guns around, like this, firing in all directions, *ra-ta-ta-ta-ta*, and then throw grenades—boom—but forget to take the pin out first." Abu Hajer didn't like to joke about those things. He just sat quietly.

Nevertheless there was something honest about Abu Hajer. He didn't try and hide how broken his heart was. After a while he started to accept me. We'd eat together on the straw mats in his living room while he and Abu Saad told each other what they'd heard on the news.

Once, while I was sitting eating hummus and bread with the Abus, my phone rang.

Yeah, suddenly it had coverage.

It was my uncle—y'know, the one who took me to the Islam Net meeting the first time. I stood up and took a deep breath, didn't know where I should go to take the call. My uncle talked calmly. Of course Mom had told him I'd hung up when she pressured me too much.

I didn't say anything about the car bomb. Just that everything was fine and that I was staying away from dangerous places. Then he started to hint strongly that there were other ways to help, that war is dangerous, and that Mom was worried. Not a surprise really, but you know it affects you anyhow. I said I'd take it easy, that I just had to finish up down here, then I'd come back home. I could hear my uncle was struggling not to get worked up. He said it wasn't our job to get mixed up in this. The Syrians had to sort it out themselves, in their own way. Then the line was cut, and his words were left hanging in the air around me. I'd already experienced how useless you can feel. What if it was wrong for those of us from outside to interfere? But at the same time, I felt a responsibility. Not just toward Syria, but toward God, you understand? That's what I was thinking.

We'd just gotten back in the ambulance and were on our way out of Salqin when some kids came running past. Abu Saad asked them what happened. They told us Dawla was about to try some people under Sharia law, so we followed the kids in the vehicle. There was a crowd of people standing in a half circle around two men who were kneeling at the base of a cliff. Their hands were tied behind their backs. They were blindfolded. A young man and an older one. We parked and climbed onto the roof of the ambulance to get a better view. I wondered what they'd done, but then I heard the word *loti*: it means "homosexual" in Arabic, from the story of Lot.

The town was mostly FSA, but Dawla was running the show. Most of the people standing around were civilians. Some people from the FSA or other groups were there too. They were watching. It was damn hot that day. The air was heavy with dust. I went closer and saw a soldier wearing a balaclava read something from a piece of paper. The two guys who'd been accused of being gay were asked if they'd ask for Allah's forgiveness. The older man did it. Went along and said that what he'd done was wrong. So he got to leave. But the younger one was adamant. He was proud. It costs to be proud.

A soldier lifted him by the hair and pulled him up a path that led to the top of the cliff. They dragged him to the edge of the precipice.

Maybe twenty meters up.

We were below. The crowd was totally silent. There were probably a lot of people who thought it was wrong, but nobody said anything. Then one kicked him in the back. His body did a somersault as it fell to the ground. A dull thud, and there he lay. He wasn't dead. The blindfold had slid half off, so we could see one eye staring at us. His body was shaking. He would probably be dead in a matter of seconds, but one of the Dawla soldiers went over anyway, put his rifle on automatic, and emptied the magazine. Someone shouted, *"Allahu akbar,"* but it wasn't convincing. There was fear in the man's voice; they shouted mostly out of fear.

Me? What I saw gave me a knot in my stomach. But it's not about what I think, is it? It's about what God does or doesn't like. I don't know what God would want us to do, how we should punish gay people.

To be totally honest, I think what people do in their own homes is between them and God, y'know? But I don't like it if they're out publicly. Then it's a problem.

It's like a virus. If you keep it contained, it's all right, but if you let it out, it spreads.

Yes, a bad influence. It's the same with smoking. Fine, smoke at home if you want to, that's up to you, but don't smoke on the street and pretend it's cool.

No, not the death penalty. You have to show it's wrong, but that was going way too far. What do you think about homosexuality?

OK.

Yes, I understand.

I didn't mean to bad-mouth your friends. I just think it's wrong.

What's sick is how the violence creeps into you. You know what you've seen is wrong, but you accept it because everyone around you accepts it. Or at least on the surface they do. Morals are a vulnerable thing. Your sense of justice is influenced by how other people act. Maybe it's cowardly not to say anything in such a situation, but there's a real chance you'd get in trouble if you opened your mouth. And when everyone thinks like that, there's an agreement that it's OK. It's how it should be.

We didn't take his body with us in the ambulance, no.

I got a motorcycle. It didn't mean I felt more useful, but it cheered me up. Motorcycles always cheer you up.

Yeah, right after the gay thing. Write that it was the next day or something, so it flows better.

No idea. The second half of October sounds about right to me.

Abu Saad had heard about a motorcycle for sale and asked if I was interested. We drove to a farm an hour outside Darkush, where we met a chubby farmer. You could see by his skin that he'd been working outside his whole life—by his rough hands, the deep wrinkles in his face, and the dust in his hair. I wondered what kind of wreck he had lying around, but then he opened the garage and showed us a flame-red bike without one spot of rust. It was a fake Suzuki. I think it was called Guzuki or Uzuki or something like that. Chinese, I think, but it was really great. He told me it'd belonged to a martyr. The farmer's son had died in battle. Well, for me it was an honor to have something that had belonged to a martyr. I realized it was tough for him to sell it. He gave me an unbelievably good price. He asked for 450 dollars, but I put 500 on the table and said I wouldn't even think of giving less than that.

Then I just had to ride it back. Over the next few days I rode the motorcycle whenever I wasn't with Abu Saad in the ambulance. I rode through checkpoints where we'd delivered food, and some of the rebels recognized me and gave me a thumbs-up. I went full throttle and felt the wind on my face as I tore through olive groves and over dusty plains.

It was easier to get online after I got the motorcycle. There was an Internet café in Salqin, for example. Tiled. Ten to twelve computers, each with a flat screen, and steps up to a mezzanine, where there was a chill zone with rugs and pillows and stuff. I was hesitant when I sat down the first time there. I didn't know what to search; I mean in Norway I searched for things on Syria all the time. But now I was in Syria; what was I supposed to search? I looked up some Norwegian newspapers. Same crap as always. Makeup tips. Advice if you were depressed. Advice if you were looking for sex. Advice for whatever. Not much to be had there. So I looked up maps that showed where the Syrian regime had advanced recently. Read about all the attacks they'd carried out. In Idlib the government soldiers had taken girls called Aysha or other typical Sunni Muslim names and used them as slaves. You really want to buy a machine gun and throw yourself into the front line when you hear about things like that.

I had to calm myself down. Went onto Facebook, and believe it or not, suddenly there was a message from Carlos. "Are you there?" I got really excited. "Yes," I replied. *"Subhanallah,"* he wrote, and then, of course, he really let me have it. "How could you leave without telling me?" I tried to explain it was best he didn't know and stuff. He wasn't feeling argumentative and said he respected our choice. He was more interested in knowing how we were doing down here. "Just tell me everything, brother," he wrote. I started to think about the car bomb and wanted to tell him about what I'd been up to. But I didn't really know what to write, how I should put it, so I just wrote that everything was OK, really vague stuff, and that I missed hanging out with him. Carlos, on the other hand, had a lot to say. He said he was struggling with his faith, with *iman*, y'know. Carlos had become religious so fast; he kinda burned out. Spiritually burned out. Then he wrote that he'd gotten a girlfriend. "But there's a problem," he added. "She's from a really Christian family." They had already complained about him being a Muslim. I wrote that if he loved her, it'd work itself out, *inshallah*. "Just hurry up and marry her." He started to write about all his problems—you know, details of his love life—but it was hard to take in what he wrote. Norway seemed so far away, and the images of the car bomb still filled my head.

When I left the Internet café in Salqin, I saw that a stage had been put up along the road, not far from where the gay man had been pushed off the cliff. Dawla was running the show now. A guy was standing on the stage with his hair pulled back, and he was laughing and talking into the microphone. I think it was a Koran quiz or something. There was candy for all the kids. They were trying to make a good impression, win over people's hearts, y'know. I stopped for a moment, then I drove home to Abu Saad's.

A few days later, I got a message from Arbi. At last. He'd been in military training up in the mountains, had gotten himself a weapon, an RPK, and had sworn *bayah*, allegiance, to Sayfullah Shishani. Now he was on his way to Aleppo, where government forces were advancing and had to be stopped. And then he wrote something that really hit home. "Brother," he wrote, "if you want to see who the hypocrites are in this war, then look at the people who are behind everyone else." That bothered me; I thought he was at the front and I was at the back.

He'd gotten to the root of the problem, while I was just trimming the branches. He probably didn't mean it like that. But he was where he was supposed to be. He was doing what we were supposed to be doing.

After reading his email, I went to a shop for weapons and military equipment. Technical combat vests were hanging outside the store. Some of them had been handmade in Syria. It had gotten that far down there; the war was so established that they had home production of combat vests. The shop was run by an older FSA guy, who held a cigarette and a teacup in one hand and used the other to beckon me in. There were weapons all over the walls. Most of them were from Turkey; that's what the seller said anyhow. He showed me a pump-action shotgun, a sharpshooter rifle, and a grenade launcher. He wasn't busy. He let me examine each of the weapons. Then he showed me two pistols, and I noticed an emblem on the back of the hammer on each of them. The seller told me it was the emblem of the Syrian military. *"Ghanima,"* he said, "spoils of war." I put them down, got a bad feeling. Who had these belonged to? Whose hands had held them? What had they been shooting at? I said I was more interested in a machine gun. The guy rubbed his eyes and found a Kalashnikov. He only had one machine gun, he said. I held it. It was lighter than the one Abu Saad had. Almost like it was a toy gun, y'know? It didn't feel right in my hands.

No, I wanted to talk to Abu Saad. Maybe he knew someone, like with the motorcycle. Besides, I'd probably have been cheated on the price.

Oh yeah, I bought something. I bought a plate to put in my combat vest so it would be bulletproof. Nobody used those things down there; the only one he had was lying around getting dusty. It was heavy, about nine or ten pounds, and I got it cheap. You should have two, one in the front and one in the back, so I had to decide where I wanted to get shot. Back or front?

We'd been in the vicinity of Dana with our deliveries, and I'd started to ask more about Dawla. Y'know, Abu Saad wasn't the kind of person to judge rebel groups and paint them black or white. He wanted me to find things out for myself. OK, I'd seen some things that I didn't like about Dawla, but I was still curious. Abu Saad suggested we drive into Dana, then I could see the Sharia court and make up my own mind.

We had to go through a checkpoint that had barriers and sandbags and huts on the side. A guy with a black kerchief around his head was on top of the huts, his eyes hidden behind a pair of aviator sunglasses. The Dawla flag was fluttering right behind him. The guy that came over to the vehicle was wearing a balaclava, and he spoke to Abu Saad for a long time. Strict operation, but as soon as we were on the other side, everything was relaxed. Dawla soldiers were standing strategically in front of the Sharia court. A machine gun here, a machine gun there. Otherwise, it all looked pretty normal. A completely normal town. People kept going in and out of the court.

Of course, I'd never seen a Sharia court before, but neither had Abu Saad. He'd just heard from his relative who'd had that bad experience with it. Y'know, Abu Saad was always talking as if he was going to show me things, like a tour guide, but he was just as curious himself.

We managed to park on a side street, where a gang of fighters were standing around a grill. Chechens—you could tell by their bodies, the way they moved, the way they talked. They were probably on break from guard duty or something. The actual court was open to everyone, but there were separate entrances for men and women. Inside I saw a huge guy wearing a white tunic and a kind of scarf—I can't remember what it's called; you know, the ones they wear in Saudi Arabia, with the ring around the top. He was the judge, I was pretty sure about that. He was just walking around. Probably having a break 'cause he was fed up of answering everyone's questions. People were lining up, y'know, with arguments between neighbors, shoplifting, theft, smuggling, selling cigarettes, everyday disputes, whatever. You have to explain practical laws to people—*fiqh*, based on Sharia, or God's laws. What's right and wrong. What's halal, what's haram. There were many false accusations, people who used the situation to get rid of somebody they didn't like, who came up with stuff. So the judge had a lot to sift through.

Yeah, there was only one judge. Well, there was another one sitting there too, but he wasn't accepting petitions. There weren't enough people who knew how to do that job, and the pile of papers was, like, this high.

I went over to the cells. They were dark with bars, so you could see who'd been arrested. A window at the opposite end of the hall let in a stream of light. I heard the sound of someone sobbing but couldn't tell who was crying. Some people claimed they had a jail in the basement as well, where they took people from other rebel groups. I don't know if that was true. When it comes to Syria, you never know what's true and what's a lie.

I really wanted to see how the actual trials worked, but Abu Saad came over and said it was time for prayer, so we went to the nearest mosque. On the way out, Abu Saad said he had mixed feelings. He'd been talking with a man and had heard some stories. "It's good they follow Sharia here," he said, "but you can't condemn people who don't know any better. You can't just start whipping a guy who's been drinking his whole life and then push him into a mosque."

Dana was more lively than the other towns. Really. There were other rules there, some people were obviously afraid of Dawla, but I got the impression the town was vibrant. Abu Saad put it this way: "In Dana, Dawla's working; it gives people stability in the middle of the war." But at the same time he didn't think it would work in Darkush. "People are different there," he said.

I noticed some small things. The barbers, for example, they also had those photographs so you can point to a hairstyle and say, "I want that style," and if you're lucky you get something similar. But in Dana, they'd blacked out the eyes and most of the faces of the models. In Dawla's interpretation of Islam—actually for most Salafists—the use of pictures is strongly forbidden. On the posters there was just an outline of a face and then the hairstyle at the top. It was the same with advertising posters. Some of the stores had TVs, but there was a cloth over the screen. All the programs came from Damascus, of course, and the women didn't wear hijabs. If music was played, they turned down the volume.

The next time Arbi sent me news, he'd been on the defensive against the government forces southeast of Aleppo. They'd managed to hold them off. Arbi had proven himself particularly courageous and had been promoted by Sayfullah Shishani to one of his personal bodyguards. "Brother, come for a visit." *"Inshallah,"* I answered. Maybe there was a place for me after all, with Sayfullah's Caucasians. But I'd promised to help Abu Saad, and I didn't want to be a *munafiq*.

Carlos kept sending messages when he saw I was online. Once he wrote that he'd done something he regretted. He'd split up with his girlfriend, so he went to a party and had a drink, and now he felt bad about it. Sometimes I thought I missed life in Norway, but the best antidote was getting a message from Carlos. Then I lost any desire for Norway. I wrote to him that as a Muslim you trip and fall many times. The most important thing is to get up again and carry on. He answered that he felt lonely in his belief now that I'd left him. I remember the message word for word. He didn't just write *left*; he wrote *left me*.

One evening Abu Saad got the grill ready at his house. Normally his wife cooked, but grilling was like a boys' night. He'd bought and marinated some meat. Saad was with us, but after we'd eaten, he was sent in to his mom, while Abu Saad and I stayed there poking at the embers with sticks. It got dark. The stars came out. It was crazy how many stars there were in the sky. All the man-made light had been bombed away. I thought about the telescope I'd gotten from Dad when I was small; it would've been fun to use in Syria. While I was looking up at all the stars, Abu Saad said he had news he wanted to talk over with me. "We're going to Aleppo," he said. "Are you ready for that?" I was back on earth in a split second. I wasn't just ready, I was hungry for something to happen. "Yes," I said.

We packed our things. It was well into fall now, October, maybe even November, and you couldn't light a fire near the front line, so warm clothes were a must. There's something about the cold there; when it finally gets cold, it goes right into your bones.

Norwegian-wool long underwear, three layers of shirts, and a Stormberg fleece sweater. I'm not really sure they'd be happy for the advertising. The very best thing was my Buff scarf, because your neck got really cold, and I could pull it over my nose if it got dusty. And a pair of woolen socks—important, you know—really thick Norwegian-quality ragsocks. I gave Abu Saad a pair as well, which he really liked. He had bad shoes, some kind of Chinese crap that were ripped at the sides, but he took good care of them, he really did. Brushed off all the wet Syrian dirt that had stuck to them. Since it had gotten cooler, Abu Saad wore a coat.

Nope, it was dark blue. He wasn't the type to wear military clothing, but he did have a camouflage cap that he sometimes wore. It was too small for him. He looked a bit silly in it because he couldn't really pull it down over his head properly.

We left early one morning, right after prayer. I heard Abu Saad talking with his wife while I waited outside. Her voice was tight with worry. Abu Saad was probably trying to say something comforting. When he came out, he stared at the ground the whole way to the ambulance. Those red clouds I like so much hung over the olive grove, and the ground was damp. We drove through Darkush. The crater in the market square was still there. Abu Saad talked about the twenty-plus people who'd been killed. It was never clear who'd planted the bomb. Most probably the government. Some people thought it was Dawla. The town was picking itself up and trying to somehow get on with life.

We drove through Salqin to let Abu Hajer know where we were going. He said he'd pray for us. He even patted me on the shoulder, still without smiling. Then we drove up past Sarmada and Dana; the two towns were about midway between Darkush and Aleppo. At a crossroads we went to the left. Abu Saad pointed in the other direction. "A car drove down that way and got blown to pieces by Assad." You had to take the right road in Syria.

Abu Saad and I were silent for nearly the whole trip. Once in a while he'd lean over the wheel and stretch his back. He never complained, but I realized his body wasn't in the best shape. His fingers were never completely still; he drummed on the wheel. He'd given me two bullets to guard in my jacket pocket. "The last two," he said.

Believe me, nobody wants to end up a prisoner in Syria.

I played a *nashid* I knew Abu Saad liked on my phone. Looked out the window. When you think you might not be coming back, you might as well take in the view.

The trip from Darkush to Aleppo is no more than sixty miles, but with checkpoints and detours it can take nearly half a day. For a whole stretch there were almost no houses. In the middle of that stretch, I saw Abu Saad looking at the rearview mirror again and again. A whole military convoy of rebels was speeding toward us. They came right up behind us and started to pass. Trucks and pickups. Massive anti-aircraft guns—y'know, the ones where one person sits turning it and another person shoots. Some trucks were loaded with heavy artillery, others with soldiers armed to the teeth. As they passed us, they pointed up to the sky. *La ilaha illa llah.* They smiled; they were happy they were going to become martyrs. Abu Saad blew the horn, and I rolled down the window and leaned out. I pointed up to God. Waved my Kalashnikov out the window and yelled that God is great.

We saw a lot of cars as we got closer to Aleppo, but they were civilian and driving in the opposite direction. They'd packed their cars full, mattresses tied to the roofs. They'd had enough. These were the things that kept me going. These things confirmed that what I was doing was right, even if many of the people were probably so fed up they didn't care if it was Assad or the rebels who won, they just wanted peace. An old man was driving along in a tractor with his wife. He'd gotten a whole houseful of furniture on his trailer. The people behind him were honking and passing. Then that was the end of the cars; they were driving in a convoy too.

Right afterward we drove past a woman with a baby in her arms who was pulling a little boy along. They had to have walked a really long way, because there was nothing on the road behind them. Things like that gnaw at you, that we couldn't stop and help people like her. Nobody can help everyone.

Our mission was to transport wounded people if the offensive began. In the meantime, we transported food from a warehouse just outside Aleppo into the town itself, to a garage being used as a depot. From there we took rations to supply the front line with food. Y'know, it was those bags from UNHCR and the World Food Program, donated stuff. Each one contained a few bags of vacuum-packed food, like astronauts get up in space. We had to get those to the soldiers.

We just had to get started and load. It gave me flashbacks to the back-breaking work I did for the temp agency in Norway. A bald rebel came with us in the ambulance from the first garage into Aleppo. He talked nonstop with Abu Saad, updating him on the situation.

Maybe he was from Ahrar or the FSA. I don't remember.

The stuff in the garage belonged to all the rebel groups. I'm sure one of the groups had the main responsibility, but things weren't all that clear.

Whatever, I didn't understand almost anything of what they said. I just looked out the window. We came over a hill and looked down on Aleppo. The town was getting closer. It's crazy big, man, really enormous. It doesn't seem to stop, and in the middle there's a little hill with a fortress on top. It's like one of those World Heritage Sites.

It was starting to get late as we came into town. We drove through the ruins of an industrial area. The bald guy made an effort to explain something in English. He said that while the rebel front was pushing forward, criminals were coming in behind them and stealing expensive machinery from the factories. They would dismantle the whole thing and transport it to Turkey, where they could sell it for lots of money. He took a long time to find the words in English, but I tried to seem interested. Before he was done explaining, we heard a helicopter above us. High, high up. "Look," said Abu Saad. A little dot fell out of the sky. It disappeared behind the buildings far ahead of us. It was the first time I heard the sound of a barrel bomb.

It's a sound that, I don't know, it hits your stomach more than your ears. I swear, you would've heard it even if you were deaf. It's like the earth itself is roaring in pain.

It was bustling when we got to the center of town. I'd been in the country, in Idlib, for, what was it, over a month at least, and it was quiet there. I wasn't used to so many people anymore. In Aleppo the whole uprising was more visible. You saw flags and slogans on the walls. Lots of rebel soldiers. There was hardly a wall without bullet holes in it. People had gotten used to the war. It was an everyday thing now.

We were stopped by two teenagers at a checkpoint. They knocked on the hood and pointed up to the sky. I smiled and pointed up too, but I quickly understood that they weren't pointing to God, but to a plane. Then I heard the sound of thunder. People shouted to take cover, so we parked the ambulance under a tree and ran off. Ambulances are targets for the air force because they know the rebels use them. People were running but were pretty relaxed. The sound disappeared and then came back, before it disappeared again and was replaced by another sound that cut through the air. I could just see the flash of the missile before it hit, less than a few miles away. It sounded like a building fell down. The bald guy grimaced.

Before I got back in the ambulance, I recognized one of the jihadists I knew of: Omar al-Shishani, the one with the long red beard.

Yeah, he'd been the leader of the JMA, but then he'd taken a few hundred soldiers and joined Dawla, and now he was on his way to becoming one of the senior leaders. Minister of War or something. One of the key people in the big picture, and he was right there. He was sitting in the back of a car, with the window down, and was looking around. We even caught each other's eye before his car sped off.

OK, so maybe it sounds like I'm name-dropping, but it was a big deal for me. It made me feel like I was finally where all the action was. Aleppo was the heart of the war. The important leaders were there, the important battles. I tried to tell Abu Saad, "Hey, Omar al-Shishani is in that car there," but he didn't look in time and thought I was messing around. "Do you really think Omar al-Shishani is just driving around?"

We took a detour around where the bomb had fallen and drove past a park full of kids who were playing. I mean, a bomb had dropped just a little ways away, and there were kids playing as if nothing had happened.

Right by the park was a cemetery. I noticed a young man my age sitting cross-legged with his gun at his side talking to a grave. He wasn't yelling like Arabs sometimes do. On the contrary, he was just sitting and calmly talking to the grave.

The sun was setting. We needed to do *maghrib* before we got to the garage where we were going to load up the supplies. We asked a guy on the street where we could find a mosque. On the way we heard two bangs, one right after the other, and I jumped. People around me wondered what was wrong; after all there were bangs all the time.

The minaret on the mosque had been shot away a long time ago. Assad aims for the minarets. The entrance was full of flip-flops. I, however, was wearing hiking boots from Norway. I was worried they might disappear if I left them lying out there, so I carried them inside with me. After prayer the imam talked to us. He waved his fingers and sounded severe. His words were steeped with bitterness. I heard him say, "Bashar al-kalab"—"the dog Bashar." Beyond that, I didn't understand much.

I was surprised how much light there was in the town itself. Out in the country, any little light quickly became a target, so I'd gotten used to night being, well, night. But the center of Aleppo was full of light and life. You could barely get around in a car some places because there were so many people out. Old hunched men would be walking down the middle of the street, hands behind their backs, holding a *misbaha*. Kids would stand on the corners listening to *nashids* on their phones.

We found the garage and unloaded the supplies, but when I went to lift the last sack, the bald guy said I could leave it. He was going to show us where to deliver the food, right down on the front line in a part of town called Ramouseh. The lights disappeared one by one as we left the center. We had to turn off the ambulance lights as well. The bald guy sat chewing seeds, flicking the shells out the window. You could just make out some collapsed buildings. It got completely dark. I don't know how Abu Saad managed to drive because he couldn't see anything; he might as well have shut his eyes—it wouldn't have made much difference. It was totally quiet as well. The bald guy said we were right on the front line. No one lived there. There'd been almost no civilians the last few miles, just guards set up in the occasional house. Then we heard the hum of a little generator. We drove to where it was and parked. I carried the sack up some steps to a windowless room with a single light bulb. There were a handful of soldiers there, each in his corner or along the walls. Some of them had lain down to sleep.

We heard cracks from the artillery. You know, Assad and the government forces don't go into a town and destroy it house by house. They pulverize entire buildings and chew their way inward. Obviously, it's nerve-racking to hear buildings collapsing one by one around you. That's the point. The psychological effect. It's like Assad wants to keep us on edge. But those guys there at the front line, they were completely calm.

The darkness makes you quiet. The darkness makes you listen.

Afterward it seemed absurd to see lights again when we got closer to the center. People, nightlife. A war going on right over there, and here you are just living your life and selling peanuts or whatever, y'know. We dropped the bald guy off, turned into a side street, and lay down to sleep on the cardboard Abu Saad had put in the back of the ambulance. I remember I slept with my shoes on, and without eating anything whatsoever. It was my turn to be short on sleep and food.

I went to bed tired and woke up tired, and in the morning we drove past the graveyard again. That same guy was sitting there. Just as quiet, his legs crossed, talking to the gravestone.

The next two or three days we delivered food and packs of water bottles to the garage in the center of Aleppo and farther south, to the front line in Ramouseh. We handed out the space food there. The most hard-core Islamists didn't want it because no one could guarantee it was halal, and besides, it came from the Americans. But the FSA people were happy to eat it. We also had bandages, local anesthetic, and painkillers with us, and believe me, we gave out cases and cases of those.

One day one of the fighters asked if I wanted a look at the actual front line. He was a Christian actually. I found out because it was time for prayer when we arrived with the food that day, and he just sat there while we prayed. He'd lived in Aleppo all his life and had just as much reason to be angry at Assad as anyone. He showed me the way. You know how they knock out walls to get from one building to the next—that's what they'd done. I crept through the holes. The Christian guy put his finger to his mouth and walked silently through a room. There was congealed blood on the ground. The furniture was scorched. In the corner was a half-burned teddy bear staring at the wall. Someone had died in this room, I thought, as I crept through the bloodstains. The Christian guy pointed at a hole in the wall, through which I saw a building on the other side of the street. A Syrian flag was sticking up from it. Sandbags were piled around the windows. OK. There they are.

In the daylight the area near the front looked much worse than how I'd imagined it in the dark. Anything metal was twisted. The asphalt was all broken up. The buildings that hadn't collapsed were full of holes. There were almost no people there. A scrap heap, wasteland, ruin—call it what you want. Then you'd see, I don't know, a sofa in the middle of the street, for example, with a soldier warming himself by a fire of furniture.

On one of the trips we heard a plane diving toward the city. That's one hell of a sound, as if the sky is splitting open.

They hit a hospital.

No, totally normal, civilian hospital. Things like that happened all the time. But the offensive from the government forces didn't happen. Or rather, it was delayed. I guess we could have waited at the front until it started, but Abu Saad wanted to get back to his family.

On the way we drove by cliffs with old caves in them that had housed people since I don't know when. Abu Saad said some of the caves were being used again by people who'd fled the war zone. We stopped at a small town called Urum al-Kubra to eat and pray. After prayer Abu Saad told me his wife was pregnant and that was why he wanted to go back. To take her to the doctor's for a checkup and stuff. I was happy, but Abu Saad looked worried. He probably had mixed feelings about having another kid in the middle of a war.

There was a place that sold milkshakes in that town, something pretty rare in Syria. Abu Saad usually paid for everything; he always made a fuss when I tried to pay. But I actually managed to pay for that milk-shake; I wanted to treat him and congratulate him on kid number two being on the way. And then, while we were standing there . . . how was it again? Yeah, like this. First I saw a pickup approaching with a Dawla soldier standing on the back of it. Kids were running behind the truck throwing stones, and I didn't quite understand what was going on. Were they aiming at the soldier? At the car? What was happening? The truck passed us and stopped nearby. Then we saw it.

I mean, you just can't do that with a body.

An Assad soldier had been tied to the truck and dragged. His head was gone. His clothes were all torn up. Just a lump of flesh full of dust and gravel. There was a dark-red trail behind him.

Abu Saad said we should go. He didn't want to see that. We got in the ambulance and left. Only after we'd driven a little way did he start to talk. "That's not following the Koran," he said. "Not Islam." He said you had to bury people with dignity, even your worst enemy. I just sat there clinging to the car seat.

That corpse: I try not to think too much about it. I'm surprised I can even talk about it at all. That dark-red stripe behind it.

Every time I think of that scene, I start to doubt humanity. What does that word mean really? Are we just animals with clothes on? Compassion had become a rare commodity in Syria.

I thank God it was Abu Saad I met in Syria. He had morals. He kept a certain dignity in all that crap. But nevertheless, he only talked about it in terms of religion, you know. He never asked what I was feeling personally.

You can get tired from seeing things. We were exhausted. We had to take turns driving, I remember, and I couldn't eat properly the next few days. The smell of the corpse permeated the air. I started to doubt whether I'd actually seen what I'd seen.

I went on a lot of motorcycle rides. I rode just to ride. The nausea disappeared if I went fast enough.

Every time we meet I have to go through a kind of security check. All the inmates have to after a visit. You sit in a room. We call it the waiting room. There's just a sofa and toilet. Some hate messages carved on the wall—*Fuck the police*, or whatever. You have to wait until someone from your ward comes and fetches you. It can take ten minutes, half an hour, sometimes over an hour if the guards are changing shifts. It's a room that really makes you sit and think. Everyone hates that room. But y'know what? I like it. Sometimes I want to push the button by the door. Ask, like, "Hey, have you guys forgotten me or what?" But I let it go. I tell myself the purpose of that room is just to wait. *Sabr.* So I think about what we've been discussing. I think of things I could have said, some details that maybe would've helped you understand a bit better.

Yeah, y'know, I was thinking about what we just talked about. The corpse dragged behind the truck. I wonder if I can add something to that. I think I was a bit, I don't know, a bit fake.

Because I thought it was satisfying, in a way.

I think it was satisfying for the Syrians. It made them happy. I saw that they could let out all the hate they felt. Their desire for revenge. I think it gave them a kind of relief.

Sure, I felt sick and I still think it was wrong according to Islam, wrong according to whatever. But I just want you to have the whole picture. Seeing that corpse being dragged behind the truck was a kind of peace for your soul. I just want to tell it like it was.

I missed talking to people from Norway. Abu Saad was busy taking his wife to the hospital and sorting things out for his relatives, so some days I was on my own. I got in touch with Arbi at the Internet café in Salqin; we were logged on at the same time. I grinned at the screen. Arbi was typing like mad and had tons to tell me. He said yet again I should come visit him in Haritan.

It's just north of Aleppo. *Just get ahold of a Chechen and ask where Sayfullah's group is,* he wrote. I promised to come as soon as I could and told him to call home. It was mostly 'cause his mom had been nagging my mom.

Yeah, I'd heard from Mom that Arbi hadn't given his family any sign of life since he'd left. *It doesn't mean anything to have balls on the battlefield if you don't even have the courage to call home,* I wrote.

I got other messages as well. Old friends from before Islam came into my life. They were asking if I was in Syria and stuff. I didn't know how to answer. In the middle of it all, I even got a message from my child-hood sweetheart, that she wanted me back.

No, I hadn't heard from her in years. I bet Mom put her up to it. Either that or it was Shaitan. I mean, what's the likelihood she suddenly writes to me after so many years? But it got me thinking. Not of her, exactly. But maybe I should try to find a wife in Syria.

I also got a message from Carlos. That was maybe the best, but at the same time the most difficult. He wrote that he was miserable in Norway. He wondered how he could get to Syria. What was I supposed to say? I was actually really happy. There was nothing I wanted more than to share what I'd been going through with Carlos. But I couldn't exactly say everything was fantastic here. I didn't say he should come, or that he shouldn't. I just asked him to think about it carefully. But y'know, I was so happy I think it showed through the Internet. When I left the café, I stood for a moment with the sun on my face and imagined Carlos there with me.

Totally awesome.

Since then I've often thought about the weight my words carried that day. I could've put him off. Frightened him. "Hey, you know what? Stay home, brother, there's nothing here for you." You get lots of time to think about things like that in prison. All the alternative scenarios, the parallel lives. But I think I just missed him too much.

On the way home I stopped at the cliff the gay guy had been thrown from. I don't know why. I just pulled over and stood there for a while. Then I drove home. Abu Saad was still out. I walked around the house alone. Syrian houses can be pretty bare. There was a bookshelf with china on one wall. Saad's plastic motorcycle was in the corner. One of the wheels had fallen off. He always spent a lot of time putting it back on, and then it would fall off again a few days later. I went out, washed some grapes at the water pump, and ate. I imagined Carlos and me down here, riding motorcycles in the sun. Laughing about everything that was different from Norway, grieving together about all the suffering, fighting side by side. While I was thinking about it, little Saad came home with a hungry cat. He gave it water, and I found a tin of tuna I'd bought. As soon as it had eaten, Saad wanted to chase it around the house. The emergency aid was over.

His friends came by too. One of them always had snot hanging out his nose and an open mouth, and he stared at me like I was from Mars. They talked to me in Arabic, and I randomly answered yes or no and hoped it fit what they were saying. I tried to play with them a bit like I used to play with Little Brother in Norway, crawling around and roughhousing, but they stopped and wondered what was wrong with me. Y'know, kids play in a different way down there. I tried to hang out with them, but they wanted to run and throw stones at birds.

When Abu Saad and his wife got back, I could tell he was exhausted, but I asked the question I'd been thinking about all day anyway: "What would I do if I wanted to get married here?" Abu Saad sat back and smiled at me. "I thought you'd ask about that sooner or later." He said it wouldn't have been a problem at the beginning of the war. There were lots of people who wanted to marry a *mujahed* foreigner. But then the men would go back to their countries. Or they died. And the wife was left alone, maybe even pregnant, but without a husband. So the foreign fighters had gotten a bad reputation.

That got me wondering why people were coming here. What was their intention? For me a lot of things had to be in place before I could marry. Language, having a house—and that's just for starters. I really just wanted to put the idea out there, but Abu Saad totally shot me down.

Abu Saad was already tired before we started to talk. He fell asleep in the living room. I put a hand on his shoulder, and he jumped up and went to lie down in his room.

I couldn't really sleep that night. Went outside into the darkness. The air was sharp and clear, and I tried to understand what I wanted, where I was going.

What I dreamed of had changed a bit. I wanted to be a martyr. At the same time you still hold on to the thought of something else. Think that you can do what other people do. Find a house. Get a wife and have kids. Live a life.

Yes, sure, you have a short-term plan and a long-term plan. War makes your head unstable. But the thought of a family—that changed my mind, made me think there's more than just taking a shortcut to the next life, that there are things to do in this *dunya* as well. Some people say that getting married and having a family is 50 percent of any religion. You know, the Prophet wanted a large *umma*, so a lot of children gives you points up there. But personally, I also wanted a big family.

No, not in Syria. Or rather yes, but not long-term. I don't know. I wanted to fight as long as I had the strength for it, do my best for the longest possible time, and when I couldn't do it anymore, then maybe I'd think about moving to Turkey. Preferably a place out in the country. At least that was the idea I had when I was driving through Turkey with Arbi.

I would've visited Mom and my friends in Norway, of course. But live in Norway? I don't know. I was born in Norway, but I never really got used to it. To me it's a society that's good at getting ahead quickly, but with no clear direction. When I got messages from Carlos and heard how he was struggling with his faith in Norway, I don't know, it felt like I didn't really have any reason to go back. I never hated Norway, y'know—you don't complain about your host—but at that particular point in time, I was fed up with all the lies and immorality. All the facades. All the loneliness hiding behind the high-tech systems. I didn't want to wake up one morning in a synthetic chaos. I wanted to wake up to the call for prayer and roosters crowing. Go to the mosque early and live a simple life in a place where you could practice Islam without people thinking you were weird. A place where you had a close relationship to your neighbor. For me that's a healthy society. Actually, I just wanted a stable life. A structure that brings peace to your heart.

A few weeks ago we learned about the philosopher Rousseau at prison school. It was the most intense discussion of the class because the teacher tried to get us to think through his arguments. But I actually liked him a lot, Rousseau. Mankind is basically good, but we fuck it up. I could really identify with that. We have to get back to something more natural.

I got almost no sleep that night, and Abu Hajer drove up really early the next morning. Now there was no doubt. The offensive against Assad had begun. We just threw some clothes in a bag and got into the ambulance. It was no joke. We drove real fast. Again and again we saw other vehicles driving in the same direction, full of soldiers. Some of them looked like they'd just woken up. A guy was sitting trying to fasten the belt on his pants on the flatbed of one truck. Other men were loading cartridges into magazines. They had to hurry; this was serious.

Aleppo wasn't quite as full of people as the last time. You could hear the crack of shots from a long way off. People were searching for cover. Most people had pulled down the shutters on their stores. The people in the streets were cheering at us. That made me proud, I remember. "May God grant you victory," they shouted.

Abu Saad prayed to God and managed to take the edge off that way, even though his fingers were drumming faster than ever on the wheel. My thoughts were going too fast for me to be able to pray properly. Someone else was sitting in my body, and maybe he was going to die today.

Abu Hajer had parked his own car and rode with us the last part of the way. He had a radio. All the rebel groups were using the same channel for communication, people were talking almost all the time—total chaos. A hundred meters from the buildings on the front line, we found a broken garage door we managed to open, so we backed the ambulance in. We were supposed to transport the wounded, so we waited for instructions.

We heard that government forces had gained a few blocks. They were advancing by smashing holes through buildings. I still have nightmares about that—that someone will smash through the walls where I'm sleeping, knock into the prison, into the cell, that the walls aren't thick enough.

Then the first message about the wounded came in: drive to such and such building. It was people from Ahrar al-Sham. Two men came downstairs carrying a wounded soldier. They were carrying him wrong; his butt was hitting the steps. They laid him down and said to wait, there were two more. The guy had been shot in the thigh and was lying there clenching his teeth. Abu Saad went to work, rinsed the wound with disinfectant, so the soldier cried to Allah. Then Abu Saad gave him a shot, two milliliters of morphine, and bandaged the wound tightly. I was told to hold his leg up high.

Then they came with another one. He was in a cold sweat and completely white in the face. Abu Saad put his ear to the man's mouth and nose. He'd been shot both in the ankle and high up in the stomach.

Nobody uses bulletproof vests there. I told you that, right?

No, they wanted to die.

A third soldier came down. He'd been shot in the upper arm. It was just hanging off, flopping around. He was walking without help. Actually smiling through it all, if you can believe it. We lacked equipment, but Abu Saad was good at improvising. He broke a plank of wood in two and laid the halves on either side of the arm and taped around them.

I remember in the ambulance the man who'd been shot in the arm was stroking the dying man's hair. Completely peacefully. I clutched the barrel of Abu Saad's gun. Really gripped it tight. Abu Saad drove as fast as he could. A couple of times I turned around to see how it was going in back. The dying man's face got paler and paler as his life ebbed away.

We arrived at the field hospital. It was in a basement and had sandbags around the entrance. They had three doctors, two from North Africa and one German Arab. They were ready with a stretcher as soon as we arrived. There was no hope for the guy who'd been shot in the stomach. He might have even died in the ambulance, I don't know. The guy with the injured leg was put on a stretcher. And then the guy with the planks on his arm, I don't know how he managed, but he politely thanked us for the ride and walked into the basement clinic.

"Yalla, akhi," said Abu Saad. No time for a break. We hid the ambulance back in the same garage and waited on the street, where Abu Hajer was still listening to the radio. The shooting hadn't stopped, but it was quieter. "Is that a good sign?" I asked Abu Saad. "Maybe," he answered. We listened to Abu Hajer's radio. Suddenly Abu Saad's eyes opened wide. "Listen carefully," he said. I didn't understand what was happening, just did what he said. Then there was a boom. It was as if the sound was coming from everywhere at the same time. The earth shook. *"Istishhad,"* explained Abu Saad. A jihadist had driven a truck full of explosives into the government forces to become a martyr. Not where we were, but a few miles east, and we could still feel the earth tremble.

Then we heard *"Taqaddam, taqaddam"* from the radio—"advance, advance." The rebels had held their ground well, and now they were counterattacking. Assad was answering with artillery. We took cover in the garage and sat against the wall there. We heard grenades whistle past as they shot through the air. Then a blast nearby, outside on the street where we'd just been standing. Shrapnel hit the wall next to me. The weird thing was that I wasn't afraid at all. I was pissed off. I wanted to shoot back. Then came the plane. Y'know, they circle around first trying to get an overview. You feel like a little insect down on the ground. The plane fired a missile. I felt the ground shake, and a few small pieces of rubble fell from the ceiling down the back of my neck. Then the plane disappeared, and a new message came over the radio. Same place as last time, more injured. I looked up to the sky for more planes. Nothing. Just gray clouds. Weather for war. No strong sun and no rain. Just gray, like the prison wall out there.

The first day was the worst. We made several trips with the wounded, but by evening things had quieted down. The government forces continued to attack, but it was only small skirmishes to divert attention from larger attacks elsewhere. In the end they gave up on that as well, and rebels emerged from every hiding place you can imagine. Just in the area around us, there must have been over five hundred fighters with dust in their beards. Tears had left traces in the dusty face of one guy. I saw Uzbeks with slanted eyes; a couple of Africans; some white people, maybe Europeans. Some of the Syrians couldn't have been more than thirteen. They asked for water, and we handed out bottles from our garage.

Some were happy to be alive. Others were upset they were alive. Some were so exhausted they didn't even know they were alive. I talked with a sniper who asked for water and noticed he smelled of piss. That's how it goes. When you're in position as a sniper, you can't move. What you need to do, you do in your pants. But it didn't just smell of piss, it smelled of fear too. Wet and clammy.

At night we slept in the back of the ambulance. The floor was covered in street-food wrappers and empty cans of Jack Wrestler. We weren't that good at cleaning up. The cardboard was covered in blood. We just turned it over before we crashed. When we shut the door, it was completely silent, no sounds of war. I lay there feeling like I'd been on a jihad, but I still thought, y'know, that I was capable of more. What Arbi said about hypocrites always bringing up the rear when there was a skirmish was still simmering in the back of my mind. There's even something like that in the Koran, that you shouldn't lag behind when there's a war. I turned to Abu Saad. He was lying there rubbing the corner of his eye, so I knew that he wasn't asleep yet. "Abu Saad." "Hmm?" "Should I be doing more?" He took a deep breath before he answered, "Listen, everyone at the front wants to die and become *shahid*. It's almost harder to find people to do all the jobs behind the scenes." OK. All right. I thought about it for a minute or two. And then, "Abu Saad." "Hmm?" "Do you think I could contribute more? Do *ribat* at least?"

Yeah, sorry. Put that on our list. *Ribat* just means to stand guard. You know, they say that one day and one night of standing guard is worth as much as one month's fasting and night prayers. Abu Saad nodded. "We'll find somewhere for you, *inshallah*."

It was completely out of the question to ride the motorcycle to Arbi. I'd be alone and unarmed. But Abu Saad was as generous as always. We loaded the motorcycle into the ambulance, and off we went.

We'd stayed two or three days in Aleppo before going back to Abu Saad's. While we were resting, I often went up on the roof and thought of Arbi, wondered if he'd become a martyr or whether he was still alive. I thought maybe it'd be good to visit his group in Haritan. Maybe that was the right place for me too. Anyway, I wanted to see how he was doing.

Abu Saad frowned at first. I don't think he liked the fact he'd be alone in the ambulance again, but after my help in Aleppo he thought I deserved time off. He drove more calmly than usual, his hands resting on the bottom of the steering wheel. We saw a huge bonfire in a field outside of Dana where Dawla members were burning packs of cigarettes. It was well into November by that time, but it could still be warm during the day, so I had the window open a bit.

As we approached Haritan, we stopped a couple of Chechen fighters who were walking along the road.

Oh, yeah, the Chechens really were everywhere. Especially around Haritan.

We asked where Sayfullah's group, Jamaat Sayfullah, was. They pointed us in the right direction, out past the town.

Along the road we saw buildings in ruins, a supermarket with broken glass everywhere; it had been fancy at some point for sure. A little after came Sayfullah's base, a large walled-in area. Tight security. After being inspected, we drove onto a large tarmac parking area. It looked like it might have been a car dealership at one point. There were still some ads hanging here and there. Farther away there was an apricot-colored villa and a small park.

Abu Saad helped me unload the motorcycle. He asked me to take care of myself. "Stick with your friend and trust Allah." Sometimes he had a fatherly tone—y'know, both caring and strict—and when I wanted to do something or other he always said the same thing: "Trust Allah." Then he left, and I felt pretty bad. I didn't want him driving around alone.

Walking into the villa, I saw some soldiers. They were sitting around a little fountain in front of the entrance. Some were relaxing in the sun. Some were cleaning their weapons or loading huge machine guns onto the backs of their trucks. Most of them were speaking Russian. Older guys. Enormous bodies. You knew these men were first-class fighters. You know, people born in the Caucasus Mountains. I asked for Arbi without thinking that he'd probably gotten himself a *kunya*, a nickname, by now. Still, they pointed to the entrance to the villa. The door was open; I just went right in.

About seventy fighters were living there, a third of Sayfullah's group, so there were people everywhere. I searched the ground floor, but no Arbi.

There were so many rooms. The second-floor landing was filled with shoes; this was where you had to take them off. And there, in the pile, I saw a pair of hiking boots just like mine. *There,* I thought. *He's here.*

I found him in the corner of a room in his fatigues cleaning his teeth with a *miswak.* He cocked his head when he saw me, like he didn't quite understand what was going on. "*Subhanallah,* there you are," he said after a moment. "Where did you come from?" His beard had grown. He smiled, and smelled quite bad. In other words, everything was as it should be. I felt whole again.

Arbi asked if I wanted to go say hi to the boss himself, sooner rather than later. He took me into a room full of older guys. And Sayfullah was sitting in there. When I saw him in videos in Norway, he looked very strict, but it turned out he was soft and gentle. He said I shouldn't feel alone here and that he'd make sure I was well accepted by the brothers. I think he thought I was coming to join the group. Then we left the old guard in peace. Arbi asked me to come and say hi to the boys. Well, *boys* is the wrong word really; they're grown men. Many of them had fought in the Chechen wars, and some had even been in Afghanistan, and by that I mean in the war against the Soviets.

So we did the rounds. "That one there's a coward." "That one's red-hot with a fourteen millimeter." "He wants to blow himself up." "That one got shot in the butt." Then he asked in Russian if the guy wanted to show us his wound and got a slap on the head in response. It was surprisingly tidy in there, but there were weapons everywhere. Of course, Arbi also wanted to show me his faithful wife, as he called it, and pulled out a huge RPK. They're also Russian, but a bit longer than the usual Kalashnikovs. "Really good in a fight," he said, "but not that practical when you're sitting in a car or something."

The villa was awesome; it had cold marble floors, and I was glad I had my ragsocks on. It was actually warmer outside than inside. Arbi showed me a swimming pool a little ways from the villa, but it was empty and being used as a garbage dump. There was an untrimmed hedge around the pool, withered flowers, and dry fountains. You could easily imagine how lovely it'd been when the garden was still cared for. When Arbi saw my motorcycle, he totally flipped. "This'll be fun," he said. Then another guy came along who wanted to test it out, tipped it up on its back wheel, and sputtered around. That started it; a whole gang came along wanting to give it a test run, but I couldn't stand the circus, so I took Arbi and rode into the town center. I felt free right then. Just Arbi and me. He pointed and explained where we should go.

First we went to a restaurant. Green plastic chairs. Plastic tablecloths. Plastic flowers on the table. "A Tajik runs this place," Arbi said, "but he doesn't like us." "He doesn't?" "Nope. He came to Syria long before the war. He doesn't like what's happening; just check out his face when he takes the order." Arbi was right; the guy was a real sourpuss. So we started to joke around with him. Called him back over right after we'd ordered and said we'd changed our minds. Arbi was like, "No, no, we'll have the chicken." And right before he'd gotten to the kitchen door, we called again and asked for something different. I think we managed it three or four times before he got mad and we both ended up with a shish kebab.

Arbi always ate fast, but now the food he wanted to get in his mouth was fighting against all the words he wanted to get out. He told me he'd already been in a lot of battles; for example, he was only one or two miles east of Aleppo when I was there transporting the wounded.

Arbi said there was something epic about this war. He talked about a hadith that says the angels hold their wings around the Levant. "Holy war on holy ground," he said. I wanted to say that there was nothing holy about what I'd seen in Syria so far, but I let it go. I wanted to believe what he said was true. Then all his stories came out.

I don't know. Like, one story was about a brother he'd talked with as they sat around a fire together. He'd said that if he had to die, he wanted to be shot by a tank. Smashed to pieces and be done with it. "And you know what?" Arbi said. "He really died that way." He said it'd been weird to carry the corpse after; his bones were so broken that the body had no skeleton and you couldn't get ahold of anything. "And you could tell he had the smell of a martyr," he said. "Like a sweet smell." They say that martyrs smell sweet. We sat there on our plastic chairs and had almost finished eating. Then I asked, "Brother, how do you want to die?" He answered without even blinking, "I'd rather be blown to bits from an airstrike." It seemed like he'd already thought it all out. I started imagining it in my head—not good when you're trying to finish a shish kebab. "Brother," said Arbi, "what's this about you not having a weapon yet?" I said I was waiting for Abu Saad to get one for me. "Screw him," said Arbi. "I'll get you one."

We buzzed around town while Arbi pointed things out like a local tour guide. "That's a good café." "They've got the world's best milkshake there." "That's the Internet café." Arbi said there was Internet at Sayfullah's, but he wanted to show me the Internet café anyhow. It smelled of warm sweat as soon as you walked in. Forty, maybe fifty foreign fighters were sitting there, all glued to their screens. The people who hadn't gotten a computer had bought a code so they could get Wi-Fi on their cell phones. Two young Syrian boys were walking around selling chocolate, but the owner chased them off. He had his own chocolate to sell. You could see that some of the soldiers had come straight from the front line; they were Skyping with their folks back home, letting them know they were still alive. Lots of languages mixed up together. Some were crying, some were laughing, some were sitting with their wives. And everyone was carrying weapons. Assad would have hit the jackpot if he'd bombed that Internet café.

After a round of prayers, Arbi took me to a bakery not too far from the mosque. "Cake!" he cried and grinned. Y'know, cake in Syria doesn't taste the same as cake in Norway.

Yeah, yeah, it'd probably be a better book if I could describe the taste, the smell, and all that, but it's not so easy to explain.

Just write that it tasted like an awesome rave was happening in your mouth.

There was a sort of harmony in Haritan. Around Darkush I'd really only seen Syrians, but here it was full of Caucasians and a few Western Europeans. Some were walking around with their wives, who wore niqabs. Some of the women even had Kalashnikovs on their backs. Where had I been? Here was where all the foreign fighters were. We even met some Swedes out on the street. "*Tjena, tjena*, hello, hello." Everything was so chill. I felt more at home here than I did in Darkush.

I thought about it. But to move, I'd have to join Sayfullah's group, and I wanted to get a feel of what it would be like first. But yeah, I wanted to be closer to where it was all happening. Closer to Arbi, of course. And closer to Aleppo.

Sayfullah's fighters were eating when we got back to headquarters, four or five guys around each massive plate. I got a spot between two huge guys. I was a bit shy, but they said I should help myself to more. *"Yalla, akhi!"* I felt like a little child between those two guys, and besides I was pretty full from the shish kebab and cake we'd had in town. But that didn't help. They gave me my own plate. "Here! Eat!" It's like that when you hang out with Caucasians. The same when it was prayer time. They spread out, and I crept in. Before I came to Syria, I thought that the choice of group was about who you want to die with, but it's also about who you want to live with. It had been a good choice not to be in Sayfullah's group at the start. I didn't really fit into the culture; they made me feel small. But to be honest, in the mosque I don't mind feeling small. That's the whole point. When you're small, Allah is great.

I think Sayfullah liked Arbi and me. He said he was fascinated that we'd left a well-functioning, rich society and come down here. He ordered people to take care of us, but I didn't feel at home among his men. It was more like, *What's he doing here?* They probably thought I was a total dork.

That plate I'd bought, for example.

Yeah, the one you put in your combat vest. They laughed about that. Said only cowards had those. So I took it out of the vest and asked if anyone wanted it. One of the Chechens seemed to be interested—"Oh, thanks very much"—and then he threw it in the garbage in front of everyone else.

There were already a couple of Chechens who thought they ought to get rid of the Uzbeks and the Tajiks and make the group a pure Caucasian one, so you can imagine how they felt about a Norwegian Pakistani with a bulletproof plate in his vest. Even Arbi seemed a little on the outside, actually, even though he was a bodyguard and Chechen and everything. Behind his stony face was a real sensitive guy. I think he was glad I'd visited, I'll put it that way.

Sayfullah gave Arbi and I our own room while I was there, and the password to the Internet—the full package. In the evening Arbi lay down on his mattress and fiddled with his cell phone. He showed me pictures of some women he was chatting with. *"Mashallah,"* I said, "but isn't that haram?" Some imam had told him that as long as it was with the intention of discussing an eventual marriage, then you could have contact with women. Which imam he'd heard that from, I've no idea. Arbi showed me some sites where you could get in touch with women who were interested in making hegira. I sent out a few messages, crossed my fingers, and waited for replies. Arbi, on the other hand, was in full swing chatting with a few different women. It wasn't exactly flirting; they were really discussing marriage.

Yeah, of course we flirted too.

I fell asleep, but Arbi woke me up in the night. "Hey, Tariq," he said. "I'm hungry." *OK,* I thought, *can't he make his own food?* He said he was a total catastrophe in the kitchen. He was wondering if I'd help him. We snuck into the kitchen. There were tons of supplies in there. "Omelet?" I asked. "Awesome," said Arbi. I found some eggs and vegetables, asked if he could chop an onion. But in the end I had to do that too, 'cause he was completely useless; he almost cut his finger and was complaining about the tears.

That was a good moment, in the kitchen in the middle of the night eating an omelet and grinning at each other. We were finally where we were supposed to be.

After a few days at the villa, Arbi said enough was enough. I needed to get myself a weapon. We left the bike and walked into town. There was a car mechanic who sold weapons. His son was there too, helping him out, his hands and face covered in oil. I felt bad when I saw things like that, kids who had to work when they were only twelve. His school had probably been bombed.

The mechanic brought out two Kalashnikovs, and Arbi disassembled them. One had a wooden butt, and the other had a metal one that folded up. He looked through the barrel for scratches. I wanted the fold-up one, but Arbi thought the wooden one was better. Less used. It was from 1969. You might wonder what it'd been through, what it'd shot at in over forty years.

It took almost an hour to barter down from $2,300 to $1,900. That wasn't a bad price, I found out. A gun like that could easily cost $2,500 some places.

Arbi congratulated me. "May you kill lots of *kuffar* with that thing," he said. *"Inshallah,"* I answered.

They'd set up a shooting range inside Sayfullah's compound. I felt the weight of the weapon in my hands before I fired the first shot. Total miss. Arbi said I had to adjust the sight. He explained something about standing a hundred meters from a target, securing the gun into something, and adjusting the sight according to where the bullet hit. I never actually did it. You needed a key to adjust the sight, but OK, I could at least hit something at close range. I wasn't going to be a sniper after all. Now nobody could mess with me; that was what mattered.

Arbi pulled out our balaclavas, and we took pictures posing with our guns. We looked like hard-core gangster psychos. You know, boy stuff. Yeah, speaking of boy stuff, I'd sent out several feelers to women. A woman in London had replied tentatively. Arbi had, what can I say, an edge. He was juggling several chats, and a couple of them were well on the way to taking the big leap.

We stayed up most nights chatting with women and cooking omelets. It almost became a ritual. The cook noticed and told us off because we took his eggs, but what were we supposed to do? We were hungry.

One day Arbi and I went to the Dawla base, which wasn't that far away.

I don't know, just to see what it was like there.

Yeah, it was the morning, and we were outside the villa talking. I sat on a wall, and Arbi was on the motorcycle, swaying back and forth, lifting first one foot, then the other. Sayfullah was in meetings, and because he had several bodyguards, Arbi got off work to hang out with me. Arbi said it was easy to read people's hearts: "Some people raid Assad's armories and get rich on *ghanima*, while others fight to protect civilians even if they have nothing but the dust on their faces." That was a dig at Dawla. Arbi was close to Sayfullah, after all, so he shared his opinions. Raiding the armories wasn't really stupid. If the rebellion was going to continue, you had to think a little strategically. Arbi spouted off several arguments. Those leaders didn't care about the lives of soldiers; they were arrogant and threw out *takfir* left and right. And they were too hard on the local population. Things like that. I agreed that the *minhaj*, the way forward, could be exasperating, but they were still our brothers in the fight against Assad.

Dawla was the big topic, yes, but not just for us. It was the big question in Syria at that time. Remember, a little over six months earlier, Dawla didn't exist. Or rather they did, but they were the same as Nusra. Conjoined twins or something. And then you're gonna tear them from each other, understand? There was a struggle for power between Dawla and Nusra, and Sayfullah chose to lean toward Nusra.

The thing was that Arbi was curious about Dawla. He wasn't thinking about leaving Sayfullah and joining them; that was out of the question. But I think he wanted to understand what was happening, because there was so much talk of disagreements between Dawla and the other groups. Was Sayfullah right about Dawla? Things like that. So that was why he wanted to check out the Dawla base.

It was in the area, yeah. Near Haritan.

Of course, I was just as curious as Arbi. I kick-started the bike. Vroom! We took off as soon as he suggested the idea.

They were staying at a fancy hotel; that was some five-star jihad. They had a nice garden, still well cared for even so long into the war. Half-hidden under a tree they had a cannon, and in the middle of the garden there was a huge rocket launcher that had left tracks of mud in the grass behind its tires.

We went over to some soldiers who were sitting eating.

Yeah, like a picnic on the grass, with a blanket and stuff. Their weapons were resting up against the wall behind them, and they said, "Come, come and eat. We haven't seen you before."

All sorts. Some of them spoke Danish—two blond guys and a Danish Arab. A couple of Belgians were sitting over here, a Frenchman there, and Chechens everywhere. Oh yeah, and a guy from Fiji. Just think—Fiji! They were eating *khobz* with chocolate spread and drinking tea, while a Syrian cook was stressing about making sure everyone had what they wanted. He was limping a bit, that cook. I bet it was a war wound.

Of course, they thought we were with Dawla. Asked which division we were in and everything. Arbi said it straight out: "We're with Sayfullah." That made them a little hesitant, but they were still open. It was all pretty chill really. "You're welcome here whenever you want."

They talked about the offensive against the Kurdish forces and said that Assad's soldiers had parachuted in just south of Aleppo. One of the rebels was hit with shrapnel in his head during the parachute attack, and when he died, he fell down right in the prayer position. They were fascinated by things like that, even though it was probably coincidence he fell that way.

When you see people eating together, talking together, they become more human, really. I couldn't quite piece it all together. On the one hand, they're so human, but then they're also extreme. You know, I've never doubted people like that have their hearts in the right place. They were humble. Sincere. But then you hear their opinions. Honestly, I didn't understand what was going on in their heads. There was a guy who was defending something; I don't know, man, I don't want to go into details. It was just this one guy after all. He didn't get much support, but he was waving around some hadith or another defending something totally indefensible.

And then you had the leaders. Arbi talked with one of them in Russian. Stuck-up guy. People were starting to stream in from all over the world to join Dawla, so the leaders weren't afraid to sacrifice a few lives here and there. They didn't value a soldier's life really. You noticed it in the men. They weren't quite committed, didn't look you in the eye when you talked to them. They weren't cared for really. They were unsure. Confused. Every time they heard a bomb in the distance, *"Subhanallah,"* but there was fear in their voices. They were too sensitive. And it was chaotic there. Really messy. Weapons and ammo were just lying around everywhere.

No, it wasn't tempting. You want to be valued, not just thrown into the front like trash.

On the way home, I saw a woman walking along the road. She was wearing a hijab and loose clothes and had beautiful eyes. "Arbi," I said, "check it out on the right." *"Mashallah,"* he said almost before he'd even turned around, and, you know, his style was to get right to the point. "Are you going to ask for her hand then?" Once he'd put the idea into my head, it was hard to get it out again. Arbi was like, "Follow her, brother," so I slowed the motorcycle down into first gear. My God, we didn't have anything better to do than to chase after a girl like that, can you believe it? I felt like a fucking stalker, but Arbi just sat behind me laughing. Then she disappeared into a house, and Arbi slapped me on the shoulder so hard I nearly lost control of the bike. "Now you know where she lives," he said.

Back at Sayfullah's villa, Arbi got hold of a Syrian who spoke good English and explained that we needed help on a mission to get a woman. He grinned but said we needed to get an older guy to represent me; he was only twenty-five, and that wouldn't do. The cook, the one with the eggs, overheard the conversation and had to chime in: "Remember, Syrian beauties are dangerous."

Everything went really fast. In the end a whole group of us went. The young Syrian brought along an older one, a sixty-year-old man, who was going to speak on my behalf. One of Sayfullah's deputy commanders also came with us, an Uzbek who spoke a bit of Arabic. So, that was my team. Plus Arbi, of course, but I asked him to wait outside so we wouldn't have any laughing fits.

I knocked on the door. A little boy opened it. We said we wanted to talk with his father. The boy invited us in to a *hadiqa*—y'know, one of those little gardens inside the house with potted plants, some chairs, and a cat sneaking around. Then the father came. He was polite, told his son to fetch some tea. It was the young Syrian who started the conversation. He said that we were from Sayfullah's group and wanted to talk about his daughter. "OK," said the father. Of course, he was thinking it was the young Syrian who wanted to get married. I hung back a little. I knew those kinds of situations from Pakistan; you don't go in full-steam, you show a little humility. The whole thing's not as strict in Syria, but I didn't know that, did I? When he figured out I was the one who wanted to marry and not the Syrian, he smiled at me and asked if I knew any Arabic. Problem. I didn't really. The daughter only had an elementary school education, and she didn't speak English. On the other hand, being Norwegian was an advantage; I think he got dollar signs in his eyes. While we were talking, the daughter came in with our tea. I was embarrassed; I felt my face burning up. But I plucked up some courage and looked at her. She had those clear blue eyes. But just a quick peek, just once; you couldn't stare too much in such a situation.

We talked about everything else, the war and life before the war. Then there was no more tea in the pot, and we had to get to the point. The father disappeared into the house and we waited in the garden. Probably about an hour or so. We sat outside and talked quietly, and I pet the cat, which had come over and wanted to cuddle.

The father said he agreed. He actually did. He came out to us, sat down again, and said we could get married. But there was one thing I hadn't considered. The dowry. He asked for ten thousand dollars.

No, I didn't have that sort of money. It'd be OK to haggle, but you have to do that over time, maybe help the family out with things, build up a relationship with the relatives.

On the outside Arbi seemed all fired up. "Hey, that's no problem, really. Sayfullah will probably be able to sort out the money for you."

I got cold feet about the whole thing. My plan was to be a martyr. When you get married, you're stuck. You're not with your brothers anymore, and if you have kids, then it's game over. Fighters with kids stop going on dangerous missions. A wife doesn't want to be left home alone. That's something about women who do hegira; they're used to the fact that they might become widows. But with a Syrian woman, forget it. Then you have to stay home, go food shopping, and do everyday things. I wasn't ready for that.

When we got back to the villa, I felt relieved. The stress was over. Arbi started to talk about another possibility, all the widows who'd lost their husbands in the war. It was considered noble to marry one of them. Sayfullah gave them housing, money, and food, everything they needed, but they were still alone. I told Arbi I was tired of all the woman stuff. Couldn't we just take a break from the whole thing? "Fine then," he said and threw himself down on the mattress to chat some more with his girls. After a while I nudged him in the leg and asked if we couldn't do something or other. "Two minutes," he said. That turned into five, ten, then twenty minutes. He was completely lost in his screen.

I might as well throw myself into my screen too, I figured.

"Arbi," I said, " it looks like we're going to get a visit from Carlos." *"Subhanallah,"* I heard from the other mattress.

I woke up early to see Arbi standing in the middle of the room, his eyes wide open. A plane was rumbling above us. Several times, back and forth. A bad sign. We heard the missile drop, and Arbi threw himself on the ground.

No, no, it really shook, but it hit twenty or thirty meters away from the villa. Arbi was like, "Good morning, Syria!" That wasn't the first time there'd been an explosion close by. I leaped out of bed. The Chechens out in the lounge were totally unfazed. They said Allah had already decided their fates. If they were supposed to die now, then all right, they were ready.

Man, that day was full of bad news. We were in Haritan, same place as before, and we kept on screwing around with that Tajik. Outside the restaurant we met a Syrian rebel. He looked at us and said something in Arabic, picked up a stick, and snapped it in front of us. Then he picked up two sticks, held them out, and showed us that they couldn't be broken. We looked at each other, Arbi and I. Then he patted us on the shoulder and disappeared.

Later we heard that Assad was offering a reward for the head of every foreign rebel. Two thousand dollars, I think, if they were alive, otherwise half that. One person in Sayfullah's group had already disappeared. We wondered whether it had anything to do with that reward. We had to keep our paranoia in check, be careful, not travel around alone—two sticks are stronger than one. Suddenly there might be some poor, desperate wretch who needed some cash. It meant the foreigners got more suspicious of the Syrians. The atmosphere got toxic. Come to think of it, that reward thing was a tactical success for Assad.

That same day a guy came to the villa with news. A bit like messengers in the old days, because in Syria a lot of the communication was like that. The messenger came with bad news, as if there wasn't already enough of that. It was from a nearby town called Anadan, where Dawla had a checkpoint. A car from Ahrar al-Sham was trying to get through with a badly wounded soldier, so they needed to hurry. The Dawla soldiers started asking a lot of questions, but the people in the vehicle eventually had enough and just stepped on the gas. Dawla answered by peppering the vehicle with bullets. Then there was revenge on all sides. Ahrar al-Sham sent people. Dawla sent people. Ten people were killed before the leaders managed to end the conflict. Fights like that, man, they're just so meaningless.

Dawla and the other rebel groups had already had many disagreements, but now it was obvious. You could no longer pretend that all the rebels were friends.

The next day Sayfullah called a general meeting. Parts of the group that lived other places showed up. We gathered in the largest room. Sayfullah stood on a coffee table. Someone had turned a couple of the lights on him; it was like a little stage. He started in Russian, but then he saw me and stopped. You know, he was convinced that I would join his group, so he said to Arbi, "You translate for him." For a moment everyone looked at me, the foreigner who needed extra help. Talk about standing out in a crowd.

Then he began, and Arbi whispered his interpretation: "Brothers, you know what we've sacrificed to get where we are today. I ask you not to pay attention to the disagreements we've started seeing between groups. I'm sure that many of you agree with me when I say I'm fed up. I can't take any more of this *dunya*. *Dunya, dunya, dunya.* I want to go to Allah." Then he explained that he'd talked with Julani, the leader of the Nusra Front, and that he, *inshallah*, was thinking about joining them. But not yet.

"Sadly," he said, "the time has nearly come when we must choose, and I'd rather go there than to Dawla. But remember, we're not on this earth for long no matter what. This *dunya* will carry on and forget us. And there is one mission I cannot turn away from, and that is the prison in Aleppo. Rebels and civilians are being held there like hostages. You don't want to know what Assad's soldiers do to the women. We will gain nothing from it in the form of riches. No weapons or money. We won't get any richer by freeing them. Many of the other groups have already given up. Now we're left with the task, together with our brothers from Nusra and Ahrar al-Sham. It's not certain I'll be with you much longer, but I hope, as you do, that we will get our rewards with Allah. So, brothers, who is with me in liberating the prison?"

Everyone stood up and roared that they were with him. Then one person yelled a *takbir* and the soldiers answered, *"Allahu akbar."*

I gradually got more and more respect for Sayfullah. One time Arbi and I saw him in Haritan. Y'know, all by himself. He disappeared into a store, and we followed to ask if we could help. Arbi asked why he was alone, and Sayfullah answered that he was just buying some warm underclothes; it made him sad to see brothers freezing now that winter had come.

I mean, think about it. He could've asked anybody to do that for him, but he did it himself. One of the fiercest military commanders around, and he's standing there looking at the shelves for socks and long underwear for his men. It reminds me of something in Islam, the thing about keeping your good deeds to yourself. Don't boast or make a big deal out of it.

No, he helped other people too. Orphanages and stuff. Y'know, not those madrassas where kids are trained to be fighters with Kalashnikovs. Just regular orphanages. But he didn't make a show about that either.

I told Arbi I wanted to join the attack against the Central Prison in Aleppo. He nodded and agreed but then said there were some problems. "It'll be dangerous," he said first. "There'll be relentless barrel bombs and air raids; even Rambo would piss his pants." And then there was the language. Everything would be in Russian or Chechen, Arabic in an emergency. Norwegian, English, and Urdu wouldn't be helpful. At the front messages had to get through quickly. And then there was the question of *bayah* as well. I'd need to swear allegiance to Sayfullah if I wanted to go out and fight and stuff. Give up my money, control, do what I was asked without grumbling about it. I was silent. I couldn't give a clear answer. Arbi stared at the floor.

One day Abu Saad's ambulance showed up.

I don't know, a week or two maybe. We hadn't really agreed on a time.

Of course it was good to see him. I felt like he was family now. He was surprised to see me with a gun. I think he was glad I was starting to take some initiative. That I was getting myself sorted out. He said hi to Arbi, who, of course, told him all about me trying to get married. Abu Saad just shook his head and laughed. You bet I got to hear about that one for a while!

He explained he'd started to deliver food from a new communal kitchen in Salqin out to the different checkpoints over there. He'd been talking with the men guarding Atme. They needed more soldiers at one of the checkpoints. It sounded like a good plan, especially with Carlos on the way. Atme was just on the border. Things were starting to come together.

We ate and prayed before we left, and Abu Saad got to know Arbi and Sayfullah's people. They were planning the attack on the prison. Abu Saad even asked Sayfullah if they needed an ambulance during the attack. Sayfullah said he'd get back to him in a few weeks—"Then we'll nearly be ready, *inshallah*." That's how things work down there. Two people meet, talk, make some kind of loose agreement. That's why the intelligence really struggles. They try to figure out structures, but what sort of structure is there really? The groups like to appear coordinated, make fancy propaganda videos where everything seems organized. But it's more like this: "Take your ammo, take a weapon, that direction over there." "Where?" "Oh, somewhere over there. Trust in Allah, *yalla*!"

A big part of me wanted to stay with Arbi, but we weren't there for each other really. We were there for the Syrians, and ultimately for Allah. Plus, there was one more thing. Arbi was a bodyguard, and I wouldn't get to do that even if I did pledge *bayah* to Sayfullah. We would've been sent to different places. They didn't let childhood friends fight side by side.

Can you imagine being at the front and watching a friend die? They tried to avoid that sort of thing.

We said good-bye. The cook came out and wanted to send me off with a tray of eggs, but I couldn't accept that. It wasn't enough we'd been eating his eggs every night; he wanted me to take even more.

Nope, we left without the eggs.

There were two checkpoints in Atme, one that faced the Turkish border and one up at the front line against a Kurdish area the PKK controlled. Or the YPG, if you want to be accurate. That was where I was supposed to stand guard.

The checkpoint was up on a hill. The first time I went up there, it was so foggy you couldn't see a thing, and then suddenly the guards were right in front of you. They'd put up three homemade tents, you know, just some branches with a tarpaulin over them. And they had a little fire.

No, no, Assad wouldn't dare fly so close to the Turkish border, so you could have as many fires as you wanted.

The checkpoint itself was two mounds of earth shaped by bulldozers, so cars had to drive in an S-shape to get through. There were two posts with Dushkas, huge machine guns. One was aimed down at the road, and the other was aimed at the PKK positions. A flag with the phrase *la ilaha illa llah, Muhammadan rasul ullah* had been put up on one of the mounds of earth. All the groups there could get behind that.

Yes, several groups shared the responsibility for the checkpoint. One day it was one group, the next it was another, and so on.

Me, no. I had my own schedule. I left with Abu Saad when he came with food, and returned the next time he came.

Why do you think that's strange?

Well, think whatever you like.

That thing about groups—I can tell you straight up I never swore allegiance to any group. Here I am, sentenced for being in a terrorist organization, so it wouldn't make any difference for me to admit it now, y'know? The PSS would probably pat me on the back and be happy my version was finally similar to theirs. But I won't pretend that I swore allegiance to any group because it seems most plausible for the plot of the book. Or because I've been sentenced for it. If I did that, then the story would be too neat. That's just how it is. Life isn't believable sometimes.

You're right there. It is weird that all the other guards belonged to a group. I was the exception.

Of course, it helped that I'd been with Sayfullah. Even if I hadn't sworn allegiance to him, it gave me points to have contacts there. It was Abu Saad who'd arranged the whole guard-duty thing; I bet he'd told them I was friends with one of Sayfullah's bodyguards and stuff. It gave me more cred really.

Because I didn't follow the same shifts as the guys from groups, I got to know a few of them as they rotated in and out. Ahrar, Nusra, the FSA, something called SRF—they were the most corrupt, totally controlled by the US. And then there were people from JMA, the ones I'd wanted to join in the beginning. Nice people, but they only spoke Arabic, so it was hard to figure out what they stood for.

No, Dawla wasn't part of it. They had their own tactics. They joined the offensives, but they didn't put people in guard posts afterward. They'd rather find some important public building, paint it black, and set up a Sharia court. That's how they got control over the law. They became the authority that judged, and the other groups used their courts too. But the whole situation started to get tense.

Between the groups. Rumors started flying about a toxic atmosphere between Dawla and the others.

People from the FSA were standing guard when I arrived the first time. They didn't exactly make me feel welcome. They stood there and watched me while they drank their tea and talked in Arabic. Y'know, not everyone was happy about the foreign jihadis. But I got talking with an Englishman, a black guy with roots in Eritrea. He explained what I needed to know.

We were supposed to check the cars that passed through. Look for weapons, bombs. People on their way into the Kurdish area had limits as to how much food they were allowed to have with them. They could only take in enough for their own family. There were also limits on gas. And they were asked if they used drugs. Most people just laughed at that question, but one person got caught with a bag of weed. I thought it wasn't really that big a deal, but the other guards cried haram, and we had to do the job we'd been given.

The bag was thrown into the fire. As the smoke spread, I could smell old sins.

He got to drive on. If it had been powder, though, they easily might've taken him to Dawla's Sharia court, where he would've really been in the shit.

For the most part it was a chill job, even though things had to be fast. Cars came through, and we had to check them properly. At night it was more tense. That was when the attacks might come. We sat around the fire and drank tea to keep warm. Something makes you feel safe when you're sitting near the flames of a fire, a primitive instinct maybe.

Abu Saad and I fetched the wood from a nearby refugee camp. UNHCR was running it. We could see the camp from the checkpoint when it wasn't foggy. A dirty place, maybe the size of this whole area of the prison here, if not bigger. Nearly no adult men there. Kids ran around playing in the dirt when they weren't in the town begging. Families were given space food and thought the whole thing was temporary, the war had to end soon.

I mostly bonded with the Nusra people. They were serious. Checked the cars properly, but were friendly and smiled at everyone passing through whether they were Kurds or Arabs. They improved the tents and made good food. The FSA people even admired them, I remember, but y'know, I was still skeptical about Nusra.

It seemed like they had a hidden agenda. I can't quite put my finger on it. Maybe I was skeptical because I grew up in the West, where you always need to be critical. There's always some underlying thing waiting to trick you. You don't quite believe things, never totally buy it, don't open up. But they were open to me. Much more than the FSA people.

One of the Nusra soldiers, Abu Omar al-Masri, was especially warm to me. Egyptian. He'd studied at the university in Cairo and said that the more he studied, the more he thought about the next life. He taught me more Arabic but wanted some Norwegian words in return. I taught him "God is good" and "fish balls in white sauce." The latter was mostly because he wanted to learn something that would make a Norwegian laugh. He thought the first thing you should learn in a new language should be something to create a good mood. I also learned how to recognize an Egyptian accent, because they don't quite get that *j* sound. They almost say a *g* instead. *Gihad*, not *jihad*.

Masri made the best tea. He was the kind of guy who tells stories non-stop. He was interested in everything that had to do with the Arab world. Told about what had happened in the other countries: Tunisia, Egypt, Libya, Yemen—the whole lot. I asked him what was so important about our job. "There aren't any attacks here. What's the point?" He explained that even if there was a ceasefire with the PKK, the conflict could flare up again. "Just wait for the peace talks in Geneva," he said. "Then it'll be good to control a position in this area."

To be honest I think there was another reason I ended up in Atme. I think Abu Saad wanted me close to the border in case things really got going with Dawla.

Yeah, he was really looking after me.

Y'know, a safer place while tensions were rising everywhere else. Because that was the burning question now. Everyone had an opinion about Dawla. But not everyone talked openly about what they thought. Masri, for example, only aired his opinions when the two of us were alone. He shook his head about Dawla. Said they'd sent soldiers to attack Assad, but before the battle was over, their own soldiers still at the front, they'd fired Grad rockets at the front line. Those leaders, they didn't care about their soldiers' lives. They probably thought the young boys should be happy to be martyrs. *"Shahid inshallah,"* and that was that.

When he had a bigger audience, usually when we were sitting around the fire eating, he avoided talking about Dawla and told stories about the Kurds. He said it was the JMA and Sayfullah's groups who'd stopped the PKK and taken control of Atme. In the middle of the battles, Kurdish women stripped naked and ran away, to draw attention or something. Masri said guys who'd seen the women had to pinch themselves in the arm. "What's happening? Is it the *hur al-ayn*, or what?" You know, the seventy-two virgins in Jannah.

Yeah, yeah, there were plenty of stories about Kurdish fighters. Some people said the female snipers cut off one of their breasts so they could aim better. Things like that. One of the guards once showed us pictures of dead Kurdish soldiers. That wasn't a pretty sight. Mouths open, as if their souls had been ripped out of them.

That was jihadist entertainment—war videos and movie clips of snitches being beaten up. After a while there were beheadings; Dawla had the monopoly on that. We showed each other the videos we'd downloaded. "Hey, check this out." *"Alhamdulillah*, may Allah take revenge on all spies." Some people had filmed things themselves—war videos, dead Assad soldiers, or PKK fighters.

The thing is, I hadn't gone to Syria to fight against the PKK. But they were sneaky. They used the rebellion as a way to take control of more territory. Opportunists. So we had to hold them back. The question was how many different fronts the rebellion could handle.

You know, we looked at the PKK as 100 percent *kuffar*. Communists who worship their leader, Öcalan, or whatever he's called, the one with the huge beard who's in prison in Turkey. And they're nationalists. There's no place for nationalism in Islam. Sorry. In Islam everyone is a believing brother or sister, regardless of nation, black, white, conservative, liberal. But for the PKK, Kurdistan comes first and then Islam. Maybe Islam. Or maybe no Islam at all. Masri once showed me a video he'd downloaded on his phone in which they'd put a flag with a religious saying onto a step so that it got trampled to pieces. They had to be *kuffar* to the core to do that kind of thing.

One night we were sent a little present up there. I had just left the fireside and lain down in my tent. The mattresses were on the ground, damp all the way through, and had this musty smell. But if you were tired enough, you slept anyway. Then a bomb exploded right next to us. The tarpaulin over me ripped. But, y'know what, at that particular stage, I really didn't care anymore. I hadn't been hit, *alhamdulillah*, and that was that. People had already taken up fighting positions when I got out of the tent; nobody was injured. The bomb had hit just ten or so yards away, but behind a little hill that had protected us.

Best regards, the PKK.

One of the brothers decided to send something in return. He pulled out the Dushka and shot over their headquarters. But the others asked him to stop. No return fire either. It was just a friendly greeting to keep us awake at night. Then the Dushka had to be disassembled and cleaned because it got full of sand. A two-hour job for two minutes of fun.

Abu Saad didn't come the following day, and I was worried. He was often late—more often late than not, in fact—but it had been over several hours. The other men were about to change shifts, and Masri asked if I wanted to go back with them to their base in Atme. We could ask the guards who took over to tell Abu Saad that I was there.

Masri was actually trying to recruit me to Nusra, but he wasn't pushy. He was indirect, was nice, and invited me for tea and let me decide. But I was on the fence. I couldn't really see myself joining his group either.

At the base it was really quiet. Masri went to make some food, so I was left with three Bengalese Brits, who offered me coffee. One of them had a suicide belt on. I asked where he'd gotten it. He said he'd made it himself with a support belt like the kind you get at the pharmacy when you've got a bad back. He'd sewn extra pockets in the front and put in several pounds of homemade explosives wrapped in plastic wrap. He pulled out the whole thing carefully to show me. It looked a bit like marzipan with shrapnel in the front. A wire zigzagged around the marzipan pancake with a fuse, and on the other end there was a firing mechanism that looked like the ones on hand grenades. "You just pull out the pin," he said. *"Allahu akbar."*

Yeah, yeah, two pounds of TNT is enough to pulverize a car, and here he had, what, ten or eleven pounds.

I tried to have a conversation, but they were just too tense. So I went for a walk outside, sat in the shade, and watched the wind in the trees. I still got a bit stressed hanging out with people with suicide belts.

The wind felt cleansing. It turned a page in a book in which everything is written. Or that was perhaps what I hoped for. But everything was the same.

While I was sitting there, two boys came over to the fence around the base. One of them was almost a teenager, emaciated and exhausted.

The other one was younger and reminded me a bit of Little Brother. They called to me in Arabic. They probably wanted money. One of the Bengalese guys came over and gave the smaller one a few coins. Then he disappeared, but the older one stayed there hanging over the fence. He was wearing a black cap and dirty clothes. A little bit too big for him, likely donated. I still remember his eyes; he had strong, light-brown eyes. His face was completely covered in dust, but his eyes were clear. I went over to him and dug in my pockets, but I only had large bills. Then he put his fingers to his mouth. *"Khobz,"* he said. I knew that word. "Bread." I made a sign for him to wait and went in to see Masri in the kitchen. Asked if there was any bread I could give away. He gave me a bagful. "Here," he said. "Take it." But when I came out again, the boy was gone. I went out of the gate to look for him, but he'd disappeared. It might sound strange, but that was the worst thing I think I experienced in Syria. Not bombs exploding or people bleeding but being too late to give bread to that boy. He must've thought I'd rejected him. That I just didn't care.

Early the next day, Abu Saad and I went on our way to Aleppo again.

Yeah, he came and got me. He'd been out talking with some people about the government offensive in Aleppo, sorting out a new mission for us. He thought I was angry because he was late, but I was just thinking it sucked that the boy hadn't gotten any bread. Everything was getting to me: I hadn't changed clothes in a couple of weeks, I was drinking Jack Wrestler to stay awake, pretending I didn't have a sore throat and that everything was fine, but in the end it was a piece of bread that broke me.

Aleppo, yes. Same job as last time, but in a different area. Abu Saad let me drive. He'd noticed that I was feeling down and gave me more responsibility so that I'd feel better. Abu Saad always knew what was going on.

The part of town we had to go to, Sheik Sayyid, had been blown to pieces. Someone had written *QANNAS* on a wall with a large arrow in the direction we were going. It means "snipers." The rebels were farther forward, so I wasn't sure it still applied. Abu Saad asked me to step on it; we sped 'til we got there. There was a person there who welcomed us and said we needed to take cover. "They're using artillery." Inside the building there were twenty or thirty rebels. Some of them had set fire to some garbage and were warming themselves around it. FSA people. We had food rations with us and drinks that we shared with them. They told us that some Dawla soldiers were holding off the Assad offensive in a cement factory farther up. They'd held their position for two days without reinforcement. "Why don't you help them?" Abu Saad asked. They explained that to get there with supplies was extremely dangerous. You had to cross a dried-out canal, where you could easily get shot. The FSA people didn't dare. There was something weird about that group; they were cowards but still in a good mood. While we were talking, one soldier snuck behind another and pulled his pants down. The whole group started to laugh their heads off. It was the first time I'd heard people laugh so much in Syria. They posed and took pictures of each other. Me too. I posed with a badass fourteen millimeter and a rocket launcher. The prosecution at my trial was obviously happy about that one. But nobody had the balls to go and help the IS soldiers. Everyone waited behind.

I went for a piss two floors up. The soldiers had their own room to go in, but it smelled so bad I had to find another room. Everything was abandoned anyhow; there was plenty of space. When I came down again, someone shouted and pointed to a little dot in the sky. *Not again,* I thought.

Not a plane, no; it was a helicopter. And then I noticed another dot. And another. There were five of them. They were heading toward us in a diamond formation. They were so high that you couldn't hear them. Then they started to drop barrel bombs. When they hit, the ground really shook; shit, nobody wanted to die a martyr when they heard a sound like that.

Hide? OK, but where? They crush everything. And when you can't hide, you panic. It works like this: first one person freaks out and shouts like a madman, then a couple more get infected, then four, eight, sixteen, and everything happens in a matter of seconds.

Abu Saad and I threw ourselves into the ambulance. Drove like mad back to where we'd come from. On the way we passed a truck with an anti-aircraft gun in the back. We just about managed to see them crank up the chase before we drove on, but the helicopters were flying too high. It was impossible to hit them.

A family of four suddenly rushed out of one of the buildings, totally terrified. What were they doing there now, so close to the front? Abu Saad jumped out of the ambulance, opened up the back, and told them to get in. There were two girls in addition to the mother and father. One of the girls cried when the barrel bombs exploded, but the parents were calm through it all. We drove them to a safer area. The father thanked us for our help and walked on into the center of town with his girls.

Abu Saad leaned over the wheel, looked up at the sky, and squinted through the dusty windshield. When he was sure all the bombs had been dropped, he looked at me. "Back again?" I nodded. Then he turned the ambulance around and drove back toward the front line.

It turned out that they'd dropped the bombs too early. The FSA soldiers were still there, just as alive, but a little less flippant. They started pointing and explaining where the Dawla fighters were holding off the offensive. They wanted us to deliver two packages with water and energy drinks to the Dawla fighters. It wasn't enough that they were too cowardly to go and fight themselves; now they wanted us to deliver supplies. What sort of soldiers were they? I was just about to say that they could do it themselves when there was an explosion behind me. I felt the force of the blast. Something hit me in the back of the head, and I threw myself on the floor. Didn't hear a thing. Just a whistling sound. A whole wall had collapsed nearby, and we'd been pelted by rubble. For some reason I picked up the stone that'd hit me and put it in my pocket. Abu Saad was there in an instant asking if I was OK. I couldn't hear a thing—the whistling in my ears was so loud—but I nodded and gave him a thumbs-up.

Reinforcements arrived. Saudi Arabian Dawla soldiers to relieve the men who'd been on guard for two days. There was a bridge over the dried-up canal, but using it was just asking to be shot. You had to run under it and look for cover behind the pillars. We helped the Dawla soldiers carry some boxes of drinks to the canal, but not any farther. Then we stood and watched them run, one at a time. There must've been nearly twenty of them. The ones carrying boxes were slower, but they managed OK. At one point there were only three men left. One of them took off and darted across. Then we heard the shot. His leg was ripped off and flew through the air. The rest of his body crumpled to the ground, arms flailing. The last two soldiers ran out and pulled him back, just below where we were standing. Blood was spurting out of his leg stump. One of them took off his belt and tightened it as much as he could around the stump, but there wasn't much he could do. They asked for help, but I didn't dare go down to them. Fear took over. In situations like that, you find out what you're made of. You imagine you're tough, that you're going to go to war and be a hero. And then you just stand there.

No, I wouldn't say I'm particularly brave.

If it had been a machine gun, the bullets would have passed through and left a wound. But they were shooting with anti-aircraft ammo meant for destroying planes and helicopters. His leg was ripped off and landed in the gravel at the bottom of the dry canal. Half a pair of camouflage pants and one black shoe.

There was nothing we could do. He died right there. I saw one of the men helping him cry over his chest. *"Astaghfirullah,"* I heard Abu Saad say. He asked God to forgive us.

I don't know. We could've at least helped him up so he didn't have to die down there.

The FSA people came and picked up the corpse after it was dark. They were so cowardly. Not that I was any better myself, but they just stayed back and hid until it was dark. What sort of soldiers were they? The Dawla fighters that had been holding the front line for two days also snuck back in the dark. The ones who'd been doing the shit jobs, the hard work. They were exhausted.

We didn't sleep that night, and in the morning there were more checkpoints than usual. First the FSA had a checkpoint, and then twenty yards farther were the Dawla soldiers, who had to check as well. Maybe they wanted to provoke each other. The trust between them had faded away. Syria was ruled by suspicion.

We'd thought about stopping to say hi to Arbi and asking if we could sleep there, but Sayfullah's base was almost empty. Not even the cook with the eggs was there. We drove on. Exhausted. Sleepy. I saw that woman I'd wanted to marry walking along the street. My skin felt dirty and clammy. I didn't say anything to Abu Saad. A lot of people were at the Dawla hotel Arbi and I had visited. A new crowd of people. New executions. Two Jordanian spies each got a shot in the back of the head. One. Two. When they were captured they found micro-cameras built into the corners of their glasses. Otherwise, they looked like two jihadists with beards, just like everyone else. I was too tired to shout. Just watched. They spat on the bodies, dumped them. That was enough. I'd seen enough.

Some of the FSA checkpoints were totally improvised. Some guys might put out four rocks and a barrel with FSA colors on it. "There. This is a checkpoint." Get it? We called them flying checkpoints. Four soldiers were standing at one of those with weapons. "Open up!" We noticed right away they weren't very organized. "These guys want something," said Abu Saad. He was pissed. "OK, what do you want?" "Money." "We don't have money," said Abu Saad. He tried not to make them angry, but also not to give in. "Grenades?" "We don't have any grenades either." "OK, open the gas tank."

They got a can and a hose. One of them got down on all fours and sucked one end of the hose until gas came out. None of them said anything. None of them dared look us in the eye. It was gloomily silent while the gas was flowing. "Got enough now?" "No, wait, a bit more." Abu Saad shook his head. After that we never filled the tank completely.

When I first got a gun, I thought nobody would mess with me. But people pull out their guns a bit faster than you; then you're just back where you started. Abu Saad talked about getting himself a suicide belt. Nobody messes with you then.

At the next stop things were more like they should be. There they asked us to turn off our lights and drive slowly. Planes were in the area. They were silent as long as they were flying high up, but then they dove down like birds of prey. You only heard the sound of the engine after they pulled the nose up again, after the attack. People said the Syrian air force didn't have enough good pilots for that type of maneuver. The ones who dove like that, they were Russian fliers.

While Dawla and the other rebel groups tightened their grip around each other's throats, I got my own house.

No, Abu Saad had asked around a little, but it was Arbi who helped me with it. He'd sent me a message that one of Sayfullah's people knew someone who knew of a house.

Well, firstly, Carlos was on his way, and I didn't want to burden Abu Saad anymore. Carlos would probably have been welcome to stay there, but y'know. Two: I didn't want to live in an FSA-controlled area anymore. It felt wrong. Three: it was time to get myself organized. And four: I wanted to live closer to Aleppo. That was where it was all happening if you wanted to be useful against Assad.

Not exactly. It was around Dana, in a village called Tawameh. But a lot closer to Aleppo, and not so far from Atme either, where I was still supposed to be on guard duty.

No, just a little house.

It suited me perfectly because I wanted to live simply. Even the first time I saw the house, I started to imagine a life for myself. There was a farm nearby where you could buy fresh milk directly from the farmer. I had my own garden, and I thought I could get my own hens after a while and have fresh eggs. And going up to the house there was one of those trellis roofs with grapes, just like at Abu Saad's place. Perfect. It was just what I was looking for. Something natural. Pure, organic food straight from the neighborhood. None of that synthetic stuff you get at the supermarket.

I imagined, well, something or other; I don't know, maybe I could find some peace there. A simple life in the eye of the hurricane.

Abu Saad asked if it was OK for him to live there too because he was going to be in Aleppo more. Anyway, his wife and little Saad had moved to his in-laws' house. He thought it was better that way, in case anything happened. He wanted to contribute more as well.

When I moved in, he and Abu Hajer came, and we had a small house-warming party. We also invited some other foreign fighters who lived in a house nearby.

Yes, I'd met them by coincidence on the street that same day. Three Algerians who were associated with Ahrar al-Sham. Like, why not? So they came over as well. Abu Hajer brought shawarma, hummus, bread, nuts, and these Arabian sweets that give you a crazy sugar high. Yeah, and sunflower seeds too, of course. The revolution would've come to a complete stop if they'd run out of that birdseed stuff.

While we were eating, Abu Saad and Abu Hajer joked about me looking for a wife. "That's why you've gotten yourself a house, eh?" "You already imagining kids running around the garden here playing?" Once they got started, they were unstoppable. Then the two Algerians started to wrestle. You know, wrestling is Sunna. We took turns.

Yes, right. But in Halden I mostly practiced striking and kicking. I'm more of a boxer than a wrestler, and these guys were doing Greek wrestling, like they'd been doing nothing else their whole lives.

No chance. I was thrown on my back and was counted out immediately. Of course, Abu Saad used the opportunity to tease me. "Look, this is the strong fighter who wants to get married!" But then he was pulled into the wrestling match himself, not by me, but by Abu Hajer. "Wait, wait," I said. "This is a battle between Sharia and democracy. On your marks, get set, go!"

No, neither of them managed to get the other on the ground.

In the end we settled down and prayed together. Yeah, and then I got a gift from Abu Hajer. A radio. It wasn't much use to me, because everything was in Arabic, but I was still proud, because it meant he'd accepted me at last.

The next day I rode the motorcycle into Dana and bought some fruit, food, and pots and pans for my kitchen. I had to learn to do things for myself now. The wad of money in my pocket had gotten smaller, so I couldn't keep being cheated on prices. I had a gold watch from when I had my business. That was worth something. But who would have the money to buy a gold watch in Syria during the war?

Some young guys had started to patrol in Dana. They drove around and were *hisbah*, Sharia police. You know, in a way Dana was Dawla's laboratory. They could experiment with their vision of society there. For me it was actually reassuring because there was less crime in the towns Dawla controlled, and during a war it's a luxury to feel safe. And then they had people who went around solving problems, like social workers. They weren't completely out of touch.

I saw a lot of Danes that day. And I heard a man speaking Norwegian to a woman in a niqab, but I didn't go over to them. Y'know, sometimes it felt like you were in a tourist trap, bumping into other Norwegians. But you don't go to Syria to form a Norwegian club, do you? I had my own house, I was learning Arabic. I was starting to become a well-integrated jihadist.

I was at the checkpoint in Atme a few more times. Sayfullah's people had started to guard there as well.

No, I hadn't met any of them at Arbi's. This was a different division. Some Uzbeks and a Tajik who'd walked the whole way from Afghanistan. He figured the war was practically over there, so he thought he'd come over to the next party. He'd walked through Pakistan, Iran, Kurdistan, Iraq, and into Syria. He nearly always wore a balaclava. Quiet guy.

There was an American there too, Abu Muhammad al-Amriki. He was Sayfullah's emir in the area. He hung out in the town itself, Atme, but came up once in a while to check that everything was OK with his soldiers. Then I'd talk to him a bit in English. I liked Abu Muhammad; he was a calm guy and fun to talk to. You know, charismatic.

There were big differences between the Syrian rebels and the foreign fighters, the mujahedin. You know, war came to the Syrians. But the Caucasians, Uzbeks, Tajiks, Europeans, North Africans, all us others— we came to the war. We had the ember of jihad that the Syrians didn't have.

I didn't get the kind of peace I'd imagined in my new house. When I sat quietly, I started tapping my fingers just like I'd seen Abu Saad do, counting in my head—one, two, three, four, five, six, seven. Time goes quickly with your fingers like that—tick, tick, tick, tick. I still do it after I lockdown here in the evenings—one, two, three, four, five. Tick, tick, tick.

I also started to wash myself more than necessary, do *wudu*. I didn't want to be unclean when I went to God. Every time I touched something, I'd say *bismillah*, wash my hands, mouth, nose, face, head, arms, feet. The whole thing. And right afterward I'd do it all over again. I don't know, I felt kinda restless, because restlessness was in the air.

Just restlessness. I don't know how to explain it. I noticed it in the neighbors, in people around me.

OK, let me give you an example. A guy used to sell falafel from a truck not far from where I lived. After a while it became my standard breakfast. Falafel and milk. In the beginning he was nice, the falafel man, packed the roll in nicely and smiled. But then, I don't know, he changed—"Here, take your food." Small details. A look. Or the kids.

When I was at home, a whole horde of kids would gather outside. There were rumors that a foreigner lived there. Maybe he had some money. I sometimes handed out bread, and I always had some candy in my pocket for them. If I gave money, I had to do it right before I left, or it was chaos. But then one day it was totally quiet. I wonder if their parents maybe told them they shouldn't come over. That foreigner, y'know. People felt something was going on. A divide, and soon it would start to get ugly.

It was a relief when Abu Saad said we had a job. I couldn't handle sitting still anymore.

The Central Prison in Aleppo.

It was one of the biggest blemishes in the Syrian War. I'd gotten a message online from Arbi a few days earlier in which he'd told me about the prison. "It's complicated, brother," he wrote. "*Inshallah*, this is where I'll become a martyr."

Abu Saad had been in touch with Sayfullah. Things were starting to happen, and he'd gotten word that Ahrar al-Sham needed help with supplies. I gulped down a Jack Wrestler and jumped in the ambulance.

We fetched masses of space food from a depot north of Aleppo. The prison was also on the north side of town, so we didn't have to drive through the city center. We drove through a field on a bumpy road and into the village closest to the prison. I thought I'd seen destruction, but here everything was totally smashed. Things had been pulverized. The pieces were even smaller. There were craters in the ground, all the houses were deserted, someone had ripped out the windows and doors to sell them. It was the FSA people who did that, Abu Saad said. Vultures.

The rebels had taken over the area in the spring of 2013, but Assad's forces had managed to stand their ground in the prison itself. It was December. Several hundred soldiers and thousands of prisoners had been there for almost a year. Syrian prisons, man, just imagine. They're already hell, but then you get a war, food shortage, and disease on top of it.

You might say that. The siege didn't make it any better, but it was still the government forces that were holding them like hostages.

The main building was Y-shaped if you looked at it from the air. There was a wall around the prison, though it was broken in many places, and on the outside of the wall there were buildings occupied by the rebel groups: Ahrar al-Sham, Nusra, and Sayfullah's group.

No, Arbi wasn't there yet, but we met one of Sayfullah's soldiers at a guard post. He pointed to where we should take the food bags, an unfinished industrial building where Ahrar was holed up. Big, empty space with soldiers huddling here and there. The windows were blocked with sandbags, and snipers lay behind them pointing their guns out. In the corner there was a homemade catapult. Real old-school, based on weight. They used it to shoot gas canisters filled with explosives. Lay them on the catapult, light the fuse, and good luck. *Yeah, yeah,* I thought, *whatever works.* They were creative jihadists, you have to give them that. They even had a huge homemade cannon, which they just called *Jahannam,* Hell.

When we'd unloaded the bags, they told us stories about the prison. Some of the female prisoners had been stripped naked and displayed in the windows. They knew their enemies were deeply religious, right. Women had been gang-raped, and they'd been there so long they'd started giving birth to the soldiers' kids. What a place to start your life.

One of the older rebels, probably over sixty, reminded me a bit of my dad's mom. The same calmness, but instead of a rake, he had a Kalashnikov. He shook his head and said they'd failed to take the prison many times. One time they had advanced pretty far, but then Assad's people started to shoot prisoners and throw bodies out the windows, so they had to withdraw.

One of the Ahrar leaders interrupted, asked if we were the ones who'd come with the ambulance. Abu Saad nodded. He said they needed help immediately at Nusra's checkpoint just before the main road to the prison. Hostages were going to be freed.

Abu Saad was right on it. We drove over and saw a cluster of soldiers and people with those vests from the Syrian Arab Red Crescent, SARC. Four SARC trucks were lined up behind the checkpoint.

I don't really know about the politics there. Red Crescent had the responsibility, but some of their people had backed out. The government forces had shot at the medical personnel several times, it wasn't anything new. So they asked if we would step in, drive right into the heart of sadism.

I looked around. One of Sayfullah's people was there. I recognized him from the base. It was one of the men who'd laughed at the bulletproof plate I had in my vest. I couldn't look like a coward now. *"Yalla,"* I said to Abu Saad.

We switched into a Red Crescent car that had the organization's flag hanging everywhere. Nusra soldiers had ransacked all the vehicles. We took some big pans of food with us to deliver. We could only hope that the prisoners would get some of it. Then the message came over the radio: "Go now." Nusra opened the barrier, and we drove into the wolves' den without a single weapon. Abu Saad told me not to look around too much. It could provoke them. "Just look straight ahead and do what needs to be done."

First we drove in a convoy of SARC vehicles. Came to the Y building and drove toward the main entrance. The door opened only when we'd come to a complete stop. Three soldiers were standing there in dirty shirts. They looked around. You could see the safety catches were off on their guns. Their fingers were on the triggers. I made eye contact with one of them; he looked like he was on some kind of drugs, or just really sick.

Y'know, I'll never have any sympathy for those people—sadistic pigs. But I will say one thing. They'd held out for nearly a year in there, with constant pressure, on their guard the whole time. People never fight as hard as when they're backed up against a wall. They taught me that. But the price you pay is that you turn into an animal. I was looking at three animals. Black eyes. Shit, they smelled so bad.

"Get the food," Abu Saad said. I went to get it. Put the pans on the ground. Then the prisoners came out. They were just skeletons. Their clothes were hanging off. One of them was gasping for air. They shuffled over to us like zombies. I helped one of them into the truck, held him by the arm, and could feel the bones under his skin. It looked as if they'd chosen the oldest or the sickest, or at least I hoped that was the case, that there weren't thousands more zombies like that in there.

We turned around and drove off.

We heard their stories after a while, but we could already read most of it in their eyes—a life without light, without food, without water, where the only thing that was blooming was bacteria.

We had three in our car. I passed a water bottle back to them while we were driving. One couldn't manage to open the top. I helped him unscrew it, but then another grabbed the bottle. He just couldn't wait. They'd forgotten any kind of manners; their instincts had taken over. They cried and drank interchangeably. Coughed up the water. Tried again, a little slower, a little at a time. Like that, yes.

Tick, tick, tick. One, two, three, four, five, six, seven. I sat on the roof of the house with a blanket around me and ate birdseed. Abu Saad was home with his family. It was New Year's Eve. Not that it made any difference; they celebrated with rockets every day there. My infidel friends in Halden would be hanging out drinking that night. No, I wasn't going back there. I had other plans; I was heading in a very different direction. I'd seen so much. I was deep into the war. I was finally ready, determined. My faith in God had become stronger and stronger. I really got it, that when your time has come, it's come. It was actually real simple. Death is just a curtain between you and God, a veil. The bag of birdseed was half-empty; it was the salt they put on it that got me hooked. Shells from the seeds were strewn on the roof under the plastic chair. Actually, there were two plastic chairs; I was resting my legs on the other one. Soon Carlos would be there.

He was on his way through Turkey.

Yep. He'd gotten that far. I chatted with him from an Internet café in Dana and asked where in Turkey he was, but he didn't want to say. He thought they were watching him, the Norwegian police. *So what,* I thought. Anyway, I explained the route. He was coming the easy way. Remember at the beginning of my time in Syria when we got supplies at the river?

Yeah, the tub they sent back and forth. He was supposed to cross in that. A day or two and he'd be here. I tried to look forward to it but couldn't quite manage. I was still thinking about the prison. Or *sijn*, as they say in Arabic. If I could've pushed a button and blown up the entire Central Prison in Aleppo, I would've done it. I really would have. Just as well for them to be free of it, I thought. Just be done with it.

I heard grasshoppers, the wind. Once in a while the night sky would light up and there'd be an explosion in the distance. Boom! I imagined Syria from above, like a map, and tried to imagine how the Syrian army was gradually moving into the rebel-controlled area. Hammering their way in through the walls. Advancing. May Allah punish them eternally.

When Carlos arrived, I realized how hardened I'd become.

No, Abu Saad got him. When I heard the car, I turned off all the lights and hid behind the door. Carlos came in first. Called out, unsure, "You here, brother?" I stood right behind him, like this, completely silent. Right there, that was a great moment. You have to remember to put this in the book. Y'know, there he was. He was completely surprised when I tapped him on the shoulder and was about to knock me out. "*Alhamdulillah*, it's you." Then he just laughed. I saw the bags he had with him. My God, it was like he'd brought his whole wardrobe. He tried saying he had clothes for us too, and that he didn't know if it was warm or cold and stuff, but it was mostly bullshit. And he'd brought some vacuum-packed meat from Turkey; he probably thought we were lying in ruins and eating gravel or something. He was actually surprised at how well I was living, even if it was just a normal little house.

Abu Saad clapped us both on the back and said it was about time we spoke some Norwegian, so he went to bed. I made some tea and took Carlos up on the roof. He was overwhelmed by how many stars you could see. "Yeah, there are some advantages when the power supply's been blown to pieces," I said.

Carlos told me he'd been feeling more and more like a hypocrite in Norway, but he'd decided that he didn't want to leave before getting his mom to convert.

Yeah, that's what he said.

Then he wanted to start reminiscing about our past and all the mistakes we'd made when we were younger and everything, but I interrupted him. He'd come down to Syria and wanted to be friends, but I didn't want friends. I wanted brothers. Besides, there was a lot I needed to explain to him. Carlos still thought there was a united front against Assad. I tried to explain those days were over. "Even if someone has a beard and believes in God, they'll still shoot you in the head if they think you're with another group." Carlos looked away. He'd come down here full of kindness, and he thought I'd be happy and peaceful because my belief was so strong. But I wasn't blissfully happy or peaceful. I was ready for war. And I wanted him to be like that too. That goodness in him—I tried to rip it out right away; it didn't belong in Syria. "This isn't some kind of *tablighi* meeting," I said, "and besides, there's a reward on your head."

Oh yeah, he tried. He concentrated and asked a lot of questions while I was crunching birdseed. But then I got irritated too, because he kinda wanted to understand everything all at once. "Hey, when will we be trained? Which front will we go to?" I told him to calm down and look around first.

"Brother, I'm looking forward to whatever happens in the future," he said.

So, she's reading it as we go along?

Yeah, that's OK, but I don't know if I've got a lot to give your editor. There wasn't a lot of happiness about seeing each other again. I'd become hardened. Y'know, before when we were dealing drugs, Carlos was the one who could reach me when I was too hard. But nobody could reach me where I was then.

You can tell her this isn't that kind of story. You can't always find a silver lining.

In the morning after prayer, I fixed milk and falafel, and Carlos was in good form. *"Subhanallah!"* For Carlos everything was fantastic all the time. What did he want with Paradise? He was already there. Abu Saad left for Salqin to talk with Abu Hajer, get the news. Then he was going to see his family and go to his farm in Darkush.

Carlos and I rode the bike to Dana. On the way Carlos asked if we could switch so he could try out the bike. I slowed down, drove onto a side street, thought, *why not?* But as soon as I'd put my foot on the ground, a couple of stray dogs came toward us. I had to turn around quickly before the other strays in the neighborhood figured out there was a party and the whole pack came barking and snarling. Carlos just laughed. I told him to shut up and take my gun. He unhooked it from my back and waved it around. "Should I shoot? Should I shoot?" But I figured he didn't even know how the gun worked. I eventually managed to turn the bike and hit the gas, while Carlos just sat behind me and laughed, the gun in his hands, like some crazy cowboy. *You laugh,* I thought. *The dogs here bite.*

No, no, for him everything was still fantastic and unbelievable and I don't know what. Especially in Dana.

Yeah, his jaw totally dropped. He still hadn't seen Syria in daylight. He was surprised that everything was so normal. It was like being in a normal Arab town. People were shopping, talking, sitting in the café. "Oh, there's a foreigner!" He pointed to some European guy. I gave him a look, but he just laughed. "Don't be so hard, brother."

We went to a café, and you know Carlos, he had such an open heart. He smiled the whole time and talked with people, made them feel good. He even picked up a few words at the café; he learned things faster than I did. But if I lacked *sabr*, Carlos was ten times worse. He wanted his own weapon right away. Well, OK. The way things were in Syria then, it was pretty crazy not to have a gun.

Yeah, I took him to a gun shop. It was a hangout for jihadists from all over the world. It smelled of sweat. Weapons and hand grenades, here you go. I wanted to buy Carlos a machine gun, but I didn't have the cash. I thought he could get a shotgun or something, just to start with. But then we found a small pistol that looked perfectly fine. That would do for now. Machine gun later. We drove out of town, stopped at a field. Now I was Abu Saad, and Carlos was me. First he tested the pistol. Bang! It wasn't much fun. So I let him try my Kalashnikov. Put out a can of Jack Wrestler for a target.

He hesitated. Everyone does in the beginning. But then three shots rang out. He was shaking like a leaf. He'd forgotten to set it to a single shot. I got a bit angry. Said that was that, now he'd tested it. Carlos wanted to shoot more. Said he could buy the bullets and all, but I told him he should save the bullets for the *kuffar*. Besides, I'd become a bit like an Arab; he wasn't going to buy me shit.

Abu Saad came and got us after a few days. I'd started to wonder what had happened to him. It was time to get an update on the situation. As soon as he came through the door, I saw a shadow hanging over his face. He said there'd been clashes between the FSA and Dawla near Dana. "Near Dana?" I asked. He nodded. It wasn't safe there anymore. He told us to jump into the ambulance.

On the way I asked if there was anything we could do. Abu Saad was silent, took a deep breath. He said we just had to wait and see how things developed. "In the meantime we should stay away from your house," he said. "It's in the middle of the danger zone now." Besides, they needed people up at the checkpoint in Atme again because several of the soldiers there had been redeployed to fight Dawla. Somebody had to hold off the Kurds so they didn't use the opportunity to advance. Abu Saad asked if we'd go up there and do *ribat*.

Carlos almost shouted yes. Of course, he was really happy. "At last! A mission!" It'd already been, what, three or four days since he'd arrived, and that was pretty much the limit of how long he was gonna wait.

We stopped at Abu Saad's farm. One day max. Carlos wanted to make friends with the sheep, of course. Pulled up some grass and fed them. In the afternoon I took him to the barber in Darkush. Said it was best to have short hair during the war; it was more hygienic. It cost him. He'd always been proud of his looks, but he understood. After fussing over his hair, the barber tried the same beard joke he did with me, but Carlos didn't really have that much of a beard to joke about. A little fluff on his chin he'd been growing for a year. Still, he was really proud of that. "Tell the barber if he touches it, I'll take his head off." He got to keep his tuft of a beard, and the barber kept his head. Everyone was happy.

We took the ambulance up to Atme the next morning. Abu Saad insisted that Carlos borrow his Kalashnikov; he'd bought a pistol for himself so he could manage with that. In any case he only needed it to protect his family and keep an eye out 'til things cooled down.

Sayfullah's people were on guard up at the checkpoint. The Uzbeks and that Tajik that always wore the balaclava. Carlos went around and said hi to everyone, overly enthusiastic and nervous.

I tried to talk to him again, explained that he shouldn't be so open with everyone. That he shouldn't eat too much; it was best to get your body used to less food. That he shouldn't fiddle with his weapon, talk too much about where he came from, what he thought, where he was going. He'd had enough. He completely stopped listening to me. He wanted to know why nobody was manning the huge machine gun, the Dushka. "Should I stand guard there, or what?" "No, no, just relax man. Come and have a cup of tea." When he eventually realized that not very much would happen, he wanted me to take photos of him. "Here, in front of the sandbags." "Take a photo here." "And another here." "And one over there by the machine gun." "And one from the side." It was weird to see the photos again in the trial, so long afterward. Y'know, you're asked to explain the photos in front of the judges, lawyers, journalists, researchers, and everyone else. Why were we there? What were we doing? Who were we with? But the only thing I could think, sitting in the courtroom with the photos in front of me, was that Carlos was wearing that jacket we'd gotten from the temp agency where we worked—y'know, where we had to haul pigs that time in Rakkestad.

I tried to answer, but I was just missing him. Thinking about the things we'd done together. Things we didn't get to do.

In the evening, I think it was one of the first days we were there together, we were standing by the sandbags looking at the PKK positions down below. I wanted to show Carlos. And while we were there, there was a sudden explosion in front of us. A ways away, but anyhow. Carlos grabbed his gun and threw himself down on the ground. Changed his position but didn't really know what he was supposed to do. The others came out too. The PKK shouted something up to us, and some of our men shouted back. *"Kuffar!"* After a while I told Carlos we could relax. I even went to bed, but Carlos stayed by the sandbags. "You'll keep watch?" I asked, mostly in jest. "Huh? It's war. Are you really going to bed?"

I lay down and used precious battery power playing *Spiderman* on my cell phone 'til I fell asleep. I don't know how long I'd been sleeping; things always happened when I was asleep up there. But anyway I was woken by two shots. I got up again. Carlos had taken cover. "I just wanted to look around a bit," he said, "then a bullet flew right by my ear, *Alhamdulillah*, and one on the other side, *Alhamdulillah*, and so I threw myself on the ground."

I shook my head. "Glad you're alive," I said.

Around the fire in the evenings we talked openly about the hatred that'd grown between Dawla and the other groups. Sayfullah had chosen his side. It'd been formalized with a *bayah*; his group became part of the Nusra Front. But not everyone was happy about it. One of the Uzbeks clearly thought it would've been better to join Dawla. The Tajik was happy about Sayfullah's choice. It was a question that divided people.

One day, Sayfullah's local emir, Abu Muhammed al-Amriki, came up. He told us about several meetings. Some Islamist groups had united and attacked Dawla in several places. "Doesn't look like anyone will be relieving you," he said. We were left at the checkpoint for maybe two weeks. News came rolling in. Quite literally. Abu Saad drove up with food, and Abu Muhammed stopped by regularly to talk with his people. The discussions got more heated. The whole group was nervous, tense. This wasn't good. Violence was spreading. Dana had been besieged by other groups that wanted Dawla out. Three Australian fighters had given up their weapons and tried to escape with their wives but had been shot on the way. Every day more people were being killed on both sides. They said it was dozens each day. One day closer to forty.

Somebody said Dawla widows were being raped by other rebel groups as they took over. Others said the widows had been well cared for. There was talk of Dawla women with suicide belts who blew themselves up. Some thought the US was controlling the whole thing. Most of it was rumor and speculation. One of the Uzbeks said that Nusra was involved in the attack against Dawla, but later that they were mediating between Dawla and the other groups. The whole thing seemed fishy.

Takfirs were thrown around left and right and center. Dawla accused the other groups of being *kuffar*, *munafiq*, and *murtad*—"apostates." Nusra called Dawla Kharijites, while Dawla answered by calling Nusra Murjites. They were referring to conflicts in Islam in the time right after the Prophet. The Kharijites were strict and thought that people who had committed serious sins should not be seen as Muslims, while the Murjites were more tolerant and believed only God can judge. At the checkpoint we talked a lot about these things around the fire. We discussed the groups' *aqida* and *minhaj*, their doctrine and their path to it. Or goals and means, to make it simple.

I think Carlos was influenced by those discussions. "Brother," he said one day, "something's going to happen here. What do you think about joining Dawla?" He thought they had better *aqida* than the other groups. "They probably do have the right *aqida*," I said, "but not the right *minhaj*." Carlos hadn't seen what I'd seen. I tried to explain, but he didn't listen to me anymore. I'd lost Carlos. "We have to protect the flag bearers of Sharia," he said. I tried to talk like Abu Saad. Said that in Islam you shouldn't take sides when Muslims are fighting against each other. But he always found a way to twist around what I said. In the end I just asked straight out, "Are you gonna take off on me, or what?" He shook his head. He wanted me to go with him. I thought a lot about something that Egyptian, Masri, had said to me once: "Every time you pick up your weapon, remind yourself why you picked it up in the first place." I hadn't picked it up to fight other Muslims.

I thought about leaving Syria. For the first time, I thought about giving up. Going away. At least as long as it was like this. I wasn't the only one. Buses of fighters who didn't want to be there anymore were crossing into Turkey. Mostly Arabs—they were deserting left and right. Didn't want to kill fellow believers.

In the middle of it all, Abu Saad showed up and weighed in.

Yes, when he brought food for us. "The time has come," he said. "You should go to the JMA and pledge allegiance to them." He thought they'd managed to keep out of the internal conflict. Besides, they were taking in foreigners.

I don't know; it seemed so distant at the time. For Carlos it was even further. He didn't want to go.

One day we were in Atme, the actual village. We had a few hours off from guard duty and went down with Abu Saad. Abu Hajer was also in the ambulance. I hadn't seen him since my housewarming party. He was as serious and stern as always, but Carlos always found a way to make people smile. Yeah, even Abu Hajer. He and Abu Saad were going to pick up a new ambulance in Turkey. "A slightly newer model," he said. *"Mashallah,"* I said. Then they dropped us off in the town center.

Atme was—how should I put it?—a neutral town. Even Dawla soldiers could be in town as long as they were unarmed.

Yeah, I think there was a Dawla base not too far away that had been stormed by Nusra or something, and the soldiers could either join Nusra or give up their weapons. So there were some in Atme. And because they couldn't carry weapons, they probably thought, *Let's recruit people.* It wasn't too difficult. A lot of people thought Dawla was the victim of all the other groups' attacks. Besides, they seemed purer because they didn't work with moderate or secular groups.

One of the men who was recruiting was a fat, dark Iraqi. He walked up to Carlos while we were sitting in one of Atme's Internet cafés. The place was really busy, full of jihadists from every group, old and young. I even heard a guy speaking Urdu there. The ceiling fan was going around slowly. It was crooked, looked like it was about to fall down. An FSA scarf hung over the counter, something the jihadists didn't like much.

Yes, Carlos got talking with the Iraqi guy. He nearly shouted, "I'm from Norway, but my father was from Chile." Great, here we go again. The Iraqi started in with his arguments about joining Dawla. I'd heard it all before. I knew it by heart. But Carlos hadn't seen what I'd seen. He was receptive. Sat there and agreed with the Iraqi.

Y'know what? If you search online, you'll find a picture of him with four decapitated heads. That's the Iraqi.

Believe it or not, in the middle of all this, while Carlos was talking with the fat IS guy, while I was sitting between two jihadists in balaclavas, while the whole rebellion against Assad was falling apart, finally there was a woman from England who was ready to come down and marry me.

Yeah, one I'd been chatting with. She'd gotten some money and everything.

Are you mad? I didn't even know where I was heading.

Outside the Internet café, we met Sayfullah's local emir, Abu Muhammad. He told us about trucks full of weapons that had just crossed the border from Turkey. "And they're coming to the FSA and Ahrar al-Sham, but also to Nusra, so together they can keep slaughtering our brothers in Dawla." He was unusually open. Said straight out he didn't agree with Sayfullah in allying with Nusra. "I'm skeptical," he said. "Nusra isn't just Nusra; there are stronger forces behind them." I'm not sure if he meant Saudi Arabia, Qatar, the US, or Turkey. Maybe all of them. "I don't want to feel like a pawn in a chess game," he said.

We were finally relieved at the checkpoint a few days later, and Abu Saad drove us to his farm. Forget about going home to Tawameh with all the fighting around Dana. But Abu Saad was busy. He had a pregnant wife and everything. He wanted to stay with his family for a few days, so Carlos and I took long-awaited showers and got some sleep at his place. I sat up on the roof looking out over the olive trees, watching some birds. I wonder if they knew there was a war in the country, or if it was all the same to them. What did they think about the plumes of smoke, the explosions, and all the corpses lying around? Did they see any difference between Dawla and Nusra? While I was pondering this, Carlos came up on the roof. He'd finished his shower and was standing there with a bare torso and a towel around his waist. He stretched and yawned. "What are you doing?" I asked. "What d'you mean?" "We're in a Muslim country, brother, put some clothes on." Then he was embarrassed, I remember.

We tried not to talk about the different groups and stuff that day. Every time we did, things got tense. We tried to be just Tariq and Carlos, like we'd always been. But we'd kinda forgotten how to do that. We prayed together, and I tried to make a little food, even though I never quite learned how to use the oil they use there.

While we were eating, I heard a large diesel engine. I went out to see what it was—a pickup fully loaded with weapons, bags, and equipment and maybe eight or nine soldiers. It was Abu Muhammed al-Amriki and the Uzbeks, the Tajik with the balaclava, and last but not least the fat Iraqi from Dawla. I greeted them and asked what they were doing at the farm. Before they could answer, Carlos put his hand on my shoulder. "I'm going with them," he said. "What do you mean?" He looked me in the eye. "I asked them to pick me up here," he said.

He went in to fetch his things, and I was left standing there with al-Amriki. "You're welcome to join us," he said. I was stunned. Said I had to find out who was shooting at whom first, that I'd rather avoid choosing sides. I asked where they were going. "First to Haritan," he said, "and then on to Raqqa." "What about the Nusra flag on the truck?" "Easier to get through the checkpoints," he said.

Carlos threw his bag in the back of the pickup. "Forgive me, brother," he said. I didn't answer. Wanted to show him I was pissed, or something. Not that it made any difference what I said or didn't say. I might as well have said something or hugged him. I could've done that. But I didn't.

When Abu Saad heard about Carlos, he looked at the floor and shook his head. That evening we had a proper talk. He repeated his advice that I should pledge *bayah* to one group. It had become dangerous for a foreigner if he couldn't answer when people asked which group he belonged to. At the same time, it wasn't that easy. Abu Saad was still talking about JMA. He'd tried to find one of their leaders, but they were in hiding now that everything was so chaotic.

"What about Sayfullah?" Abu Saad asked. He said a route through the Dawla-controlled territories to Haritan had opened. "Maybe that's the best place for you now. You know them, they know you, and that's a luxury." Well, that was true. *Bayah* to Sayfullah would've been a good move with things as they were. No matter what, it might be a good idea to get over there. Sayfullah knew more about what was actually happening, especially at the leadership level. On the ground it was impossible to know what was true with everything being said; people were killing each other on the basis of rumors and suspicion. Besides, I wanted to ask Sayfullah why people from his group were deserting. And I wanted to ask Arbi to get in touch with Carlos. He wasn't listening to me now, but maybe Arbi could get through to him.

Abu Saad was thinking about all the front lines that were being abandoned now that the rebels were fighting each other. He was willing to go to the front so it didn't get any weaker. He'd hinted to his family about it, he said. He thought Sayfullah might also give us advice about where soldiers were needed.

The next day we left for Haritan. First we stopped at my house. More moderate rebels were standing outside the Sharia court in Dana smoking cigarettes, almost as if they were making a point of it. The actual court was riddled with bullet holes. Several buildings were covered in soot, and burned-out cars were abandoned in the road. No more Islamic State in Dana.

When we got to my house, I was glad to see nothing had been touched. There was no sign of fighting in the little village. But the house just wasn't the same. The air wasn't the same. I packed my things. The motorcycle was outside. I pushed it into the house and locked the door.

The main road to Haritan was closed. We had to take smaller roads up, down, around. There were so many checkpoints—new checkpoints, colder stares, trigger fingers ready. All the checks took a long time. It got dark while we were still on the road. We turned off the headlights and drove in the darkness. I squeezed the stone in my pocket, the one that'd hit me in the back of the head in Aleppo.

Then someone shined a flashlight at us. Abu Saad slowed down, and when he stopped I saw guns pointing at us from both sides of the truck.

"Where are you going?" "Which group are you with?" "Who are you?" Abu Saad started to explain. We were working for several groups but were independent. *"Fisabilillah,"* he said, "for Allah's sake"—that's what you say when you're independent. That was fine for Abu Saad, but not for me, not for a foreigner. That they didn't believe.

They pulled us out of the car. "On your knees!" We dropped to our knees in the ditch. It had been raining, and the wetness seeped through our pants. There was a field in front of us. It was totally dark. The only thing we could see was the wet, red earth lit by the flashlight. Then I felt the barrel of a gun against my head. Here? Now? I'd thought I'd die from one of Assad's bullets. Who were these people? Were they bandits robbing us? Were they rebels? Abu Saad said I should stay calm and let him talk us out of this. I couldn't breathe. My body got cold. They wanted to check the vehicle. Of course, they found our weapons, but no more than that. In my pocket they found my wad of money but put it nicely back. *OK, so not highway robbers,* I thought. I heard Abu Saad talking to them. Quiet voices. Then the barrel disappeared from my head. I was lifted up. "Sorry," they said. "We have to be careful." They said Dawla was sending suicide bombers to checkpoints. We were told to drive slowly on. "Flash your headlights once in a while to make yourselves visible," they said. And so we drove on.

I asked Abu Saad what he'd said to make them let us go. "I made them understand that we were traveling together," he said. "Yeah, but how?" He paused. "I told them they'd have to shoot me first."

We drove slowly. Flashed the lights. There were so many checkpoints, and at each one machine guns were pointed at us. It would have been over for all of us if anyone had been even a bit jumpy—finished. Whenever we were stopped, Abu Saad immediately said, "We have two guns in the back." It was late by the time we arrived at the apricot-colored villa.

The guards were stricter there as well, but one of the soldiers recognized me. People were gathered in a large room on the second floor; a lot of people wanted to talk with Sayfullah now. He greeted us quickly and continued talking. Arbi was nowhere to be seen. But the cook was there. He whispered that Arbi was stationed at a factory.

We found out that people had been killed in Haritan as well. The shops had shut, y'know, a little like in a Western movie when everyone closes shop before a shoot-out. So there wasn't much food around either.

In the end Abu Saad asked the question on everyone's mind. Totally banal, but important. "Who shot first?" Sayfullah said Dawla had. They'd provoked the other groups, picked a fight. He didn't want to spread hatred, he said, and refrained from answering a number of questions, even though he probably knew more. But he made it clear he thought the Dawla leaders were making a big mistake. I'm not sure how useful his comments were. I would've preferred to talk to Arbi.

We had to get some sleep. The villa was full, mattresses strewn all over the floor. People couldn't live spread out anymore.

The next day one of Sayfullah's soldiers asked us to help him move. His things were in a small village called Kafr Hamra, a short drive away. People said Dawla was advancing toward that area. They needed a route for getting reinforcements to areas they still held. Abu Saad reluctantly said yes. Kafr Hamra was a key position for Dawla, so it was only a matter of time before they'd take it. Sayfullah was uneasy too; the orphanage he was running and several of the widows he took care of were there.

We made two trips into Kafr Hamra, loaded up, and drove back to Sayfullah's base. Then, on the third trip, we started to hear shots from the neighboring village. Dawla was on the way. We didn't want to risk getting killed just to help somebody move. The civilians were panicking; people didn't know where to go. On one side Dawla, on the other different rebels, and, as though that wasn't enough, Assad's forces were advancing from the south. They used the opportunity to push forward and take positions on a mountainside a few miles away. It was a little too far for snipers, but you can be damn well sure they were sitting there with binoculars and popcorn enjoying the show. Ha ha, look at those idiots fighting each other down there.

It was a total mess. It felt like everyone was shooting at each other, and the road behind us, the one back to Haritan, had apparently been closed off again. Remember what al-Amriki had said about not wanting to be a pawn in someone else's chess game? Well, chess was nothing compared to this. In chess you start from one side, and everything is black and white. In this game the enemy could be anywhere, and someone who was the same color as you could suddenly shoot you down.

Twenty or thirty soldiers were at one of the checkpoints. We stopped to ask what had happened. "They've taken control there," they said and pointed to the neighboring village, maybe half a mile away. There was only one road from that village to Kafr Hamra. So it would all go down on that road. That was where they had to come from.

You could hear them cursing at each other on the radio. "You're America's bitches," shouted Dawla. "Damn Jews," someone yelled back. You know, one of the rumors was that Dawla was an Israeli invention. The usual: if there's something you don't like, you blame it on the Jews.

Then we heard there were civilians with gunshot wounds stranded between the two villages. People whose houses were between the front lines. What an awful place to have a house right then.

One of the leaders—I don't even know which group he was from—took the radio and talked with the Dawla people on the other side. "We've got wounded civilians," he said. After a bit of back and forth, he made some kind of agreement with them. The civilians could be brought out. They wouldn't shoot.

There were a couple of vehicles there, but they had Dushkas mounted on them. We were singled out. Someone said we should get the wounded;

we had an ambulance, after all. You know, as soon as they said it, some-thing felt wrong. The words were dark and heavy. Abu Saad shook his head. "It's madness," he said. "They're gonna shoot us."

People stared at Abu Saad. Everyone knew how dangerous it was, but we were expected to go. That's the logic of war. I could tell lots of thoughts were running through his head. You know, in the Koran, it says that if you save a person's life . . .

Yeah, all of humanity, right.

Fifth sura, I think.

I don't know if that's what made him get behind the wheel, or whether he felt pressured. But he made it clear that he'd go in alone. He didn't want me with him. I got in beside him anyway. What was I supposed to do? It was Abu Saad, after all. We were in this together. He looked at me strangely. "You stay here," he said. I'd put off pledging *bayah* to Sayfullah again and again. I'd held back when the Dawla fighter lost his leg. I hadn't gone with Carlos. This time I had no choice.

He looked at me for a long time. It was as if he was saying good-bye right then and there.

We started the ambulance. People looked at us, faces I'd never seen before. Maybe they were thinking they were hypocrites, they should've volunteered. But we'd been given the mission. We had to face the fear. We drove off slowly. Abu Saad held the radio while we rolled forward. Sweat was streaming down his forehead; he had to wipe it with the back of his hand a few times. It was harder 'cause the road had a barrier run-ning down the center. They'd blocked the left side with a gravel mound, but that was where the house and the wounded people were. So we had to drive around. All the way to Dawla, turn, and back on the other side of the crash barrier.

I was scared. Abu Saad was scared. It felt like the whole ambulance was scared. After everything we'd been through, it was like the ambulance was a part of us. It was like the engine was complaining; it didn't wanna go that way. The sky was gray. War weather. It had started to get dark. One of the electricity poles on the road had snapped. It was hanging in the wires like a wounded soldier being carried by two comrades. I could hear my own breathing.

It was quiet at the end of the road. Large, empty buildings. A Dawla soldier was looking out. He watched us turn around and drive back on the other side of the road. Then Abu Saad put the radio on the dashboard. "So far, so good," he said, but his hands were still shaking and his fingers were drumming against the wheel.

The people were lying behind the house. Badly wounded.

Yes, civilians. But two uninjured soldiers were also hiding behind the wall of the house. They were pinned down, as they say. Couldn't go anywhere without being shot. We couldn't take them with us; that would've broken the agreement.

We looked at the wounded. Where to start? One was shot in the stomach. He had cramps, probably internal bleeding because there wasn't much blood on the outside. Another was almost dead already, and one was shot in the foot and was bleeding a lot. We probably weren't thinking too clearly; we didn't know who to get first. We lifted the man who'd been shot in the stomach. A bad lift, didn't get a proper grip. He was heavy, I remember, made noise as we jerked him up off the ground. Then we walked—one step, two, three.

It must've been three or maybe four steps.

One, two, three. Three or four steps, that's right.

No, let me go on, I'm OK.

There's a kind of dull sound. Almost like someone clapping.

We drop the man, or maybe Abu Saad loses his grip. I turn. Several shots. I run, but I don't know, like, I don't know where to go. Where could I go?

I try to get to the ambulance. I take a step, but my foot just isn't there. I hit my head on the bumper. Then everything goes black, but I still hear several shots around me. Clap. Clap.

The last thought I have is we should've known. We should've known. And then . . . nothing.

It was completely dark when I woke up. Pain was everywhere all at once. I didn't know where I'd been shot because there wasn't a part of my body that didn't hurt. I really thought I was dead. Or dying. Somewhere between this life and the next. I've actually never felt myself so close.

To Allah.

I felt the angel of death approaching, but he went past me. It wasn't me he'd come for.

I started to realize I was alive. I cried and cried. I tried to look down at my body; it wasn't a pretty sight. My foot was twisted to the side. Like it wasn't part of me anymore, just jutted off in the middle of my calf.

I thought Abu Saad had left because I couldn't see him from where I was. I thought he'd managed to run away. That I'd been left behind. I missed Mom. I hoped everyone at home was thinking about me.

I tried to sit up, but I couldn't. I laid my head on the ground again. The earth was cold, my body was cold. I started to pray to Allah. What else could I do? I lay, waiting in the dark, in the smell of wet earth. Of Syrian earth. Of blood and gas. And everything was so eerily silent.

Then I heard some quiet movement in the gravel. I looked around. An angel was coming toward me. I can't think of him as anything other than an angel. It was an angel who was crawling toward me. When he saw I was alive, he put a finger on his lips. Another came over. They were rebels, both of them. I heard them whisper to each other. They quickly got on either side of me, lifted me up, and pulled me away. That one foot was just hanging, dangling. All my will was gone; I couldn't pull myself together. They hid me behind another house, a little more protected. And then the pain really hit. Imagine someone grabbing the flesh of your calf and pulling and pulling and pulling. They shoved some pills down my throat. I tried to work up enough spit to swallow them. I was covered in mud, and my pants were totally stiff from dried blood and muck. Everything felt so raw, I remember I really perked up right then. I was still losing blood. One of the guys who'd saved me put a belt around my thigh, right up at my crotch, and pulled it tight. Then he put his jacket under my head. *"Sabr,"* he said, *"sabr, akhi."* Then they went out to get someone else. Maybe there were others still alive.

After a few hours, I heard a vehicle. The lights were off so it took a while before I realized it was the other ambulance. The one that Abu Saad and Abu Hajer had gotten at the Turkish border. And there was Abu Hajer standing right over me.

No, absolutely not. He didn't have any idea we were out there. He didn't recognize me at first either. "Abu Hajer," I said. Then he stopped in his tracks. "*Subhanallah*! Is that you?"

Y'know what? I don't believe in coincidences anymore. I've seen too much to believe that anything happens by chance.

They'd gotten a new, clearer agreement with Dawla, promising them safe passage. He got me into the ambulance and drove me back to the checkpoint in Kafr Hamra. But he didn't take the detour past Dawla. He drove straight over the gravel mound. They were ready with a stretcher, and they carried me over to a pickup. Man, it felt so good to lie in the back of that truck, unbelievably good. I was rushed to a hospital, one of those underground ones in Haritan. That's where I saw lights for the first time that night. There were a lot of wounded people there, and in the corner there was a body bag.

The pain got worse and worse. I think it'd been, what, eight hours since I'd been shot, and my foot had been dangling there and twisting from left to right.

There was only one doctor at the hospital. He came to me, cut off my pants. The nurse put a hand on my forehead and asked what I was called. "Abu Silah," I said, "or Tariq."

She put an IV in my arm while the doctor looked at my leg. First I got morphine and then something else. The room started spinning, everything was flying. I started to see swollen, twisted faces. I recognized this. It felt like LSD, but I didn't know what they'd put into me. I saw all the images one more time. Abu Saad and I driving. His hand on the radio. All the faces. The ground. I remembered Allah. I was so close to Allah when I was lying there on the ground. So close.

Then I felt hands touch my leg. Good hands. I looked down at my shredded pants. They were full of blood. My shoe too. The people holding my leg looked like aliens. They pulled on my leg and twisted it into place. But it didn't hurt. They put a blanket over me, and everything felt good. I was warm. It was gonna be OK.

The high started to fade, but things were still floating around, and at one point I saw the nurse standing over me. She looked me in the eye. Out of the blue she asked if I'd marry her.

Yeah, it's totally true. In the middle of all that.

Don't ask me. I didn't really believe it myself. I tried to make an effort to follow what she was saying. She said she had a daughter—I dunno, maybe she'd lost her husband in the war or something. She thought I was cute. That's what she said anyway. Why then? I was dealing with more than enough with just the pain. I couldn't think clearly. She smiled at me and left. I think her shift was over because I never saw her again.

Everything went quiet. I looked up at the fluorescent lights. One of them was blinking. The room felt empty. Where was everyone? Where were the guys now? Arbi? Carlos? Had they been told? On one side of me there was a badly wounded soldier who was sleeping. On the other was the body bag. The three of us were going to make it through this night, each in our own way.

Abu Hajer was looking at me when I woke up. I could see it in his eyes: Abu Saad was gone. But only when he actually said it did it really hit me. Man, that hurt. Abu Hajer, he was used to all this, he'd seen so many people die. I waited 'til he left, then I pulled the blanket over my head and cried like never before, 'til I was totally out of tears.

Because the hospital was underground, I didn't know what time of day it was or how long I'd been there. I looked at my knee. It was as big as a football. The leg still didn't seem like part of me.

Arbi came.

Dunno.

No, he didn't know Abu Hajer. But maybe some of Sayfullah's people figured it out.

Arbi wasn't the kind of guy to show his feelings. He tried the best he could with his stoic face, but he wasn't exactly going to stroke my hair and tell me everything was going to be OK, if you know what I mean.

"Dawla's totally lost it," he said. I tried to tell him it wasn't 100 percent clear that Dawla had shot me. "Whatever, they're nuts." I told him Carlos had gone with Abu Muhammed al-Amriki to join Dawla. "Are you kidding? Carlos?" He said it was already a given Abu Muhammed would leave, but for Carlos to go with him, that really pissed him off.

Arbi said he'd talk to Sayfullah and get me to Turkey, sort out an operation there so I could join them afterward. "I dunno," I said. I didn't want to be a burden for anyone, didn't want to be in anyone's debt. But Arbi, y'know, he felt alone where he was. He insisted. He was going to take care of me. "I want to go home," I said. "Are you crazy? You'll never make it home on that leg there. We have to get it fixed." He said it as if it was for me, but I know he was scared of being left alone. He didn't want me to leave. "I'll get Sayfullah," he said. "Brother, it's going to be OK." I couldn't stop him.

He left and Abu Hajer came. He said we had to leave for another hospital immediately. Bombs were being dropped in the area, and I needed another hospital with better treatment. Then I told him too. "I wanna go home." He suggested going to a hospital in Turkey and coming back, but I told him again, "I wanna go home." He nodded.

He took me out. I saw Sayfullah's convoy outside. He got out of the car just as I was being put into the ambulance. We looked at each other briefly, like he was asking, *What are you doing? I came to get you, didn't I?*

I shut the door. We drove off.

Arbi wasn't there.

No, never. Not in this life.

The other hospital was underground as well.

North Aleppo.

They doped me up and put my leg in a cast. But the most important thing wasn't what happened to me there. People were just pouring down into the hospital. The war was over for me, but not out there, y'know?

I heard a child screaming. Its mouth was a gaping hole and its voice was twisted. It screamed in a way I've never heard anyone scream before. The mother was there too. She was panicking, badly wounded. I think she was taken to another ward. I got up, completely forgot my own pain.

Shrapnel wounds from Assad's barrel bombs. Of course, he'd use any opportunity to carpet-bomb the city. I swear, all the screams in Aleppo were in the mouth of that one child.

I don't know. I didn't stay long.

Abu Hajer came to get me again and said we had to move on. I got to call home. Said I was wounded, but that it was OK. I was on my way home and needed someone to meet me in Turkey. My mom was so happy. It reminded me of the soldiers in the trenches during World War I who were so pleased when they got wounded and could go home. Except that it was Mom who was happy in my case.

We were stopped several times on the way, by Dawla and the FSA. Abu Hajer said that if we were stopped by the FSA, then we're from Ahrar al-Sham, under such and such commander, but if Dawla stopped us, we were with them, under so-and-so. I learned the answers by heart. It worked well. But actually what really made a difference was the suicide belt Abu Hajer had started wearing. It's like a VIP pass down there. OK, if you shoot me, I'll blow everyone up, go ahead. It's strange to say it, but that belt actually made me feel safe. Before, I thought those things were horrible, but now it was our guarantee of safety. The guards let you through faster; they wouldn't bother people wearing suicide belts.

Abu Hajer was supposed to take me over the border at Azaz, but it was closed. The Turks had seen how chaotic it was on the other side and had closed the crossing. So we went to a town called Jerablus. Dawla had taken control there and driven all the other groups out. They'd painted over the FSA flag and put their own next to it. The battles were over, things had quieted down, and the border was supposed to be open.

It was Friday, so we went to the mosque. I sat on a chair outside. The imam gave a sermon about how great Dawla was now that they'd gathered good brothers from the whole world. I bet half the people in the mosque bit their lips when he said that.

After prayer, Abu Hajer asked if anyone knew when the Turks were going to open the border, but most of them thought it would be a while. He was in a hurry because he had to go back to Aleppo. In the end he found a young guy from the Red Crescent who said he could take me over at another border. "It'll work out, *Inshallah*," he said. *"Inshallah,"* I answered.

I cried again when I said good-bye to Abu Hajer. It was hard to hug him because of the suicide belt, but I took his hand and just about squeezed a tear out of him too.

Abu Hajer turned his ambulance around and drove off in a cloud of dust, back to the madness, while I limped over to the Red Crescent vehicle and out of Syria.

While I was in the waiting room at a Turkish police station, an old woman came up to me. There I sat, a stinking cripple on crutches with dust in my beard. The woman looked at me through these incredibly thick glasses and spoke to me in Turkish. Then she tried to hand me something. It was a coin. I waved it away, said it wasn't necessary. But she took a step closer and put the coin in my hand. A Turkish coin. I couldn't refuse, so I thanked her and put it in my pocket with the stone from Aleppo.

PART 3

"The sun is shining through the big window. The warmth is seeping in, but not out. Sometimes I feel like we're on a cruise ship slowly sailing through time. Full of people with weird stories, each in his own cabin."

Should I continue reading?

"I've made friends with the trees. Especially that birch tree right outside the window; it's not quite fully grown yet. We're both young, on the way to becoming adults. It's out there when I'm sad, and it's out there when I'm happy. It's out there on the numb days too. Sometimes I look at that tree and imagine what it'd be like to just stand completely still out there. Feel the wind blowing and hear the sound of the leaves. In front of me on my desk there's a kettle and a clock. I try not to look at the date. On the right there's my beard trimmer and a tin of coconut oil that smells fresh and makes me think of all the places I could've been. There are sheets of paper hanging on the walls. Prison schedules from Monday to Sunday. A plan for the reflection group Think It Out. Exercises from the physiotherapist for my weak leg. Prayer times and dhikr. And at the very bottom, a photo of my dad smiling at me. A bird just landed in the birch tree. I just wanna go outside, but then I remember the window and the walls, and I stay listening to the sound of the ventilation system.

The sound of the refrigerator. Soft torture at a low volume. You can't escape it. Sometimes I put on the TV just to drown out the noise of the ventilation system, and I see the pictures, babies and children who are crying and dying. This time I can't do anything to help other than cry together with them. OK, now I don't want to write any more."

There, that's everything I have.

Seriously?

I was worried about what you'd think.

I tried to write something about that too, but it was no good. Or rather, it wasn't very easy.

Y'know, my life stopped when I came to prison. So for me it's as if they're still alive. I met a guy in here and I was like, "Hey, you remind me of my friend Carlos," and then I thought I'd call Carlos one day, but there's no phone where he is now.

A little while ago I was in a support group meeting. Something they call Breaking the Cycle, where you sit around a table in a room with white walls and talk. One of the questions that came up was, How do you change your social network? And then we took turns answering. "How will you change your social network?" When it got to me, I said, "Y'know? I don't need to change my network." The moderator looked at me strangely. "Really? Why not?" "They're all dead."

Arbi joined Dawla.

Yeah, that was my question too.

Arbi wrote me and said Sayfullah had been hit in the head by shrapnel from a grenade and become a martyr outside the Central Prison in Aleppo. It must've happened around the same day I came home to Norway—what, maybe a few days after I'd looked him in the eye outside the hospital. Arbi wrote that a lot had happened since I left, and after Sayfullah died, he changed his mind about Dawla. When he was with Dawla, he felt he was with *sahaba*, the Prophet's companions.

I dunno. I think he was influenced by the people around him. A lot of Sayfullah's soldiers joined Dawla after their leader was killed. They started fighting more and more against the Kurdish groups. It was one thing to watch for attacks from the PKK, but actively fighting them, taking slaves and shit, I never understood that. But Arbi and I got closer; y'know, he opened up more toward the end. He knew it wouldn't be long because of how Dawla sacrificed their soldiers in Kobane. When he wrote to me, he wrote straight from the heart. He died the way he wanted.

Drone.

American.

Carlos became a sniper. He was on the front line when Dawla took Tabqa.

It was an airbase outside Raqqa where Assad manufactured tons of barrel bombs. I think it was great he helped drive the government forces out. I'm proud of that. I saw what those barrel bombs do.

Yeah, I regret that. Even though Carlos could be an idiot, I shouldn't have been so hard on him. But that's what happens. You become hardened.

Y'know, I often dream of Carlos, the same dream again and again. He's walking right in front of me, and I'm following him. I try to make contact with him, but he just keeps on walking. I try to reach him again, but he's always one step ahead. He never turns around. I never see his face. He just walks and walks and walks.

Yes, he lasted a while, but then he disappeared too.

Nobody knows.

Almost a whole year went by between when I got home and when they took me into custody. First I was in the hospital for a few weeks. My leg was green with infection and looked like a doner kebab that's gone way past its sell-by date. The doctor said three and a half centimeters of the tibia was missing.

The bone, yeah.

Mom didn't ask too many questions. She was just happy I was back home. Sometimes she says she wishes she could hug the man who shot me in the leg. Then she smiles. We don't get much deeper than that about Syria.

Everything seemed so good when I drove into Halden and saw the fortress again. But it got very quiet. Way too quiet. Norway is a pink sleeping pill.

My friends were there for me at first—Ali, Kushtrim, some people from the Oslo crowd.

Sometimes they fished for stories about Syria, yeah, sure.

I told them exactly what I thought. Nusra is working with *kuffar*. Ahrar is wrong in its understanding of faith. Dawla is killing Muslims.

Of course, they wanted to hear something else because they were heading down there themselves.

They never said it straight out, but I could tell. They let me understand. Especially Ali. You know, it was like when Arbi and I were getting ready to go. You get into a state where you almost don't talk to anyone about it, just do what you've gotta do, and then, one day, you're gone.

A few months after I got home, IS established the caliphate. It was summer 2014. A lot of my friends went down there at that time. Ali disappeared. Kushtrim disappeared. Burim from Oslo disappeared. Their parents were going through the same shit my mom had experienced.

Arbi and Carlos were still alive at that time. They wrote a lot of good things about IS. To be honest I was sympathetic toward the caliphate when it was established. I thought it would bring Muslims together. At last, you know. It gave people hope. That's what I thought—as long as they do it from the heart and build a good system. But I had mixed feelings, especially when several of my friends went down there. I know they left with good intentions, but they didn't know who they were dealing with. They believed in God and thought their faith would automatically lead them down the right path.

We all saw how it developed.

They're not coming back either, no.

But maybe you remember Liridon, the Albanian who moved to Sweden to play soccer?

I met him here in prison.

No, he's a guard. When I saw him, I was like, "Shit, what are you doing here?" and he was like, "Well, I'm working here. What about you?"

You know, when I saw him I remembered tons of stories from when we were small that I forgot to tell you. Things from elementary school. We were pretty rowdy, Liridon and I, the boys who went to gym class with our plastic bags. But he made it.

There was a lot of talk in Halden: who'd left, why they'd left, who'd come back. People talked about me, but not to me. Not that I was that easy to get ahold of. I mostly stayed home with Mom and Little Brother. After a while I went to the mosque. One of the leaders came to me. He was harsh. Said that what I'd done wasn't good and complained that they'd had problems at the mosque because of me. *Yeah, problems,* I thought.

Most of the people from the mosque kept their distance. I tried not to mention Syria. They put a chair for me at the back, next to an old Somali guy. He was happy he wasn't the only one sitting on a chair. "It's been a while," he said. "Where have you been?" "Syria," I said quietly. "What did you do there, brother?" "Jihad." Then he shook my hand and smiled.

Finally the police came and got me. I knew how it would go. I'm not sure I wanna bother talking about the trial and all that shit. I was sentenced. Eight years. Done.

Participating in a terror organization and associating with terror.

Yeah, like planning a terror attack.

It's almost automatic. If they think you've been with IS or Nusra, then you've kinda planned terror against the Syrian people, y'know?

The plan was to appeal, but then there was the terror attack in Paris. Game over, I thought. Who'd acquit me after that? So I dropped the appeal. Maybe that was stupid.

You know, the trial is over. Done. I can't change my sentence even if I dip my story in honey and cover it in glitter. I don't care what they believe or don't believe. The doubt will be there, whatever. And that's fine. Doubt away. I only want to say what happened in my head along the way. When it comes to the absolute truth, I'll let God take care of it.

To be honest, I sometimes fantasize that Abu Hajer might show up in Norway as a refugee. The whole way, y'know—by boat across the Mediterranean and up through Europe. And when he'd arrive in Norway, he'd find out I'm sitting in prison. He'd completely flip. Tell them how it really was. That would be awesome. And I would just smile and say, "Well, I told you, didn't I?"

No, I would've got some sort of punishment no matter what, because even if I hadn't given *bayah*, I was close enough with Sayfullah's group, and when he swore allegiance to Nusra, his group was automatically put on the terror list. It's a bit complicated. My point is just that it would've been good to be taken at my word.

I was most bitter at the beginning when I was in custody and struggling to sort out my thoughts. That was in a different prison. One afternoon we were walking around in the exercise yard, under the watchtower. It was sleeting and winter and dark. A Somali guy came over; I think he was barely twenty and was probably inside for drugs or something. "What was it like there?" he asked. "Hell." I was brief, didn't go into details. He rolled a cigarette. "If I . . . I wondered if . . . um . . ." He didn't even know how to ask. Then he finally got it out that he wanted to go to war for the Muslims. "What's your intention?" I asked. "Um . . . what do you mean, intention?" "What's the reason you wanna go? Do you wanna help people? Do you want some action? Do you wanna be famous? Are you just fed up and want to die?" The guy was shocked. He hadn't thought about it. But of course he took the first option. "Help people." Bingo. Good start. *"Mashallah,"* I said, "but why not collect money, food, clothes? That's what they really need." "Only women collect clothes," he said. "So you want to go there to show that you're macho?" "No, not like that . . ." You could really mess with his head, y'know? But I didn't discourage him, and I didn't help him. "If you want a shoot-out down there, you'll find a way without me helping you," I said in the end. I was moved to another section because of that particular talk. They should be commended for that, the prison authority. They were paying attention. And they have good reason for that, because the prison is full of people who are curious about IS. People who sympathize. It wouldn't be difficult to recruit people if that's what you wanted.

Because they hate.

They hate the police. They hate their parents. They hate the state. They hate Western society. But first and foremost, they hate themselves. They feel like they're never good enough. So they want to do something good, but they don't know how.

You have to remember prison is a spiritual place. You feel small when you're sitting in a cell, and when you're small, you open yourself up for something big. You look for God. It's easy to get people to pray. They need the peace that religion and prayer can bring. You should know that Islam has helped me find a better path. But many of the people who start practicing Islam in prison are also looking for politics. That's where the hate comes in. They walk around like powder kegs. I'm holding a match. But I don't light it. I don't want to rip a son away from his mother. I don't want that on me come Judgment Day.

I can give you an example. In the section I'm in now, there are twelve people. Seven of us are Muslim, even if not all of us are equally devout. One day I came out to the common area to see the guys gathered in front of the TV. Before I saw what was on, I noticed that the guard was staring nervously at me, like he was watching what I'd do. One of the guys explained, "Three bombs went off in Brussels." They didn't say more than that. The guys were silent. They thought maybe I was happy about what had happened or something. Positive? No. It's wrong to attack civilians. But I can understand it. I know where it comes from. Someone should have made a list of how many civilians the West has blown to pieces. By the way, do you know how many people the Norwegian military has killed in the last ten or twenty years?

No, me neither. Isn't it sick that we don't know that?

Anyway, I didn't say a thing, just listened to what the TV reporters were saying. But two of the guys in the section started to argue. One of the Muslims said something like "Look at that," but in a positive way, y'know? He seemed kinda impressed. Then one of the non-Muslims reacted: "Hey, if you're gonna talk like that, you can just go back to your cell." "Me, go to my cell? Why don't you go to your cell?" They continued to rile each other up, and in the end the Muslim said, "Y'know, fuck it. I'm happy about what happened, I hope more of them die." I just sat totally silent. I remember I was supposed to meet you right after. We were still talking about the Murree Cadet School.

I try to separate religion and politics now. I try not to hate. You know, hate is like drinking poison and waiting for your enemy to die. I think that was from some game on PlayStation or something. In the middle of the game, one of the characters said it. I like that idea. You can really understand the meaning of that sentence. Much clearer than when someone says you have to forgive, period. You forgive other people for your own benefit as well, or maybe even mostly for your own benefit. There's a hadith, I think, that says that you should forgive every night before you go to bed because it could always be your last night, and you don't want to take any hate from this life to the next.

Time helps. Talking about things helps. It's just too much to bear everything alone.

I tried that, but it didn't work for me. Y'know, it was a female psychologist.

No, no, I don't have anything against talking to a woman. I just felt like it was hard to open up, like she'd never understand what war is. But they have a really good prison priest. Tall guy with a slightly bowed back. He looks stern but is actually the nicest person. Sometimes he knocks on my door and asks if we can have a chat. Then he takes me into the priest's room, where there's a painting of Rome and a statue of Christ. He usually starts talking about himself first. He was a chaplain in the Bosnian War, so he understands. We've known the same fear. We believe in the same God. He's the one who always tells me, you know, that silence becomes your friend after a while. "Hang in there," he always says when we're done. "Be strong." Then time passes, and suddenly he shows up again. Knocks on my door.

I feel totally mixed up. Like, I want to keep my beliefs, but at the same time I miss the old life. Not the crime, the drugs, or anything, but the feelings. Music, for instance. One day I heard some Indian music from one of the cells in the section. I thought I recognized it. "Is that Kishore Kumar?" You know, the music my father put on in the car after he came out of prison. Then I asked if I could see the CD and found the song that my dad liked so much, "Aane Wala Pal." Whenever I hear it, I'm right back in the car with Dad, stretching my neck to look over the dashboard at the road in front of us.

The guys in the section are OK. Prison is like a brotherhood too. You take care of each other.

One evening before lockdown, four of us were sitting in a cell. It was a farewell party for one of the guys. He'd put on a CD of Albanian love songs. You know, Balkan instruments are made to make people cry. One of the guys lit a cigarette. We talked about the future. Said that despite everything, we live in Norway and there are opportunities. The guy who was being released was planning to get married right after he got out. "What are you going to wear on your wedding day?" someone asked. "Well, first I'm gonna get beaten up by my dad, and then I'll think about what I'm gonna wear." We laughed, but when the laughter died down, nobody knew what to say. The Albanian music kept playing. I drifted off. Looked out the window, saw those red clouds. Then someone clapped me on the shoulder. "*Inshallah*, Tariq's gonna get married when he gets out too." The guys, y'know, they know how to make me feel better. "Hey, we'll come dance at your wedding. Sorry, maybe that's haram? Is it OK if we dance at your wedding?"

"Sure," I said. "Just dance."

AFTERWORD

In 2016, I spent more than one hundred hours with a rebel fighter who had returned to Norway and is now in prison. *This Life or the Next* is a novel based on his story. However, it is important to note that both the source and the author have fictionalized events to a certain extent.

Demian Vitanza
Oslo, December 19, 2016

VOCABULARY

Ahrar al-Sham—A moderate Salafist rebel group in Syria. Not on the UN or US terror lists.

Akhi—My brother. Used to address fellow believers in Islam.

Alhamdulillah—Praise be to God. Used to show thanks. May be broken into three words: *al-hamdu lillah*.

Allahu akbar—Allah is the greatest. The expression is often translated as "God is great."

Al-wala wal-bara—Loyalty and disavowal. Love what Allah loves, and withdraw from anything Allah does not love. Especially used by extremists to legitimize disavowal of infidels.

Ana turidu—You need. The pronoun (*ana*) is usually omitted.

Ana uridu—I need. The pronoun (*ana*) is usually omitted.

Aqida—Creed, doctrine, or school of thought in Islam.

Astaghfirullah—I ask forgiveness of Allah. May be written as two words: *astaghfir ullah*.

Aya—Sign or verse. Used for verses in the Koran.

Ayat al-Kursi—The Throne verse in the Koran (2:255).

Bayah—Allegiance to a leader or scholar. After the Prophet Muhammed's custom (Sunna), when his followers gave *bayah*.

Bid'ah—The introduction of new things in Islamic ritual practice, something that does not follow the Prophet Muhammed's custom (Sunna).

Dawla—State or country. Used as an abbreviation or slang for IS/ISIS/ISIL.

Dhikr—To be reminded of Allah, often through the repetition of phrases or reading of Allah's ninety-nine names.

Dhuhr—See *salat*.

Dua—Prayer for something or someone, preferably after *salat*.

Dunya—This world. The earthly life.

Dushka—Large machine gun, Russian model.

Fajr—See *salat*.

Fatwa—Judicial statement given by a legal scholar, often as an answer to a question. A *fatwa* expresses the legal scholar's interpretation and is only advisory.

Fiqh—Islamic law.

Fisabilillah—For Allah's sake. May be broken into three words: *fi-sabil-illah*.

Fitnah—*Fitnah* is something that may lead to something negative for an individual or a society. The term has several meanings and is often translated as "temptation," "rebellion," "inner struggle," "dissidence," or "deviation."

FSA—Free Syrian Army. Established in July 2011 by dissidents from the Syrian army, it was initially one of the main rebel groups in Syria, whose aim was to overthrow Assad. The FSA is an umbrella term for many loosely organized subgroups.

Ghanima—Spoils of war.

Hadiqa—Garden.

Hadith—Accounts of what the Prophet Muhammed said and did.

Halal—Allowed in Islam.

Haram—Forbidden in Islam.

Hegira—Migration for Allah's sake.

Hijab—Veil, curtain. A headscarf for Muslim women.

Hisbah—Religious police. The word literally means "accountability" but is used in the sense of having to stand accountable for one's actions according to Islamic law. It is usually used in connection to trade and business.

Hur al-ayn—A woman with beautiful, dark eyes. Often used for the virgins that are supposedly waiting in Paradise.

Iman—Religious belief.

Inshallah—God willing. May be divided into three words: *in sha Allah*.

Isha—See *salat*.

Istishhad—To carry out an act of martyrdom. The word is often used by extremists to describe the actions of a suicide bomber.

Jamaat—Association or group.

Jannah—Paradise.

Jihad—Originally meant "struggle." In an Islamic context, *jihad* means "to aspire to attain Allah's favor." The expression is often used to mean war for the sake of God.

Jilbab—A word used in the Koran for cover when you are outside. A long, loose capelike garment that covers the whole body except for the hands, feet, and face.

JMA—Jaish al-Muhajireen wal-Ansar. A jihadist group established in the summer of 2012, consisting mainly of non-Syrians.

Kafir—Infidel. The plural form is *kuffar*.

Kharijites (Arabic: Khawarij)—"Those who break out." A group of
    Muslims who were originally followers of Ali, the fourth Caliph,
    but who distanced themselves from him and later the political and
    religious demands of the Umayyad (the first Islamic dynasty). The
    most extreme Kharijites consider it sinful to not take part in battles
    against the authorities and believe people who do not should be
    excommunicated and even killed. Many Muslims who are critical
    of IS compare IS to the Kharijites.

Khobz—Bread.

Kuffar—Plural form of *kafir*, infidel.

Kufi—Prayer cap. Also called *taqiya*.

Kunya—Arabic tradition in which you receive a nickname according to
    your relationship to a child. For example, Abu Ali (father of Ali),
    Umm Maryam (mother of Maryam). Also used as a nom de guerre,
    or wartime name. It is common to invent one or be given one if
    you do not have a child.

La ilaha illa llah—There is no other God but Allah.

La ilaha illa llah, Muhammadan rasul ullah—There is no other God but
    Allah, and Muhammed is His prophet. See *shahada*.

Madkhali—Follower of Rabi al-Madkhali, a scholar from Saudi Arabia.
    Al-Madkhali promotes a type of Salafism that emphasizes obeying
    and not rebelling against the authorities.

Maghrib—See *salat*.

Mashallah—So good that Allah has willed it. May be divided into three words: *ma sha Allah*.

Minaret—The tower connected to a mosque from which people are called to prayer.

Minhaj—The path to a religious goal.

Misbaha—Prayer beads.

Miswak—A twig from the *Salvadora persica* tree used to clean the teeth. Used and recommended by the Prophet Muhammed. Also called *siwak*.

MMA—Mixed Martial Arts.

Mujahed—The person doing *jihad*.

Mujahedin—Plural form of *mujahed*.

Munafiq—Hypocrite.

Murjia—A group that opposed the Kharijites on questions related to sin and who may be considered a Muslim. The group believed, in opposition to the Kharijites, that only Allah has the right to judge a Muslim, and that even if a person committed a serious sin, he did not thereby lose his status as a Muslim.

Murtad—Apostate.

Mushrik—The person who practices *shirk*.

Nafs—Used to refer to a person's inner being, the soul or the self. To take control of your *nafs* may be understood as not giving in to your own desires.

Nashid—A song with a religious message that is sung without musical instruments or accompanied only by a drum. The songs usually praise Allah or the Prophet Muhammed, but there are also *jihadist nashids* that romanticize holy war or martyrdom.

Nazar—A round Turkish amulet shaped like a blue eye.

Niqab—A face veil.

Nusra—Jabhat al-Nusra. A Syrian Salafist group with ties to Al Qaeda. The group was started in 2011 by envoys from the Islamic State in Iraq (the forerunner to ISIL and IS) and was formally established in January 2012.

PKK—Kurdistan's Worker Party (Kurdish: Partiya Karkeren Kurdistan), a left-leaning Kurdish party with its base in Turkey.

Qannas—Sniper.

Ribat—To stand guard at a border.

Sabr—Patience.

Sahaba—The Prophet Muhammed's followers.

Salafism—A puritanical doctrine within Sunni Islam that follows a literal interpretation of the Koran and *hadith*.

Salat—The ritual prayers that Muslims perform five times a day. They are called *fajr* (between daybreak and sunrise), *dhuhr* (at the sun's highest point), *asr* (between *dhuhr* and sunset), *maghrib* (after sunset), and *isha* (in the night, when any sunlight on the horizon is gone).

Shahada—Islam's doctrine.

Shahid—Martyr.

Shaitan—Satan or the Devil in Islamic theology.

Shalwar kamiz (Urdu)—Traditional Pakistani baggy pants and knee-length shirts.

Sharia—Path. In a legal-religious context, the word means "path that leads to salvation," or Islamic law. The idea of law is expressed in two ways: *Sharia*, God's law; and *fiqh*, interpretation of the law. See *fiqh*.

Shawarma—A type of kebab.

Shirk—Idolatry or polytheism.

Sijn—Prison.

Subhanallah—Praise be to Allah. May be divided into two words: *subhan Allah*.

Sunna—The customs of the Prophet Muhammed. Used as a guiding principle for a Muslim's way of life.

Sura—Chapter in the Koran.

Tablighi—Member of the Tablghi Jamaat movement, a Sunni Islamic nonpolitical group that focuses on missionary work and revival and emphasizes a return to the original Islam.

Takbir—The Arabic phrase *Allahu akbar*, meaning "God is great." Often used as an expression of faith or to express determination or defiance.

Takfir—To pronounce that another Muslim is an infidel. The person who does this is known as *takfiri*.

Taqaddam—Forward.

Tarawih—*Salat* after the *isha* prayer. Only performed during Ramadan.

Tawba—To repent and turn around. Used to describe repentance and returning to Allah by renouncing that which He forbids and doing that which He has commanded.

Umma—Community, people, or society. Especially used of the Islamic faith community.

Wudu—The ritual washing before prayer.

Yalla—Let's go, hurry up. (Also spelled *yallah*.)

YPG—The People's Protection Unit (Kurdish: Yekineyen Parastina Gel). YPG is a militant Kurdish group that operates in the north and northeast of Syria.

ABOUT THE AUTHOR

Photo © 2017 Tine Poppe

Demian Vitanza is a playwright and novelist who has conducted numerous writing workshops, including one for the inmates of Halden Prison in Norway. He is the author of *Sub Rosa* and the award-winning novel *Urak*. *This Life or the Next* is Demian's third novel and his first to be translated into English.

ABOUT THE TRANSLATOR

Photo © 2017 Sofia Thresher Ouenniche

Tanya Thresher holds a PhD in Scandinavian Studies and Literary Theory from the University of Washington and worked as a professor of Scandinavian Studies at the University of Wisconsin from 1997 to 2010. Her scholarly interests include modern Norwegian writers and Scandinavian drama, in particular the works of Henrik Ibsen. She currently lives in the United Arab Emirates with her family.